C000088152

JOSEF'S LAIR

JOSEF'S LAIR

a novel by
Robert J. Brodey

Copyright 2015 Robert J. Brodey
All rights reserved.

ISBN: 0994065507
ISBN 13: 9780994065506

For my son, Sevan, and his generation. You are never too small to achieve great things. Even at the playground.

-

Eternal gratitude to my awesome and talented wife, Lara.

-

And to my family and friends. Without you, I'd be someone else.

CONTENTS

BOOK ONE

THE GIFT

"Memory is what makes our lives…Our memory is our coherence, our reason, our feeling, even our action. Without it, we are nothing."
Luis Buñuel

"Many lives, Arjuna, you and I have lived. I remember them all, but thou dost not."
Bhagavad-Gita

1

EXCAVATION

The air was thick with the musty scent of sweat and cigar smoke. Spilled rum wet the paved floor. And though his memory was clouded, he clearly recalled how Hector had led him into the room packed with a hundred people, maybe more. There was pushing and shouting, as the Cuban was greeted by his many names -- *¡Hola brujo! ¿Qué dice, médico? ¡Saludos santero, compañero, curandero!* Shirtless drummers glistened with sweat, pounding out rhythms on bata drums gripped securely between their legs. People danced, singing songs in praise of the mighty *orishas*. Through an open door loomed an altar with tureens draped in fabrics of red, blue, and yellow with matching beaded necklaces. Plates of food were laid out for the deities, a feast to celebrate the exchange between the living and the immortals. There was an electric charge in the air, a kinetic energy that comes from being surrounded by people of faith.

Josef felt himself standing in the midst of a dream, his sight hazy and forming halos around the lights hanging from the high ceiling. He had come all the way from Israel in the summer of 1979 to dig, looking for proof of a connection between the Arawak Indians of Cuba and the great Mayan civilizations of Central America. But he was also a PhD student looking to temporarily escape home and the burden of Israel's uneasy place in the world. The present was overly complicated and far too messy to untangle. Josef preferred to lose himself in the things that had already lived, completed their natural life cycle, and were now waiting to be found so they could be placed safely under glass. Lost cultures and static artefacts, after all, didn't squirm or breathe or question. But the Afro-Cuban religion Santería couldn't be escaped. The parties celebrating the *orishas* permeated the residential walls of neighbourhoods that sat outside the colonial streets of Havana. Remarkably, religion persisted in a country where God -- or gods -- officially didn't exist under the rule of *La Barba*, Fidel.

Hector tapped his prominent nose thoughtfully and left Josef's side. It was he, with his broad shoulders and unwavering gaze, who had emerged from the crowds at the airport to greet Josef. He had been hired by the Havana University to escort him to the apartment that would be home for the next six months. With his arms loaded with Josef's belongings, Hector led the way through the terminal and whisked Josef into a mint coloured '59 Chevy. He directed Josef to sit beside him in the front seat, shifted into gear, and drove off, the Chevy sputtering down the deserted street. From the shadows, he turned to study Josef curiously, paying scant attention to the dark road beyond the yellow beams cast by the headlights. Josef rolled down the window and faced outside, watching the zinc-roofed houses speed by. He closed his eyes and let the warm night air wash over him. When they pulled up to a neat row of nondescript buildings in the quiet suburb of Loma Pequeña on the outskirts of Havana, Hector single-handedly collected all of Josef's things, including his duffle bag and his crate of books, and climbed the four flights of steps to the modest apartment with concrete floors and slatted windows. Josef wordlessly handed him some money, but the Cuban gave a halting gesture. Then he bid farewell, leaving Josef thankfully to himself.

As the party continued, curious neighbours, black and white, young and old, peered in through the bars of the living room window gawking at the unfolding spectacle. A regal man with skin like coal and a high sleek forehead moved slowly like waves lapping the shore. He was dressed in white -- from hat to shoes -- and wearing a dozen beaded necklaces. His eyes met with Josef. He smiled only for an instant then turned away, lost in the pulse of the drums. An old woman smoking a cigar took a swig from a bottle of rum. With cheeks puffed, she sprayed alcohol in the face of the man in white. He bowed solemnly, "*Aché para tí.*" To Josef, this was all quite otherworldly, and he had to remind himself that he was the one who had decided to dig in Cuba. He was on their turf and had to accept their beliefs and customs, even if he didn't believe any of it.

Josef had come to Cuba seeking anonymity and the peace that comes with working in solitude. For the first time in his life, he wasn't responsible for anyone but himself -- most importantly his aging parents. But the magistrate, moustached and sweating profusely in his tiny cubicle at the sprawling Havana campus on San Lázaro and Calle L, had insisted he hire half a dozen locals to work alongside him. "We're not contagious," he had explained. "Hiding in a cave won't make you a better person. Solitude makes a beast of a man! ¡*Qué tristeza*!" Josef had dismissed the bureaucrat, explaining how he had always excavated alone and that would not change just because he was digging up Cuban soil.

"Yes, yes. Have it your way," the magistrate had said, politely removing the paperwork from his desk. "A suggestion, though. Perhaps excavate elsewhere -- maybe in Antarctica, where there are no people to get in the way of your work."

The labourers sent by the magistrate arrived out in front of Josef's apartment building like a ragged band of revolutionaries. There was a total of seven, despite the magistrate's assurances of six paid staff. In Spanish, Josef expressed his gratitude for them coming -- even if they were two hours late -- and explained that he would pay them their full wage for the month even though he wouldn't require their services. Satisfied with the arrangement, they discussed amongst themselves what they would spend the money on -- rum, some chickens, new clothing for their children. It was an orderly affair, as they formed a small queue in front of Josef. Each patiently waited his turn to receive money, before walking away happily. However, when all the others had counted their money and left, one man remained, smoking his cigarette thoughtfully. Josef hadn't even noticed that Hector had been among the cast of paid characters gathered around. His steady gaze seemed to be that of a self-possessed man, a man of the sea, who could see what lay beyond the horizon.

"Thanks for your contribution," Josef had offered awkwardly, before handing over the last of his money.

"I haven't done anything, yet," Hector had responded, refusing his wage. "Why pay people to do nothing?"

"I'm just following the rules."

"You'll make people lazy," Hector countered. Josef shrugged. Hector's eyes followed him patiently. "I suppose you don't think that's your problem. Just remember, every action has a reaction. You never know, maybe you'll make Cuba an island of beggars."

"Then I won't pay you," Josef offered. "That'll make one less beggar."

Hector fixed his gaze on Josef then smiled broadly and held out his hand. "I'll hold on to your money as a future payment."

"A payment for what?"

"Let the future decide."

———

After sorting through a mountain of official paperwork, Josef had begun excavating archaeological mounds, large pockets of earth indicating concealed pre-Columbian dwellings, in the middle of an abandoned field a few kilometres from his apartment block. He hauled up buckets of earth from metre by metre pits, hunting for hidden artefacts. By eleven in the morning, however, the savage heat would drive Josef from the site and only in the waning light of evening would he return to finish the day's work. For weeks, his shoulders aching, his hands bloodied and blistered, he moved from test grid to test grid, extracting soil samples and sorting through the debris. He discovered remnants of seeds and fish bones, which hinted at a potential Arawak settlement but were far from conclusive evidence. What he sought, digging carefully through the layers of sediment, was pottery associated with the early Central American cultures. His hypothesis, which had garnered enough interest from the Cuban government to grant him entry, was centred around some mysterious ceramics discovered in Guatemala's Petén jungle. While Mayan art was obsessed with human figures, particularly their deified rulers, the Olmec civilization of Mesoamerica was preoccupied with the magical qualities of animals. The Guatemalan pottery in question reflected neither tradition, which led Josef to believe they were crafted by the hands of the Arawak Indians of Cuba, who would have been in contact with the Mayans hundreds of years before the arrival of Europeans. Josef had always been fascinated by the links between seemingly unrelated histories and the forces at play that allowed some narratives to get passed down while others were permanently deleted from the human record.

Josef had been in Cuba nearly a month when he noticed an old man with leathery skin and a straw hat sitting in the shade of a Ceiba tree surrounded by grazing cows. He looked up toward Josef and waved. Each finger on that hand resembled the knotted wooden stick resting on his lap. Josef walked between the cows, their tails restlessly swatting back and forth. The old man grinned, revealing the toothless cavity of his mouth. He made to stand but relaxed when Josef waved for him to remain seated. He took Josef's blistered hand and shook it. "You've been working on that site, digging for the past a long time," he said. "I'm afraid, my son, you're wasting time and burning in the sun." He leaned into the stick and hoisted himself to his feet. In his other hand, he held an old machete. Gesturing with it like an ancient buccaneer, he pointed to an unseen location and led Josef away through waist-high grass. The old man appeared to float as he cut along an invisible path, down a slight decline, and around a corner through another field. He stopped at a grassy mound in view of the sea and the rusted remains of a ship that appeared to have run aground long ago. It was a place familiar to Josef; he had walked past it countless times. "Russian ship," the old man said, disdainfully, pointing his machete at the beached vessel. "Filled with cans of terrible Russian food. Russian crew, too. I wouldn't let them drive my car -- if I had one. There wasn't even a storm. The captain was drunk."

"Vodka," Josef offered. The old man nodded solemnly. With the machete, he stabbed the ground, as if to prove a point. He looked up with a faint smile, his milky eyes fixed on the visitor. Josef reached down and scooped up a handful of earth. To his amazement, jewel-like shards of pottery had come loose.

"The earth is jealous," the old man had said. "You have to know how to ask it to yield its secrets."

His chance meeting with the old man had been a turning point for his research, providing him with a new and promising site to dig. Josef remained consumed by the solitary process of excavating and sorting through the debris. After dark, he would pore over the documents on Mayan, Olmec, and Epi-Olmec sites throughout Mesoamerica. He studied the texts -- from El Salvador to Mexico -- examining all imaginable sites with the devotion of a cabalist studying the Torah in search of clues. Of particular interest was the Mayan centre of Tikal, with its ball-courts, stelae, and magnificent acropolis and temples. He remained utterly intrigued how this sixty kilometre square site of monumental architecture had remained concealed from sight for centuries by the tropical forests of El Petén, in north-eastern Guatemala. The forest had literally closed itself around an entire civilization like a cloak, and it was the archaeologists who had rescued it from the wilderness.

Life in Cuba flowed around Josef in the same way a river moved around a rock in its path. He was accustomed to being alone, but he took comfort in the rhythm with which Cubans moved, attracted to the heated street-corner debates that reminded him so much of Jerusalem. On the way to and from his excavation site, music poured out of windows and doorways, sometimes the fast cowbell beat of Salsa, other times the complex and hypnotic rhythm of African drums. The music was an open invitation to join in.

Josef's memory settled back on the Santería gathering in the same way an accident can play over and over again in one's mind, in the desperate hope of finding some small detail that would reveal what could've been done differently to change fate. He recalled distinctly a moment when something in the bata drums changed, and they became more frantic. Those dancing around Josef were like the swells of the sea whipped up by a fierce wind. Cigarette and cigar smoke choked the air. The man dressed in white hissed something in Spanish and began spinning round and round. There was something addictive about the beat of the drums, and Josef could feel himself letting go, swimming in the pulse of the bata drums. Soon he began moving his hips followed by his feet and shoulders then his hands. He moved the same way as everyone else, caught in the same hypnotic repetition. Then as he danced, freed by the movement of his body, a strange feeling overtook him. His head grew light, his feet rising weightlessly from the floor. For a single moment, his sight was no longer his sight, his body no longer his own. That's when the appearance of a woman, sultry and radiant with eyes shaped like perfect almonds, snapped him from the dream.

———

In all likelihood, the old man had spoken of Josef to others, because within days of their conversation, children began gathering around his trench. They came to look, talking amongst themselves, at first shyly, then with greater confidence. They laughed and pushed one another close to the hole where he worked, as if to offer each other up for service. It was all very amusing, and when Josef asked if any of them wanted to help dig, most shook their heads and nervously stepped away. But within every group of children, there was at least one brave enough to try something new. In this group, it was an eleven-year-old girl named Laicy. She, alone, asked the sorts of questions that confounded adults. *Why was the sky blue? What was love? Why was Europe considered a separate continent from Asia?* Every day after school she returned to the site, still dressed in her blue and white school uniform, and got right to work alongside him, unconcerned with getting dirty. She became a constant in a world of variables: different faces, heat, wind, and rain. Her glowing black eyes, beige skin, and crescent smile radiated an amazing warmth. One afternoon, as Laicy and Josef sorted through a tray of debris, he found an exquisitely preserved ceramic shard with small intricate designs etched into its polished earthen surface. It certainly wasn't the find of a lifetime that every archaeologist dreamed of, but it was a valuable clue. Seeing his pleasure, Laicy coaxed him to his feet and made him dance with her in circles, kicking up dust, as she sang in Spanish. When they finally let go of each other's hands, they fell to the ground, breathless and laughing.

"*Bella*, where's the steel brush?"

She pointed toward the trench, and he immediately clambered down the wooden ladder. On hands and knees, he felt around in the cool damp earth. The brush was nowhere to be found. He reached up into the little nook dug into the wall and, concealed in the shadows, a scorpion lashed out with its stinger. When Josef emerged from the trench cradling his hand, Laicy insisted on taking him to her father.

"Is he a doctor?"

Laicy didn't answer and, before Josef could resist, she led him away.

Together, they crossed a field and slipped beneath a barbed wire fence. Josef held his injured hand, which was growing hot. He could feel his heart racing, as the poison made its way through his body. Though it was late in the afternoon, the air remained heavy. Thunder clouds approached in the distance, laden with the epic downpours that nearly beat the Cubans into submission. With the rain's inevitable arrival each day, people would look up with a forlorn gaze and run for cover as if under attack, huddling together in tight bundles beneath the canopy of trees. The pelting rain stung bare skin like a barrage of pins and needles. It made such a racket against the zinc roofs that all thoughts were swept away but for those praying for the rain to end.

Josef and Laicy walked across a narrow overgrown path leading through a cluster of crudely constructed cinder-block houses. On either side, behind fences, goats gnawed shrubs while locals plucked vegetables from their small plots. Children played, shouting and running in and out of the shadows.

Out front and behind houses, American roadsters sat on blocks like dinosaur remains being readied for their resurrection in museums. To one side of the boulevard that sloped into a creek, tall weeds and wildflowers rose and fell, bending with the shifting wind. A young Cuban stood waist deep in water, his back erect, his eyes fixed in defiance of his own fear. Two older men stood with him. One grabbed the collar of his shirt and ripped it off. The other forcefully tore the back off his shirt, exposing his brown skin. Still, the young man stared ahead, jaw clenched, body tensed against each effort to shred his clothes. Josef clearly remembered stopping, bewildered by what he was seeing. Laicy gently tugged at his arm and led him to a house at the end of the street. To Josef's amazement, the old man whom he had met weeks earlier in the shade of a Ceiba tree was there, sitting on the porch. Laicy slipped inside the house. With a pleasant grin, the old man addressed Josef as *el extranjero*, the foreigner. "Have you found what you were looking for?"

"Archaeology requires the patience of a hunter."

"So does the line-up at the bank," he said disdainfully, pointing his walking stick in the general direction of Havana.

Remarkably, Laicy returned with Hector, who was wearing baggy slacks and a shirt unbuttoned to the navel. She took Josef by the hand and led him inside the house. There was an old TV with broken knobs and a hanger for an antenna. Old tattered chairs of all imaginable shapes and sizes faced it. Somewhere beyond sight, a radio played. A calendar on the wall was opened to September 1979 with Xs drawn through the days like the wall etchings that marked a prisoner's days. In the corner, behind the front door, sat a coconut with a face painted on both ends, looking in opposite directions. Hector broke the spell and introduced himself, making no gesture of acknowledgement that they had already met on two previous occasions. Josef awkwardly extended his uninjured hand. Hector shook it, then turned it palm up and studied the tattered and blistered surface as a geologist would a rock. "City hands," he said, grimly. He looked at Josef a moment longer then beckoned him to the back of the house. "Papá," Laicy called out. "Make sure the spirits don't come down on him. He isn't ready."

"I know."

They passed the kitchen filled with shadows and old dying appliances, including a lock-arm refrigerator and a broken electric stove that had been outfitted to burn wood. Through a concrete doorway, they entered an ornate and colourful room at the centre of which stood an altar. There were plates of food and bottles of rum and wine. A dozen or so elaborate ceramic and wooden tureens were adorned with colourful fabrics. Black dolls, one in a blue and white dress and another in yellow and white, stood among the objects of veneration. Hector was pleased by Josef's look of bewilderment and laughed aloud. He drew up a stool and beckoned him to sit in front of the altar, before lighting a cigarette. Josef already regretted having returned with Laicy to her home. What he needed was a doctor, and he was growing impatient. He cradled the inflamed hand, feeling weaker with each passing minute.

"Everything I believe is before you," Hector had said, pointing his cigarette toward the shrine. From the altar, he retrieved several containers and began to mix their contents together.

Hector smoked in deep thought, allowing the blue veil to drift from his nostrils in an unhurried fashion. The silence was as profound as any Josef had experienced digging in the Sinai Desert. Suspended like dust, words remained mysteriously out of reach. Hector's dark eyes were piercing. With his beige skin, the blackness of his hair, and his long proud nose, Hector could have easily blended into Jerusalem's bustling streets. To Josef, he appeared like a shaman pictured in the pages of *National Geographic*.

Hector finished mixing the ingredients in the container and smeared the paste on the scorpion bite. In a few short minutes, Josef felt the wound cooling, the poison magically being drawn out of his body. With that came a sudden reversal, a growing sense of trust in Hector -- the santero.

From his shirt pocket, Hector withdrew another cigarette, lighting it with the smouldering nub of his spent cigarette. "There are so many things you can't know about Santería," he finally said.

"I was raised not to believe in anything I didn't understand."

"Of course," he said thoughtfully. "Then let me share a few things to help you understand. We have only one supreme God -- *Olodumare*, who lives far far away. He is the god of the Bible, the Torah, and maybe even the Koran. But we also believe He has many children -- the *orishas* -- who involve themselves in our daily affairs. We have direct access to them. Now that is true democracy!"

"Perhaps."

"Maybe the most important lesson Santería has to offer to the world is the need of finding balance in life. Extremes aren't looked on favourably. 'Hot heads,' people who are too reactive, need to be cooled, and 'cool heads' need to be 'centred.' A balanced relationship is one where two people give to one another, and through this exchange both increase their *aché.*"

"*Aché?*"

"*Aché*, the divine power that allows us to accomplish our ambitions. We're the children of God, Josef, so we carry a bit of God in us. Some have lots and others only a little. Making offerings to the *orishas* helps increase *aché*, so we can move ahead in life. You can't underestimate the importance of finding balance in life. Some of the deities are protectors. Yemayá," he said, pointing to a black doll in a blue and white dress, "is the *orisha* of maternity and the oceans. Changó is the brave warrior in red. Then of course, there is Obatalá, the deity of whiteness and purity and of eternal balance, who resides over the head. You will find Osain in the forests and Ochún by the rivers and streams. Don't look so impatient, Josef. I'm coming to mischievous Ellegua, whom you saw sitting behind the front door. He stands at the cross-roads, an outsider existing between worlds."

"It's a painted coconut."

"Be careful," he grinned. "If I had to guess, your path is the trickster." Hector pointed his cigarette at him. "Ellegua is the *orisha* of destiny and looks toward the future and the past, toward the living and the dead. He's a child, and like all children, needs candy and toys on his birthday. But don't let that fool you, because he's also a trickster that preys on the weaknesses of others."

Josef couldn't sustain the intensity of Hector's gaze and looked away. They sat in silence with the darkness growing outside the window. Neighbourhood dogs began a chorus of barking, which lasted until the thunderstorm closed in, bringing with it spectacular bolts of lightning and unbroken sheets of rain. Hector retrieved a bottle of rum from the altar and fetched two glasses. He poured the first drops of rum to the floor before filling Josef's glass. Hector moved his stool closer to his guest, so they could talk above the din of the rain.

"I saw a young man at the creek," ventured Josef. "They were tearing off his clothes."

"You act like you aren't curious about us, but you can't help but be curious. It's in your nature." Hector tapped his grand nose. "So the boy in the creek…Should I tell you everything or should I make you work for it?" A grin escaped him. "You're young. You still want to know everything yesterday. But you're also an anthropologist, so you tell me."

"I don't know. Some kind of initiation? Maybe his clothes represent who he was." Then with more confidence, "So they were stripping away his old identity to prepare him for a new one."

Hector was pleased: "And for the next year, he must dress only in white and no one can refer to him by name, because he's in between -- no longer who he was and not yet who he'll be. Those who are in between are both very powerful and very vulnerable. They exist outside the social order, which makes them dangerous to the order. It's like you, Josef. Laicy tells me you're half Jewish."

"Only the bottom half."

"You can't always hide behind jokes. Tell me about your parents. I'm curious."

"They're antique dealers," Josef offered.

"And they survived the war against the Jews? I'm sorry. I know I'm prying...But, I'll admit, I like to pry."

"My mother is a French Catholic. She married my father, who is Jewish. They both ended up in a concentration camp."

"I'm sorry. Really." He paused. "May I ask when your birthday is?"

"January 1st, 1945."

"New Year's Day," Hector erupted into laughter. "Everyone born on New Year's Day is born with a gift!"

"So my gift was being born at a Red Cross camp?"

"What I'm talking about transcends mortal walls," he said, smiling with infinite satisfaction. "Next time we meet, be prepared to tell me about your gift."

Hector emptied his glass of rum then spoke, as if to himself. "It's an honour to be stung by a scorpion." Josef looked at him sceptically, but Hector smiled, anyway. "Normally I get paid two chickens," he said. "But the future has decided the payment."

———

The lens of Josef's memory focused once again on the large gathering, where the drummers drummed and people danced, drank rum, and sang songs honouring the *orishas*. The sultry woman with almond eyes was there, dancing on her own. Their eyes met briefly, before Hector waved him over to the adjoining room. Josef took one last look at the Cubana, before crossing the room. He nearly collided with a nervous-looking woman in glasses, as she quickly approached. "You have to leave," she insisted. Josef smiled, embarrassed and uncertain how to respond. She was still clinging to his sleeve when he broke from her grasp and stepped into the room where Hector awaited him. Hector approached the altar with its tureens and food offerings and picked up a pair of old wooden maracas. Vigorously, he shook them, his lips moving in private conversation as his gaze affectionately moved over the pantheon. He called Josef forward. "Greet the *orishas*. You can say a prayer if you like." Josef took the maracas, rattling them without faith. That's when the woman with wild eyes again descended upon him. "What seems to be the trouble, Fabiola?" Hector interrupted. She looked at Josef accusingly and whispered something in Hector's ear. His face grew tense and then he grabbed Josef by the arm and pulled him out through the doorway at the back of the house. A primitive altar sat outside near the wash basin, with flowers and food offerings placed before it. A candle burned. Among the objects, a shoebox.

Hector directed Josef to a stool. "I need to read your shells," he said.

"I'm a Jew. An agnostic half-Jew, at that."

"*Por favor, sientas.*" Hector sat himself down authoritatively and immediately pulled out a dozen divination shells from a black velvet pouch. Josef remained standing.

"I don't want to know my future."

"What about your past?"

"I know my past. I lived it."

"Then you have nothing to be afraid of." A cigar was lit for Hector, and he puffed on it until the tip glowed red. In a moment, he mumbled something and threw the shells to the floor, which fell in what appeared to be a random pattern. In a halo of smoke, he leaned over the shells. With a sweeping hand, he drew up the shells, said a prayer, and tossed them. Again, he leaned over and analyzed their position on the floor, puffing more clouds of blue smoke. Through the acrid veil, Hector shook his head, concerned. The shoebox in the altar appeared to rattle of its own volition. Hector looked up then threw the shells again. It became clear by the speed and vigour with which he mumbled that something important was happening and that the dead were sending important messages to him. Then, after drawing a finger along his nose, Hector gave the final word of the divine. "The dead are here in large numbers." Josef shook his head with incomprehension. "You need to leave."

From inside, the drums built in intensity. Josef stood. "You invited me."

"But Josef—"

"I'm staying."

Hector looked worried. "If anything happens, I can't protect you." Then, with resignation, he gestured for Josef to return to the party. As Josef moved toward the door, the shoebox again rattled.

When he rejoined the gathering, Josef scanned the room. And there she was dancing, a glass of rum in her hand. He was immediately accosted by Fabiola. "*Tienes que ir!*" she insisted.

Before he could say anything, the woman with eyes shaped like almonds swooped down, looped her arm through his, and led him away. "*Está conmigo,*" she said to the other woman. She introduced herself as Tatiana, handed him a glass of rum, and kissed his cheek. "Don't listen to her. My sister can be quite excitable when she 'senses' bad things coming."

"What kind of bad things?"

"Dead bad things," she grinned.

Warmed by the rum and consumed by the ebb and flow of the music in the company of the beautiful Cuban, Josef felt like he belonged there. But as he danced, the music worked its way through his bloodstream like the poison of a scorpion bite, slowly taking possession of him. There was something different about the drums, which seemed to flow between worlds, creating secret passageways that either ascended or descended toward heaven or hell. Josef turned to face the man dressed head to toe in white, who was dancing in the thick of the crowd. Then, in a sudden startling jerk, the Cuban's head fell back, and he spiraled to the floor. When he again rose to his feet, he had transformed, his glossy eyes wide open, caught in a trance. He opened his mouth to speak, and the voice of a frail old lady spoke in an unknown language. No one else noticed his altered state, so Josef tried to ignore it and turned his attention back to Tatiana. They danced, and soon he found himself drawn into a dream-like rapture. The rhythms moved in circles, diverging until they began to converge again, meeting and crossing over, then diverging again. There was a commotion elsewhere in the room as more people spun and fell, possessed by the *orishas*.

Josef's own heart kept time with the drums. And as he succumbed to the music, the drums echoed something more ominous like the sound of exploding bombs. He shivered, as he passed through realms, moving backward. His body moved of its own volition, and he was unable to jerk himself from the spell. The room that once appeared one-dimensional and flat now had depth, possessing an infinite number of subtle layers, like doorways, through which to enter. The feverish energy in the room overpowered him, and the drums grew so loud, they enveloped and swallowed everything. Hector burst into the room, shouting, "The Dead want something!" He held up the shoebox from the altar and flipped off the lid. Hector roughly took hold of something in the box. Above his head he held a pigeon. "This is an offering for you!" he shouted, looking to the heavens. In a single motion, Hector grabbed hold of the pigeon's head and twisted it off, spraying a mist of blood over the room.

Josef tasted the warm blood on his lips. Then he was struck by a violent flash of light. His eyes were open, yet he saw a quick succession of images that flickered from another time, another place. It was as if the wires of history had been crossed, and he was now seeing with someone else's eyes. Josef tried to focus on Hector at the front of the room, but his vision narrowed to the point of blindness. It seemed impossible, but he could hear someone else's thoughts echo in his head. Josef slouched to the ground, drowning and slipping beneath the surface. Everything remained distant and unclear, generations away from the original impression. Shapes lurked in the shadows of his mind's eye. Then, from the haze, he saw it.

A series of explosions send dust and wooden beams from the ceiling. The thunderclap is followed by the whistling of more incoming artillery. In the veil of black that falls heavily after each successive flash, the earth heaves from its foundations, as if God is about to end it all. There is fear, but no terror or pain. No running. No escaping. Bombs fall from the sky, followed by short bursts of machine gun fire. Ratatatat. Ratatatat. There is frantic noise from down the hallway. *Achtung. Achtung*, a voice calls. For a moment, he holds his hands before his eyes. They are soaked in blood.

A brick wall appears. He knows what he must do. He digs, removing layer after layer, creating a safe place. A bomb explodes and a beam falls from the ceiling. He braces himself then continues digging, gripping chisel and hammer. Over his shoulder, he sees a picture of a madman hanging on the wall above the desk. A pale young woman stands behind him wearing a prisoner's uniform and a bright coloured badge. She must be injured, because she is also covered in blood. She sobs. He wants to tell her to shut up, that she could get them killed, but she is afraid, and he can't blame her. Another bomb explodes, sending more clots of cement and dust raining down. God has left this place, and time itself is coming to an end.

The drums had fallen silent. Faces appeared above Josef. Hector was among them, his expression full of worry. He turned to the others gravely. "I think the Dead found him."

2

THE ANTIQUE SHOP

J osef awoke and was immediately struck by a fear that could only be understood as primordial. It was a general sense of dread made worse by the uncertainty of where he was at that very moment. His eyes searched the darkened room for clues. There they were, glimpses of familiar objects tucked in the shadows: his typewriter, the old rattling refrigerator, a photo on the wall of his parents. At the far end of the room, street lights bled through the improvised curtains. Josef shuffled to the window and pulled back the tired sun-bleached bed sheets. Outside was the luminous dome of Ramban Synagogue and the sleek bony arch suspended over Hurva Square.

Then it came back to him: The Jewish Quarter. The Old City. Jerusalem. He fell back in his chair by the typewriter and surveyed the desktop covered with books and journals stacked neatly like skyscrapers. On the wall hung his PhD diploma, a fancy parchment that revealed nothing of his colossal failure to find the missing link between the Arawak Indians of Cuba and the Mayan civilizations of Central America. He looked up and found something to smile about, a series of photographs pinned to the wall. Laicy had taken them on their drive to the airport and sent them to keep him company, as if knowing of his profound solitude since returning from Cuba. Hector had been right, as he so often was, when he said children possessed the profound power to observe. There were pictures of Josef's surprised look as Laicy poked him in the ribs; blurry images of Hector's wife, Cecelia, screaming and laughing during a shrieking competition; photographs of the old man hunched over sleeping, and an image of Hector behind the wheel of his ancient Chevy.

The night before he had left Cuba, Hector had exercised his magical influence over Josef, convincing him, without uttering a single word, to give away all his earthly possessions. Everything but the clothes on his back. And the whole family was in on it. On the way to the airport, Laicy wore a pair of his shorts, which made her little brown legs look like sticks, while his camera hung around her neck. Her grandfather, who had already begun nodding off beside her, wore Josef's favourite blue jeans. Cecelia proudly sported one of his button-down shirts, her colourful Santería necklaces concealed beneath the collar. And Hector now owned two pairs of Israeli work boots and a diving watch.

It had taken Hector five times to start the car and even then it sputtered and choked, crawling along the road like a wounded insect. When they finally turned off their street and headed down the tree-lined boulevard, they had to drive on the shoulder to let the growing line of traffic behind them pass. "Any slower, and we'll be going backward," Josef had joked, only half kidding. In that instant, Hector's smile had faded, and he stepped on the brake. "Maybe you'll miss your flight."

In the airport parking lot, Hector had poured some rum on the ground to honour the *orishas*, while Josef lamented having to leave behind all his archaeological findings.

"We're proud people," said Hector. "We love our country, our music, our heritage, our land. What's Cuban must stay in Cuba."

"But what about Santería?"

"The saints, well, they belong to everyone."

Hector, Cecelia, and Josef had raised their glasses in salutation to Hector's dad, who was fast asleep in the back seat of the car, then drank the amber rum. Cecelia poured another round. Hector lit a cigarette and said something very strange: "We're all as much dead as we are alive." Cecelia was impatient: "Is it really necessary to talk like this now?" Josef leaned toward Hector and asked if he was speaking in metaphors. Hector sounded distant, as if possessed by an *orisha*: "We owe a great deal of what we are to those who have passed." He paused, perhaps to allow Josef a moment to consider the weight of his words before continuing. "The living and dead are one. You have to believe in your visions and continue on your journey."

When they had staggered across the road to the airport terminal, Josef was flooded by a deluge of memories: The children sitting around his trench watching him work, the Santería celebrations, the inexhaustible rhythms of the bata drums continuing on and on through the night, the trips to Havana with Hector where they wandered the streets, staring up between the rows of buildings, watching people lean over the balconies or hang clothes to dry in the fierce Cuban sun. In the back streets, children played kick the can between the traffic. There was a certain intensity of madness in Havana. It had a soul like Jerusalem, dark and troubling, and yet it felt like the centre of the world. Sometimes, they found themselves standing in the *Plaza de la Revolución* gazing at the world moving around them. Other times, they would stroll the sea wall of *El Malecón*, Yemayá's restless ocean spraying the roadway. In the near distance, the Morro Castle guarded the harbour.

Even now, Josef could walk back through every moment at the airport, before his departure, when the passengers moved frantically back and forth across the terminal, the air heavy from the pressing crowds, as families re-united or were saying their final good-byes. At the check-in counter, the attendant informed Josef that his flight was already boarding and that he should hurry, if he didn't want to miss it.

In the lineup for security, Hector had presented Josef with a black doll in a blue and white dress. "In moments of weakness think about Yemayá's strength. She's the *orisha* of the seas and will protect you wherever you go."

"I'm sorry," Josef had said. "I have nothing for you."

"You've given me companionship and respect. That's more valuable than anything. Remember, Josef, we don't dream alone." The security officer signaled for the next passenger, and Josef took another step forward. Hector looked toward the officer and then back at his friend. Together, they had allowed conversations to unfold as they did, carrying them over for days and sometimes weeks. Neither of them had ever figured that their time together would be whittled from months to weeks and from weeks to days and now minutes to seconds. Hector pointed to the top of his head. "Rely on Obatalá, but don't be afraid to use your feet to walk and your hands to dig. Use your tools," he implored, pointing toward Josef's worn satchel, "to reveal what's hidden."

Suddenly aware of his surroundings, Hector had hushed his voice and spoke more softly, his dark eyes awaking old fears within Josef. "You have many gifts, but you must learn to use them all." Hector clutched Josef's sleeve. "You possess a power I may never have, the power to cross shores -- to see the world -- but with that comes a responsibility to suspend judgment and observe."

"I hate the feeling you know something I don't," Josef had said, rattled.

"I wish that was the case, my Josef, but the truth is if your visions come back, I don't think anyone can save you." Hector drew a finger along the length of his nose, nodded his head, and reflected sadly, "*No es fácil.*" Laicy gripped Josef around the waist, crying. "Please Mr. Levi, don't leave. We can protect you." He kissed her forehead.

As he passed through customs, he raised the Yemayá doll above his head and called back one last time, "*Aché para tí!*"

So Hector had been right all along. The visions had found him, just as he predicted. And all the lessons he had learned in

Cuba -- about finding balance in life and using his head to accomplish goals -- somehow seemed lost. Perhaps he was not yet ready to be as Hector imagined him, a world-walker, a half-Jew that moved freely between worlds, a trickster like the *orisha* Ellegua with the clarity of vision to observe the future and past, the living and the dead, without judgment. That's why, when the visions of the prisoner in the death camp first found him back in Israel, he had driven deep into the Sinai Desert to escape. But the visions couldn't be fooled that easily, and they found him there, too.

The air was spiced with exhilaration and tension, as an army patrol fanned out into the late afternoon crowds along Ben Yehuda's cobblestone street. At Café Shalom, Josef saw him wade through the masses, wearing red denim bell bottoms, a tight t-shirt, and aviator shades. Saul was easy to spot, standing a foot taller than average with broad shoulders and thick Herculean muscles that he liked to watch flex when he was lifting things. For a moment, Saul searched in every direction, as if in preparation for an attack. He waited for Josef to stand and greet him. "Brother," said Saul, embracing him.

"Liebowitz. Where's the uniform?"

"What uniform?"

"You know, the Shaldag special forces fatigues, beret, black polished boots. The machine gun that you sleep with under your pillow."

"I quit."

"Bull."

"I'm a civilian now, Josef. One of you unarmed monkeys, who shits his pants when a firecracker goes off." Saul sat himself down and absently picked up a knife from the table and twirled it between his fingers.

"Mossad hired you, didn't they."

"Nope."

"Saul, you have a smart-ass answer for everything, so when you say 'nope,' I know something's up."

A bountiful brown-eyed waitress approached the table.

"Any bombings to report?" Saul asked.

"Not today. Maybe in an hour."

Saul grinned and stroked his dark handsome face. "When do you get off?"

"With my boyfriend."

Saul immediately shut down the charm and curtly ordered two beers.

When she left the table, Josef pointed to Saul's red pants. "I thought Mossad only recruited agents that don't stand out? You know, the unassuming types."

"Like you, you mean."

"I'm just saying, those pants can't fly under the radar."

Saul reached over the table and fondly rattled Josef by the shoulders. "So, seriously man, how are you keeping? God, I miss you. You gotta come out and play more."

When the waitress returned with the beer, Saul ignored her and snatched the beers from her hand, passing Josef a bottle, before raising his in a salute. Josef tipped his bottle and allowed a few drops to spill on the ground.

"More Cuban witchcraft? You know you broke your parents' heart when you had that initiation into *Pablo*."

"It's called Palo, and I never told them about that."

Saul had to laugh. "I did."

"You're a shit disturber, you know that?"

"You're wound so fucking tight these days. I want the old Josef back, damn it. The one that burned his high school diploma after eating hash brownies."

"Those were good," Josef admitted.

"The one that drank his face off and ran butt-naked through Tel Aviv. Hell, I'll even take the ten-year-old Josef playing hide-and-go-seek in the back streets of Haifa. You may have been a French-speaking doormat, but at least you knew how to have fun."

"Mr. Kurtz. He dead."

"You used to be funnier."

"That was a few wars back."

"Remember, I was the one fighting the goddamn towel heads, while you were in Cuba digging up dead things." Saul studied him in silence, rubbing a massive arm that bulked beneath his t-shirt. "All kidding aside. I'm not trying to be an ass, Josef. You know that. You're like a brother. And when I challenge you, I challenge myself. I need to test what I believe and confirm I'm right."

"And what you do is always right."

"What I *did* wasn't pleasant. But it had to be done. Listen, if you want to know what's wrong with the world, I'll gladly show you. You could use a real world education."

"You never change… '*Out of date, but loyal to his own time.*'

Saul laughed, and continued the thread from *Tinker Tailor Soldier Spy*: "*At a certain moment every man chooses: will he go forward, will he go back?*" Then Josef joined in so that they were speaking with one voice, "*There was nothing dishonourable in not being blown about by every little modern wind… Better to be an oak of one's generation.*"

They clinked bottles and polished off their beers. Saul was about to order another round when Josef pointed to his watch. "I told my parents we'd be there at four."

"And we know how they get if you show up at 4:05. '*Merde, Jo-sef. We though- someting happen-ed!*' '*Call if you are go-ing to be tarde.*'"

"Don't take the piss out of my parents. They're the only family I've got."

"What do they want to see us about, anyway?"

"Probably want to leave all their money to you, Saul."

"But they don't have any."

"It's the thought that counts."

Just then a most captivating woman passed by. Josef shifted in his seat, his eyes unable to break from her. Her eyebrows fell in beautiful arcs above her dark piercing eyes. Then, in the stream of human traffic, she disappeared. Saul noticed his attention had been stolen and turned to look but saw nothing.

"What's wrong with you? You're a million miles away." Josef sought the woman out in the crowd but couldn't see her in the blur of movement. Then something stirred behind him. Saul gazed over Josef's shoulder and directed him to turn.

She smiled and said her name was Asena. Josef stood nervously and introduced himself.

"You look so familiar," she said. "I had to find out where we've met."

Saul rolled his eyes then introduced himself. She ignored him, gazing at Josef before wagging her finger. "Hebrew University?"

"That's it! Archaeology."

"I teach psychology. You're always eating lunch in the courtyard under the same tree at the same time – rain or shine. I could never forget that punctuality. That dedication to routine." She quickly qualified her words: "And I don't mean that as an insult."

"None taken."

"Josef excavated in Cuba," Saul interrupted, with a laugh. "Couldn't even find his own shovel!" Josef pulled up a seat and directed Asena to sit. He hardly noticed Saul throw down a handful of shekels and walk away, his bright red bell bottoms swishing loudly. Josef called out, "Congrats on the new job, Mr. Mossad."

"Don't forget, four o'clock." Saul called back, without turning around. "So good luck getting laid in the next ten minutes," he shouted, loud enough for the surrounding tables to hear. "You really need it."

"Your friend should look for the volume control on his pants," Asena commented to Josef.

"They are pretty loud."

"Rock concert loud."

Josef looked in Saul's direction, but he was already gone. "Listen, this is killing me, but I really do have to go."

"There's that punctuality again."

"Can I call you?"

"Let's put your clockwork to the test. I'll come back tonight at 7. If you don't show your face by 8, the wedding is off."

Josef couldn't contain his grin. "I like your sass."

"But it's only free Tuesday nights."

Josef arrived at his parents' antique shop, a loaf of bread in hand. His father and mother stood by a desk in the dim light among the antiques of teak and brass talking to Saul. A fine moss of dust covered every surface, and if you placed a hand on anything among their collection, it would leave a perfect impression in the dust. Nearby, a medieval suit of armor stood guard, holding a battle axe.

His father wore a wool vest and French cap. When he saw Josef, he removed his thick glasses and pulled out a handkerchief to wipe the moisture from his eyes.

"You're late," he said in French.

Saul coughed to cover a laugh.

"Sorry papa." Josef handed the bread to his mother, who smiled gratefully and kissed his cheeks. More recently, her age had been showing. He never said it, but he was fond of her pronounced crow's feet, which radiated like sunbursts from the corners of her grey eyes. For Josef, it was proof that she -- unlike his father -- had always found joy despite the terrible circumstances of her early life.

"How's business?" Josef queried.

"The Arabs have ruined everything," grumbled his father. "Maybe, Josef, you can lend us a few bucks. Now that you're working at the university, you can afford it."

"Of course. Feeling OK lately?" His father had been taking a cocktail of pills for heart, high blood pressure, depression, and insomnia ever since Josef could remember.

"Awful."

"*Maman* says you've been self-medicating again."

"I know more than those lousy doctors. If I didn't do something, I'd already be dead and buried."

"I'm worried about your health, papa."

"You're worried," he said, with a sigh.

"Anything new?" Josef gestured to the closed door at the rear of the shop.

"The hunt continues."

His father replaced his glasses and put an arm on Saul's shoulder, admiringly. "He is built like Mount Hermon! And did you see?"

"Yeah, papa, Saul is no longer in uniform."

"But Saul, who will protect us?"

"Don't worry. He's Mossad now."

Josef's parents glanced at one another, with an air approaching concern.

That wasn't lost on Saul. "Your son is joking, Mr. Levi. My former commanding officer retired and opened a business, so when he found out I was leaving the service, he offered me a desk job."

Josef's parents looked relieved.

"What line of work?" his mother asked, probing, as she began sorting through papers on her desk.

"Furniture manufacturing in Ashkelon. So I'm back and forth a lot. There may even be some international travel involved."

"Conveniently located near the Mossad HQ in Tel Aviv."

Saul ignored him. "It's good. I deal with clients, manufacturers, and the collections department."

"Are you an enforcer or something?" chided Josef. "'*Pay for that chair, or I'll break its legs.*'"

His father wasn't impressed. "Josef, you can't make fun of a man who dedicated his life to protecting this country."

"I always thought he served himself first."

Toward the back corner of the room, a cabinet door was ajar, revealing row upon row of canned goods. Josef's father saw Saul eye the emergency food store. "In case," is all he said. He began re-arranging furniture, a habit, as if moving a lamp from this table to that one, would somehow drive more customers in through that heavy front door. Whatever his parents were doing, it wasn't working. Their antique shop was losing money every month.

"So Josef says you wanted to discuss something with the both of us. Should we talk back there?" asked Saul, pointing to the door at the back of the shop.

"No," Josef's father said, bluntly.

His mother was more conciliatory. "Our life's work has led us to some troubling information."

"How so?"

"I don't need to remind you Europe despised us," his father said, his voice low and thundering.

"Of course," agreed Saul.

"We couldn't wait for someone to seek justice for all the evil committed against us. We have the right to seek justice in the name of our suffering. If we don't remind our oppressors," his father continued, "then they'll forget, and it'll happen all over again…"

His father became lost to the present, as he travelled back into memory. "…Every sound, every banging door, created panic in the heart. So much uncertainty. You'd think you were going to drop dead of fear before the Nazis got their hooks in you…"

"We know, papa," said Josef patiently, but he was already exhausted from the lecture, which was the same one he had been listening to since he was a boy.

"Our lives were so different before the war," added his mother.

"*C'est fou.* We lived, teaching our neighbour's children, preparing them for a bright future. And then those endless summers in the Pyrénées. We swam in ice cold streams and cooked over an open fire. When you breathed, that was it. That breath was life's meaning. We had lived, and that's what made the concentration camp so unbearable. Freedom is worth everything. And we had everything until Europe stole it. Before we were taken to Le Vernet your mother and I had considered escaping over the mountains into Spain. Something stopped us, though. The reason, it escapes me now."

She answered for him. "We were convinced as French citizens that the country would protect us."

Josef knew his father was getting upset, because he began mixing up Hebrew and French. "*C'est vrai. La solution finale. Pas possible. Nous sommes Français. Mais 23,000 Juifs Français ont été déportés à Auschwitz.* We were part of the fabric of French culture -- we worked in their factories and governments, in their *système social.* We flourished when France flourished and died for France when they called on us during the Great War. *Mais la législation antisémite et la persécution des Juifs* forced us from teaching. We could no longer educate the children, teach them to read and write, to think for themselves. The legislation of Petáin and Laval ended our dreams. And why? Because we were Jews," he said, spitting out the words with anger. "And my parents died because their parents *sont Juifs.* Your big sister, too. It's a terrible history, a despicable one. And I'd never return to France, not in fifty years, not a hundred, not a thousand years -- *jamais.*"

But his father wasn't finished.

"The young people who didn't live through the war don't understand. Jews needed a safe place to live where they wouldn't be persecuted by the Russians or the Nazis, or American and Romanian fascists, or Spanish Monarchists.

Pogroms awaited the Jews who'd survived the Holocaust and were returning to Kiev and Kracow. The monsters didn't want to return our stolen property, so they slaughtered us. No, we needed a safe place to live, and that place is Israel. We were persecuted for over two thousand years. Enough was enough. How many more times would we have to be burned in our homes and synagogues, before we decided as a people to stand up and choose our own fate. We needed to return to our homeland, a homeland that would protect us from more tragedy."

"And this is why we can never retreat, even an inch," said Saul.

Little by little, his father was returning from the past.

"I'll never forget the boat ride over," he said, thrusting his hands into his vest pockets. "We were packed like sardines in a can. It was the Warsaw Ghetto on the sea."

"It was worth the journey," his mother added, looking up from the papers she was organizing on the desk. *Idle hands,* Josef thought.

"But lately, something has been lost."

"Papa, what are you getting at?"

He remained speechless, so Josef's mother spoke for him. "Perhaps he feels like the dream of Israel is dying."

"I think it's too soon to make that prognosis," Saul said, confidently.

Josef's father took off his glasses and looked at Saul. "What do you know about Central America? Particularly, Guatemala."

"Nothing," offered Saul. "I could point it out on a map, and that's about it."

"Good," Josef's father said, replacing his glasses. "Very good."

"Why?" Josef piped in.

"Something isn't adding up there. But we can't talk about it. Not yet."

"Not even a little taste, Mrs. Levi?" ask Saul, slyly.

Josef's mother offered a brief smile. "I don't think even you could swallow it."

3

THE GODDESS ASENA

Jerusalem swept by in a blur, as Josef sprinted back toward Ben Yehuda Street. He glanced down at his watch. 7:50pm. His parents had insisted he stay for dinner, despite his plea that he had a date. Then they insisted he stay for coffee afterward. Why was it so hard to tell his parents he had to go? He remembered: guilt. Just around the corner from Café Shalom, Josef ducked breathlessly into a restaurant and locked himself in the bathroom. He unraveled paper towel to pat dry the sweat beading on his face, chest, and underarms. Then he looked in the mirror and offered himself some encouragement: "This is no big deal."

When Josef approached Asena at the café, she was even more beautiful than he remembered. She looked like a Spaniard, her long black hair flowing over her shoulders, her brown eyes bright, as they followed him across the patio. She stood and kissed both his cheeks, and, in the cool darkness of evening, they ordered food and a bottle of wine.

He couldn't explain it, but he immediately felt at ease in her presence, and in his excitement, he would burst into laughter and talk so quickly that even he failed to understand what he was trying to say. Thankfully, Asena didn't hold Josef's enthusiasm for her against him. For over an hour, they feverishly discussed their favourite writers. They agreed on Gabriel García Márquez, Jerzy Kosinski, and Zora Neale Hurston, but a rift formed with the mention of Hemingway. "His writing is just too male," she argued. "His women are all cardboard cut-outs. No depth. He clearly didn't understand women at all."

"But he revolutionized modern fiction," countered Josef.

"Actually? I think the Brazilian Machado de Assis penned the first modern fiction with *Epitaph of a Small Winner*. And that was in 1880!"

"I can't judge something I haven't read."

"I'll lend it to you. I found the 1952 First English Edition at a used bookstore in Brooklyn, and I swear that story changed my life."

Josef raised his glass. "Then to Machado!"

"Machado!"

Over dessert, Asena told him of the summer she spent living with the Bedouins in the Sinai Peninsula. The Bedouins, she explained, kissed the earth three times to thank God. "Those were idealistic times," she said. "We believed anything could happen if we wanted. Living in peace could simply be willed. I still believe that." She told Josef that she studied psychoanalysis in New York in 1975. "You and I have a lot in common. All Western thinkers are archaeologists. Darwin was in search of the genealogy of the species, Marx, in search of the origin of economic and political conflict. Then there was Durkheim, the hunter of the fabled organic culture. According to them, everything originated somewhere and moved somewhere else. But I don't believe that."

"No?"

"When I lived in New York, I joined a group of Vietnamese Buddhists who'd escaped the war. I related to their view of the world, but it collided with my work in psychoanalysis, and I just couldn't reconcile the two worlds. Freud's disciple, Jung, on the other hand, was more my style, so I went to study at the Jungian school in Zürich. But even in Zürich, I couldn't find free thinkers. Like Jung said, 'Thank God I'm Jung and not a Jungian.'"

"Were you born in Israel?"

"New York. When I was growing up, my parents had always told me things like, 'Jews don't abuse their children'; 'Jews take pride in education and intellectual pursuits;' 'Jews aren't poor'; 'Jews find strength in their unity.' For years my parents talked about moving to Israel, because it was just *so* holy, and they dreamed about living among their own people beneath the unifying force of the Covenant. They weren't religious nuts or anything, they just really identified with being Jewish. Of course, when we moved to Jerusalem they were shocked. There were Jews driving buses, Jewish street cleaners, and Jewish street vendors selling fruits and vegetables and cheap knock-offs of expensive watches. In the back streets, there were poor Jewish squatters and even Jewish prostitutes! Nothing prepared them for the move, leaving a posh neighbourhood in the States, surrounded by wealthy, hardworking Jews, only to join the collective fear of an all-out war with the Arabs and check-points at every street corner. And, of course, there was their belief of a Jewish unity," said Asena, grinning with eyebrows raised. "It didn't take long for them to figure out that unity is simple for a minority within a country dominated by others. The majority antagonizes; the minority sticks together. But when that minority becomes the majority, well then the population no longer has an outside group to define itself against. Unity gives way to competition for power."

"So what did your parents do?"

"They stuck it out for a couple of years but eventually bought their house back and returned to the upscale neighbourhood, where Jews weren't prostitutes or bus drivers or toting machineguns in the streets. They tried to return to their life as it'd been before Israel, pretending everything was the same -- that Jews were intellectuals and lived in harmony -- but they knew and I knew that Jews were just the same as everybody else."

"Do you think you belong here -- as an American?"

"Who really belongs anywhere? Or who doesn't belong anywhere? What gives one person more of a right to call somewhere home over another? How many years or generations does someone's family have to be in a place before they're considered part of the landscape? Belonging is a state of mind. Nationality is about maps and nothing else. Maps are fictions of the mind. I hate maps."

In the cool night, Josef walked Asena home through the Russian Compound. They passed through the gates of the Old City and entered the Arab Quarter. A group of children ran by screaming, playing in the narrow filthy streets. They walked past Arabic signs for Halal meats, past the slabs of goat and lamb hanging from hooks, the air heavy with the scent of cumin, garlic, cinnamon, and smoke from the wood fires of sidewalk vendors. A shop keeper beckoning passers-by to look at his newest prayer mats called out to Asena by name. She returned a greeting. And between the drifting smoke, others, with brooding and intelligent faces, peered out from the dusty shadows.

"So you spent time in Cuba," Asena said. "You must speak Spanish then."

"And French, English, Hebrew, and German."

"Promise you'll give me Spanish lessons!" She said, clutching his hand. He didn't let go.

"*Por supuesto*," he blushed.

"So what was Cuba like? How did it smell? How did it feel?"

"It was beautiful, a blur."

She looked at him curiously and was about to speak when a group of Arab men emerged from a doorway and moved toward them. Josef drew her toward the other side of the road, but Asena pulled him back.

"*Salaam alaikum*," they said, greeting her.

"*Alaikum salaam*," she said in return, kissing each man three times. She introduced Josef and then began conversing in Arabic. He stood silently, awkwardly, beside her, before the conversation wound down, and they parted company with the Palestinians.

Josef glanced over his shoulder.

"Don't worry, Josef. They're friends. We play music together."

She directed him down a side street.

"You speak Arabic fluently," he said.

"Not really. To be fluent, you have to understand the subtle nuances of a culture, and there's a lot about Palestinian culture I still don't understand." They arrived at the archway on *Sh'ar Ha'arayot* and *Bab Hutta* and came to a stop outside a steel door. "Would you like to come in?"

"I'd really like to see you again."

"You're a strange one," she said, smiling widely. "You've got doubt on your tongue, confusion in your eyes, but more importantly, you've got love in your heart. You've got some learning to do, but I like you." Asena looked toward their clenched hands then stole a kiss. She gave his hand a tug and pulled him in through the doorway. They stumbled up the darkened staircase into the front room, his hands grasping her face, their soft lips pressed together. For a moment she moved away, lighting candles around the apartment. He took her in his arms, his hand moving along the warm skin of her belly beneath her shirt. Asena's nipples grew stiff as he cupped her soft flesh. His hand slipped down the front of her jeans, and for only a moment he slid between Asena's legs, feeling the moisture gathering there.

Asena's hand moved behind him, grasping and pushing him up against her. She sighed deeply so that he felt he
couldn't desire anyone, or any moment, more. The candles
flickered as she brought him to his knees. He pressed his lips
deep into her and wrapped his hands around, feeling Asena's
silky skin, tasting it. Asena pulled her shirt off, revealing the
slopes of her breasts. He was overwhelmed by the need to
kiss below and began unbuttoning her pants, feeling vertigo
as they slid from her hips. For an instant, Josef imagined she
was an altar, and he was on his knees worshipping her. He
pressed his face into her soft belly and drew down her underwear. Asena stood perfect and naked before him. She ran
her hands through his hair and pulled him even closer, as his
tongue chased down her stomach toward the mound and her
parted legs.

She brought herself down by his side. For a moment, she
pulled away, staring like the moon through the darkness. Then
Asena pulled Josef to the floor. She peeled away his trousers
and slid between him so that he no longer knew where she
ended and he began. And he was suddenly inside her. Asena
kissed his face, lips and neck. Her hand traced lines across his
chest. He took hold of her and placed her hand against his
heart so she could feel the source of his desire. On her back,
she stretched long, and his hands were free to run along her
golden stomach to her round breasts and dark nipples.

In time, she rolled on top, her hips pushing up against
him as he rose to meet her movements. He was alive, bathed
in her scent, her breath. Then Asena began slowing, her body

hot. A beautiful moisture gathered at the base of her spine. Her head fell, and she began shuddering, whispering Josef's name over and over again. He couldn't hold back any longer and cried out *Moon* as he released himself into her.

It was still dark when he stumbled through the corridor of Asena's apartment in search of water. Only part of him was awake. The other was wandering the desert, staggering beneath the midday sun. As he went toward the back of the long narrow apartment, he was startled by something looming in the far corner of the room. There was something so simple about Asena's altar, and he sensed the same love and devotion Hector had for his shrine. He stood silently, absorbing the sense of every object she had placed there so carefully. On the upper right-hand shelf, on a bed of earth, were three cloth paintings representing the Trimurti. The first was that of the Hindu God of destruction and restoration, Shiva, with an erection, lying beneath the foot of Kali, around whose neck was affixed a garland of skulls. Draped from her waist, she wore a girdle of serpents, while blood dripped from her hands and protruding tongue. The painting opposite the dominated Shiva was that of Vishnu, the Preserver, four-armed, carrying a club, a shell, a discus, and a lotus. Centred between Vishnu and Shiva was the image of the creator of the trinity and of the universe, Brahma, the four-headed God that possessed the essence of all gods.

Josef carried his gaze to something familiar. On the upper left-hand shelf was a golden menorah, eight candles plus one, for the eternal light of God. The frozen wax from past years trickled down the sleek arms of time. The shelf directly below housed a bronze and bleeding Jesus on the Cross. From those amber eyes, he sadly gazed off somewhere over Josef's shoulder. His expression was that of agony and triumph over the flesh. Beside Jesus, a photograph of the Chilean poet and musician Victor Jara, smiling with guitar in hand. On the lower right-hand shelf, a postcard from Mecca was propped up against an ancient handwritten copy of the Koran. To the left of Mecca sat a Buddha, his right hand resting on his knee, his fingertips touching the ground to affirm his right to be beneath the Tree of Enlightenment. The Buddha wasn't alone on the shelf. He shared it with a Haitian sculpture, its disc-like face round as the moon, its serene figure possessing both male and female qualities.

So what then lay at the centre of all this? There, in the midst of a pantheon of religious symbols, rested a photograph of Asena with her arms wrapped around her parents and grandparents. Beside it was a mirror just large enough for Josef to see his own reflection, as if including him in her family portrait. He had to smile. In less than 12 hours, Asena had stripped him down and exposed his inner workings as simply as someone opening a clock cabinet to reveal its cogs and springs. He already knew he had found love, but he also recognized it was not always going to be an easy kind of love.

4

O JERUSALEM

The early morning light washed over Asena's altar that now occupied a corner of Josef's apartment – their apartment. For months, Asena and Josef had seen each other with the frequency of an addiction. The intensity of Asena's presence had only heightened his sense of danger and desire for her. She seemed to be a doorway into a different world. She was Cuba, relaxed, humorous, and even a little mysterious. It wasn't a shared history that brought them together, as much as an attraction to the vastly different worlds they had inhabited before their chance meeting on Ben Yehuda Street. Every day they learned more about each other and themselves, though he said nothing of the visions. He escaped into her love, convinced it would conquer everything, including the death camp that continued to haunt him. She introduced him to her Arab friends at the coffee house, where they spent long hours arguing over politics and singing accompanied by a guitar. Asena taught them the English lyrics to Bob Marley songs, which they sang with full hearts and broken accents.

They even danced horas, laughing as they spun in circles. Josef didn't tell her, but getting to know Asena's Arab friends had renewed his faith that peace was something that could be shared between Palestinians and Jews.

Josef and Asena would often meet on campus, sitting in the shade of his favourite tree in the courtyard to share a meal and discuss anything and everything. Asena's appetite for him was like a disease and more than once she dragged him into the caretaker's closet to fool around in the darkness among the damp mops and industrial sinks. Sometimes she would hover above, patiently exploring the crests and ravines of his body, while he remained lost in the movement and scent of their sex. Other times, she worked with hungry efficiency bringing herself to climax before Josef had even settled into a rhythm. At the best of times, Asena was unpredictable in her desires and needs – but she always knew what she wanted, which made her even more attractive to Josef. That's why, when the time came, it had been an easy decision to move in together.

———

Asena was nestled comfortably beside him in bed when the phone rang. Josef pounced on the handset. From the way his father gruffly said Josef's name, he knew there was no immediate crisis and lay back in bed. It was the usual call, complaining about a myriad of things: the price of butter, the faucet that Josef still hadn't fixed, the lack of regularity of Josef's visits, and his bowel movements. "Saul came by yesterday," he added, as if to remind Josef that he hadn't. "Just to check in on us."

"What time is it?"

"Five thirty."

"Papa, why the call when the rest of the world is still sleeping?"

"They've been up in Australia for 9 hours. In Canada, they're just going to bed."

"Is business OK?"

"Maybe, Josef, you can help with rent next month."

"Of course."

Then his father said something unusual: "You know, our work has taken a turn. There have been some new -- disturbing -- revelations."

"Is this the same thing you mentioned when Saul and I came by the shop?"

"*Bien sûr.*"

Josef could hear his mom in the background, "We're delivering the documents this morning. It's going to come out in the papers. Soon."

"It's a powder keg, Josef." His father cleared his throat loudly into the phone, forcing Josef to hold the receiver away from his ear.

"But Papa, are you two OK? I mean, should I be concerned?"

"No," his mother assured him.

"Don't be so sure," his father retorted. "There's going to be a political firestorm."

"You know politics has never been my strength."

His dad had a habit of sighing, as if the weight of the world made it hard to breathe, and just now he did it again. "This isn't just politics, Josef. Lives hang in the balance."

His mom added, "The Nazis have tried to bury all their secrets—"

"--Or burn them. And the troubling part is they aren't the only ones."

Asena stirred. Josef kissed her forehead and mouthed, *I'm sorry!* She rested her head on his chest, looking up with her beautiful tired eyes.

"That's what makes our discovery so disturbing," his mother added.

"Tell me what's going on."

"We can't," his father said.

"Out of an abundance of caution," chimed his mother, sweetly.

"What, you have people tapping your phone or something? Should we be calling the police?"

"Absolutely not," growled his father.

"Listen, I have to go," Josef said, impatiently. And it was true, he had a long drive ahead to the Sinai. "I'll visit soon."

His dad sighed to make his final point. "There's never enough time. Until it's too late."

Asena couldn't take it any longer and stepped out of bed and stomped across the room. Josef took a moment to admire her. Even after all these months, he still took pleasure watching her nakedness. Her mane-like hair. The arch of her back.

Her lean powerful legs that reminded him of a thoroughbred. She looked back. "You wake this cookie before its baked, and you don't get any cookie."

Josef's father sensed he had lost his son's attention and hung up. Soon after, Josef set about the apartment collecting his tools, which he carried out to a dusty Land Rover parked nearby: shovels, brushes, a mesh sifter, water, and enough food for a small army. A sticker on the window read: ARCHAEOLOGISTS ROCK. On the far window, Asena wrote something in the dust, before coming around the other side, where Josef was looking for something among his tools. "*Sukkar*," she said, calling him by the Arabic word for sugar. She held out his chisel but indicated she wanted a kiss for it. Josef obliged. In his hand, he held a baguette. Asena rolled her eyes. "They aren't going to starve to death in one day."

"If you'd survived the camps, you wouldn't see food the same way, either."

The ritual of taking bread to his parents had actually begun when Josef was nineteen and even endured his "lean" years while writing his doctorate. Josef's father had likened it to an eatable peace offering after Josef had moved out of their family flat, while his mother simply considered it a kind gesture. Asena, on the other hand, would probably have her own psycho-analytic spin on it, perhaps that Josef was trying to make up for something his parents had lost at the concentration camp in France.

"My parents may be a pain in the ass," said Josef. "But they're my pain in the ass."

Asena leaned in for a kiss. "And you're mine."

Before driving south to the Sinai, Josef began the short walk to his parents' antique shop. He passed Asena's words written in the dust of the Land Rover window: GIVE PEACE A CHANCE.

"Asena, you're such a bohemian."

She flashed him the peace sign.

It was all quiet, as he walked along the Cardo, a stone's throw from Zion Gate and the Armenian Quarter. In the distance, an old stone building with a sign mounted above a heavy wooden door read *Objets Trouvés Antique Store.* 50 paces ahead, a stranger dressed in religious robes with a hood approached the shop door carrying a weighted basket. The Figure tried the door, but it was locked. He pulled at the un-yielding door once again, paused, then placed the woven basket down, removing a bag of oranges. As he walked away, an orange dropped from the plastic bag. The Figure picked it up and playfully popped it into the air with his elbow before catching it. From inside, Josef's parents appeared in the door-way. His father, dressed in his usual wool vest and French cap, stood stooped with age beside his mother, who gripped a thick envelope. She saw Josef and waved. Josef held up the bread. They both smiled. When the Figure saw the el-derly couple in the doorway, he began to run. Something was wrong. Josef dropped everything and raced toward them. His dad looked down at the discarded bag. He tried to pull his wife back. A flash of light. Heat. A terrible sound. And every-thing was obliterated.

Josef buried his parents side by side on the Mount of Olives. And so it was that they would remain together for eternity in death, as they had most of their lives. Mourners -- neighbours, friends, and those who worked with them -- gathered together among the thousands of sun-washed headstones that climbed the desert hillside. Beyond, the Old City walls crowned ancient Jerusalem. The Golden Dome of the Rock glistened like a jewel in the afternoon light. "They were inseparable," Izer whispered to his wife. "After everything they'd been through, you could only hope they would find some peace." The aging rabbi, who led the service, spoke of his mother having been declared a righteous gentile for her work. Thus she had the honour of being buried on the mount. He pointed toward the smashed Jewish tombstones littering the hill. It was the work of the Jordanians, he reminded those gathered. They had desecrated the dead after taking over Old Jerusalem in 1949. The Jordanians wanted to erase their memory, but it was people like Josef's parents, he said, who had dedicated themselves to preserving the past that would live on in memory.

Asena seemed confused by the rabbi's words, given Josef's parents had been antique dealers. "How had they preserved the past?" she whispered, but Josef was too stricken to respond.

Those gathered placed rocks on his parents' tombs, as a symbol of memory, and slowly dispersed. His parents' oldest friends, Rachel and David, approached Josef. David remained unsteady on his feet. "More than anything," he said, "your parents wanted you to work with them—"

"David, now's not the time."

Josef smiled faintly. "I was never much for the antique business."

David was about to say something, but Rachel gently pulled him away by the arm. When everyone was gone, Saul was left standing alone, a shadow among the tombstones. He approached and embraced Josef, who buried his head into the shoulder of his closest and most trusted friend. Saul, too, appeared undone by the sudden death of Josef's parents.

"Where have you been?" Josef sobbed. "I've been trying to reach you."

"Chained to a desk."

"I need you to find who did this."

"Josef, I won't rest until we get to the bottom of this. Swear to God."

"You know you were the son they wished they'd had."

"Don't say that."

"But it's true."

Asena warily watched Saul make his way out of the walled cemetery. Then, as Josef knelt by his parents' grave, Asena rested a hand on his shoulder and watched over him.

"I didn't do enough to help them," he moaned.

"You were a good son," she whispered. "Never question that."

"Bring them back."

"No one can."

Out front of an old low rise apartment building, Hasidic Jews were clumped together in groups carrying on emphatic conversations. The faint sound of pop music clashed with the muezzins' call to prayer drifting over the city. In the front hall, a sheet hung over a mirror. A table filled with food occupied half the living room. The mood was somber. Josef stood like a ghostly apparition, an aged version of himself. Rachel and David stood nearby, talking. Asena brought Josef a cup of coffee and made her way over to Rachel and David.

"We haven't met," Rachel offered.

"You must be Josef's girlfriend, the psychology professor. We knew Josef's parents when they were high school sweethearts."

"In Auch," David said. "Before the war."

"That's in the south of France, right?"

"Not far from Toulouse."

"I'd like to visit there someday," Asena said. "It would be good for Josef to know where he came from."

"Abraham wouldn't want that," said David.

"But Josef's mother would. She wants some of her ashes scattered there – on French soil -- at the camp. That's where her daughter died. She wants to be with her."

"I didn't know Josef had a sister."

"She died before he was born."

"That's why Abe would never go back," David added. "He always said the world outside Israel couldn't be trusted. They turned their backs on us when we needed them most.

Turning us away by the boatload, forcing us back into the arms of the Nazi death machine—"

"Please, David. We're at Shiva, not one of your debates—"

"I do understand," Asena responded. "And I know this isn't the right time or place to get into this, but we've become too comfortable in our role as victims. We wear it like a badge, excusing every terrible act we do, because we are victims."

"What are you talking about?" David sputtered.

"Really, I don't want to get into this." However, Asena couldn't help but speak her mind. "...It's just that we now hold all the power and land. When I think back to the first millennium, when we were together in Spain, things were different. Hebrew scholars and Moorish intellectuals, and even Christian mystics shared the libraries of Grenada. We shared so much -- words, ideas, philosophies. There was no land to fight over. Our liberation came from peace and understanding. Now look at us, Jewish and Arab genealogies are marred with each other's blood, and there'll be so much more blood if we continue to fight for tiny parcels of land in this ever-shrinking territory. When do you suppose it'll ever end? When the Jews kill all the Arabs? Or when the Arabs kill all the Jews?"

"You know so much yet so little--"

"She's right," said Saul, who was carrying on another conversation nearby. "War in Israel will end when our dominion is complete. Or, if we let people like Asena into power, it'll be the Arabs who *shall inherit the earth*. And we'll be enslaved or more likely slaughtered."

"And all the peace accords in the world couldn't stop that from happening," David added.

"There's no such thing as a war to end all wars," Asena said. "It's a myth."

Josef approached, and the temperature in the room immediately dropped. "Everything OK here?"

"Yes, *Sukkar*." But Asena couldn't resist getting in the last word: "I was just receiving a political education from a hawk in dove's clothing."

———

For a week, they sat Shiva. Guests came to pay their respects, bring food, and to say prayers for his parents. Every day, Josef moved as if through a terrible dream. He couldn't keep track of time and forgot to eat until darkness had fallen. At the strangest moments, he would cry, spontaneously and without warning. He didn't return phone calls or pick up a single newspaper. His sleep was so disturbed that Asena had to rub his back like a child to relieve the tension that wracked his body.

On the eighth day, Josef sat against the wall opposite Asena's altar. He was still grieving and unable to eat, yet somehow he found solace in the chaotic mosaic of the altar. As his gaze shifted from window to window of her pantheon, he became aware of each object and its purpose for being there. Each icon grew in significance by virtue of its relation to the others. The temporal meaning of the menorah weighed against the eternal nature of the Hindu gods. The destruction wrought by Kali, her tongue forever dripping blood, flowed up against Vishnu, the preserver of the Trimurti, the preserver of life-giving and death. The bronze and forlorn-looking Christ symbolized His suffering for humankind. The Buddha, himself, looked on cheerfully toward the Haitian moon figure of eternal fertility and balance. His gaze came to the mirror sitting beside the photograph of Asena with her parents and grandparents. He couldn't help but look at his reflection. But mirrors, like life, could be cruel. When he saw himself, he appeared terribly disfigured. That's when there was a knock at the door.

"What do you have?" Josef demanded, when the police detective appeared at his door. The middle-aged agent wearing an oversized blazer strode through his door, dragging along behind him the stench of booze and bad cologne. He made himself comfortable on the couch, while Josef paced the room.

"You're making me nervous," the detective said and indicated he should sit. Josef hesitated then sat, though his feet continued to tap the floor. Asena hovered nearby and sniffed the cologne in the air like a bloodhound, making funny faces to try to get Josef to relax. The detective jutted his chin arrogantly and placed his briefcase close to his side. He pulled out a file folder of documents. "Well, the bomb wasn't even powerful enough to knock the door off its hinges," he offered. "It was just bad timing -- for them."

"Well, my parents are DEAD. So you're saying it was a homemade bomb? The work of some amateur with a grudge?"

The detective found that amusing and lit a cigarette. "I didn't say that. German plastics. Sprengkörper DM12. A timed detonator. It was a professional package."

"So who are the prime suspects then? I mean who's on the radar?"

"Radar? There's nothing on the radar. It's a blank screen. No finger prints. No known threats made against them."

"It has been two weeks. The trail's growing cold. Hell, it'll be frozen by the time you get off your ass."

The detective shrugged.

"Detective, I'm not asking you to walk on water. I'm asking you to do your goddamn job."

"If it looks so easy, take my badge, and YOU do my goddamn job." The detective smoothed the creases from the sleeve of his jacket. "Well, there's nothing left to discuss."

"Unbelievable. Israeli's finest! Where did they find you? A Cracker Jack box?"

The agent ignored him, put the file back in his briefcase, snapped it shut, and readied to stand. Without another word, he waited for Josef to escort him to the door.

"So what about the envelope?"

"What envelope?"

"My mother was holding a brown envelope when she was killed."

"There was no envelope," the agent assured him, before heading down the corridor.

"I was there! I saw it!" Josef shouted after him.

Later in the evening, Josef and Asena stood on the balcony overlooking the city lights. It was a cool clear night and the stars of the Milky Way formed a perfect arc above them. Josef remained torn, stricken by his parents' death and despondent with the killer's escape. All around, clinging to the ancient city, an unspeakable sadness. Asena sighed before speaking. "So what are you going to do?"

"About what?"

"About your parents."

"You mean, because the police won't do anything?"

"I'm worried you can't let it lie, *Sukkar*."

"My parents gave me life," he finally said, "and everyone who helped them survive gave life to me, too. Do you understand how that weighs on me? I wasn't fortunate enough to have been born outside the Holocaust. I wasn't born in a quiet suburb of New York—"

Asena's eyes flashed wide with fury. "Stop using that against me. I refuse to carry the burden of not suffering through war. I was lucky, yes. But just because we come from different places, doesn't mean you can draw the curtains on me and say *you wouldn't understand how I feel*. It's a cheap shot. I can see what's happening." What she said next hit him like a fist. "When will you stop feeling guilty for not suffering like they did? It wasn't your fault, Josef. You didn't make the camps. The Nazis did."

"I know," he shouted.

Asena took a deep breath and calmed down. She picked up his hand and stroked it, before gently pulling on his nose.

"You should follow your own path." Josef looked up at the night sky. The Morning Star, Lucero, shone brightly. "I owe it to my parents to spend some time digging around. If the police won't get their hands dirty, maybe I need to."

"But you don't know the first thing about this stuff."

"I've watched my parents at work all my life."

"Your parents were antique dealers."

"I carry the war inside me," he finally said.

"But it was never your war to fight. I can't bear to see you tear yourself up over this." She pulled him close. He sunk into her comforting arms. "Promise me you won't quit archaeology."

"I—"

"Promise me, Josef."

"I promise."

5

THE HUNT BEGINS

Josef drove the long desolate road through the Negev Desert to the Sinai. He was going there to dig. He was also hoping to escape the unbearable emptiness left from the loss of his parents. Quickly, though, he returned to Jerusalem but couldn't find the courage to tell Asena why. Then, in the middle of the night, the death camp came back for him. It was the same nauseating dream over and over again that had laid blissfully dormant for months until the bomb, in a horrific flash, had killed his parents and reawakened the visions. He could hear someone else's voice in his head. As he tried to fight it off, his sight itself was hijacked, stolen so that he could not see beyond the terrible dream. The vision became wilder, exploding chaotically, like the frantic strokes of a painter's brush.

A hand grips a dagger and lunges at someone's throat. A flash of light, and he sees his eyes, wide and full of the horror. Blood flows down the knife's edge, an offering to God.

And then the body falls heavily at his feet. Behind him, a young woman whimpers, crying like an animal caught in a trap. The lightning flash of artillery momentarily illuminates the pale young woman with the haunted gaze. The aftershock sends the earth shifting under their feet. From between the barracks, he sees the crematoria chimneys plume, sending smoke signals to God in heaven. Even amid the chaos, hierarchy holds, and officers shout at the guards as they race from the Inner Station and fling armloads of documents onto an enormous bonfire. Others stand around the pyre singing songs of German glory, their voices full of revelry. Bodies swing lifelessly from the gallows. In the near distance, prisoners are lined up and shot, tumbling into a giant pit like a thousand secrets to be buried.

He hides in the shadows. How many stories would he have to tell to explain how he got here? Then he pushes the girl through the open courtyard and into the darkened corridor of the Inner Station that shudders with each successive artillery strike. Officers call out and shove the guards, telling them to hurry up and burn the place to the ground. He drags the girl with the number tattooed on her wrist through a doorway and locks it behind them. For a moment, he stares at the brick wall then stabs it with a chisel. He uses the hammer to loosen the bricks so that he can pull them out like broken teeth. Hand over hand he digs. A bomb explodes, sending a beam crashing from the ceiling. He braces himself, then drives on, digging deeper into the wall. What is he doing? Another bomb explodes sending clots of cement and dust raining down.

There's something on the floor beside him. What is it? He tries to control the vision, steering his way through, studying the detail. He pulls the final brick from the opening in the wall. Another bomb falls, and he can hear the young woman crying. He wants to tell her to shut up, that she is going to get them killed. But she's afraid, and he can't blame her.

His heart pounds so loudly that he imagines the whole world hears and sees what he is doing, kneeling on the floor, digging. He picks up a photograph from the floor. What is he doing with it? Slashing it. Why? Concentrate. Murder.

The sound of incoming artillery. A deafening blast.

Josef bolted up in bed, his chest heaving. Asena stirred and rubbed his back. "Is it that pinched nerve again?" She kissed him and soon drifted off again. He dressed and silently slipped down the stairway to the street below. As the sun rose above the Mount of Olives, flooding light over the Old City, he approached the yellow tape marking the entrance to the antique shop, a loaf of bread in his hand. The heavy wooden door and thick stone walls had suffered only minor damage from the bomb. Among the flowers piled up along the wall, a dozen loaves of bread in various stages of decay. Josef laid the bread among the flowers. He had returned countless times to the scene of the crime, but he had not been able to bring himself to go inside.

For a long while, Josef sobbed, before gathering himself and entering his parent's antique shop. The floor was still wet and littered with the broken remains of old furniture. Shadows gathered in strange forms around the stacks of antiques, and he couldn't help but feel the presence of his father in his wool vest and French cap sitting and reading a newspaper in the dim light, complaining about his sight or the price of imports. The back of the shop appeared unscathed, and Josef could hear the detective's words -- that the bomb hadn't even been powerful enough to blow the door off the shop. The medieval suit of armor holding a battle axe stood guard over the desk with a calculator and a pile of invoices. Josef shuffled through the papers but saw nothing of interest. He turned his attention to the steel door at the very back of the room. He tried the handle. Locked. The faint sound of voices came from within.

Josef turned back to face the room crowded with antiques, then saw what he was looking for. He returned to the door with the medieval axe, raised it, and expertly clobbered the door, knocking the door handle right off. The door swung open. His father's shortwave radio crackled with news: *In Jerusalem, orthodox Jews staged a violent protest against an archaeological dig at the alleged site of the City of David...In other news, Nazi architect Albert Speer, 76, died of natural causes during a trip to London...*

When Josef entered, he heard the tapping of typewriter keys and his mother's voice, hurried footsteps, a filing cabinet being opened and closed, his father clearing his throat. On every wall hung framed newspaper articles announcing the end of the war in Europe, the arrest of a handful of Vichy leaders, and the capture of other notorious war criminals. There was a map of World War II with red pins marking the death camps scattered over Europe. Bookshelves stretched from corner to corner of the room. Each shelf was labelled: History, Political Science, Death Camps, Homeland. There was no fiction on their shelves to be found. His parents didn't believe in fiction and felt it betrayed the gravity of their life's mission. Over-stuffed files documenting the lives and histories of Nazi war criminals still at large covered every imaginable surface. Despite the numerous cases in his parents' hands, their centre, Liberté, had never turned down a dossier if it meant a chance to bring a Nazi to justice. Hunting Nazis was the only role Josef ever clearly understood his parents in, and every shekel they earned selling antiques, they sunk back into their quest for justice. It was the only time they actually seemed satisfied, as they investigated and made phone calls to police chiefs and politicians from Buenos Aires to Sweden to South Africa. Despite being an archaeologist, who dug up the past, Josef had always remained troubled that they lived so thoroughly in the past. On the wall hung a faded photo of a beautiful woman -- his mother -- taken in Auch just outside the main cathedral before the war. He pulled it from the wall and cleaned it with the sleeve of his shirt, before walking over to his father's beloved shortwave radio. He rested a hand on its cool black surface, looking for some kind of comfort. *I am an orphan.*

With no obvious place to start, he leafed through the documents on their desks, looking for clues to the contents of the brown envelope his mother had been carrying the morning she was killed. Eventually, he cleared his father's desk so that he had a work space free of his parents' clutter. Then, from the shelf, he pulled out a stack of books on concentration camps. There were countless volumes, countless images of the horrors that took place in camps with names like Chelmno, Belzec, Treblinka, Sobibór, Buchenwald, Dachau, Auschwitz, Mauthausen, and Sachsenhausen. And, of course, there were all the atrocities that occurred along roadsides, in fields and forests, and in people's homes by the *Order Police* and the *Einsatzgruppen*. These were the stories of rape, looting, torture, and mass murder.

In no time, Josef went to a very dark place, absorbed by the frozen images of emaciated Jews with vacant stares being herded off cattle cars under the watchful eye of the SS. Some of the officers appeared happy and were smiling. Most looked like they took their job of erasing the Jews from Europe very seriously.

To escape the stark apocalyptic images, Josef busied himself emptying the garbage cans. He swept the floor and then organized files and re-shelved books. There were handwritten letters strewn by the typewriter. A half-typed letter sat in the carriage, a note from the grave. It read: EVERY LIFE COUNTS. THAT'S WHY WE'RE DESPERATE NOT TO FORGET, TO LEARN THE WHEREABOUTS OF THOSE RESPONSIBLE FOR THESE CRIMES AGAINST US.

He saw his parents in their final moments, as they stood together in the doorway, the heat flash enveloping them. He was there, powerless to stop the figure with the bag of oranges -- and the bomb concealed in the basket. In the midst of this memory, Josef was overtaken by the feeling that had first found him in Cuba during the rapture of the drums. His head grew light, and he felt a chill over his body as he slid toward a slit-like opening into another time and place. He resisted the vision that threatened to possess him and considered calling Asena for help. Instead, he fled the centre. He walked the narrow streets into the Armenian Quarter and out through the bullet-ridden entrance of Zion Gate, slowing when he sensed he had eluded the vision. He followed the great walls of the Old City all the way around, passing the Wailing Wall. When the Dome of the Rock came into view, he stopped. He needed to be close to the rock where Abraham nearly sacrificed his son Isaac to prove his faith in God. He needed to renew his faith, because it wasn't strong. Perhaps if he could uncover the source of Abraham's commitment, he too could be rid of all his doubts and fears. In time, Josef passed Damascus Gate and the bustling Arab markets and re-entered the ancient city through Jaffa Gate.

It was with considerable hesitation that he returned to the office. Despite his efforts to clean up, the office remained a catastrophe. Every conceivable surface was piled high with folders. He sorted through the mountains of documents, looking for any clues that could be linked to their murder. In the background, the radio played. *Two Palestinians died and dozens seriously injured in clashes today in the West Bank. Three Israeli soldiers remain in hospital. Two bombs packed into hollowed loaves of bread were discovered in a bus travelling on Route 18 in Jerusalem. The bus was immediately cleared and the bomb disarmed.* A dossier sitting next to his satchel caught his attention. He picked the file up but found it empty. Just as he was about to throw the folder among the discarded documents, he discovered a single sheet of paper tucked inside. In his mother's handwriting it merely said, **Übel?**

Josef puzzled with the word and wondered aloud why his mother would have created a file to hold a single word. That wasn't like her. She was a meticulous researcher. He studied the word a while longer, as if its meaning would emerge on its own.

It occurred to him that Übel was a name, though not of a person but a place. He approached the enormous war-time map mounted on the wall. He pushed aside the mounds of documents and scanned the map with pins marking the death camps scattered throughout Europe during the war. Beside every pin was the crucial facts about each camp -- when they were opened, who commanded them, how many died, and when they were finally liberated. For countless minutes, he carefully studied the map but couldn't find Übel. Maybe Übel wasn't a place, after all. He continued to search, country by country, region by region. Poland. Russia. The Ukraine. Romania. Czechoslovakia. Hungary. Yugoslavia. Germany. Austria. Belgium. The Netherlands. Luxembourg. France. Spain. Italy. Greece. Turkey. The war had spread like a terrible plague over the continent and then beyond. He paid close attention to Austria, suddenly sensing a strong association between these names. For several tedious minutes, he examined Austria inch by inch, though found no trace of Übel. He turned his attention back to Poland and Germany.

Then, just as his eyes grew heavy, Übel, almost invisible against the heavy black border with Austria, appeared no more than ten kilometres away from the town of Stenedal. He immediately called several war crimes centres and learned that, indeed, Übel had been a small death camp and the only one, in fact, that had existed inside Germany during the War. He touched Übel, as if a coaxing hand would yield long held secrets.

In the weeks that followed, Josef returned to his parents' centre. Sometimes, he would sit in his father's chair and absorb the room with all his senses -- the smell of dried pages of wartime documents, the sound of the radio crackling with news of a country perpetually on the verge of war, the hue of the yellow lamp cast over the room. When he was done staring, lost in memories of his parents, Josef would dig through the office like a good archaeologist, careful to note what belonged where. Somehow he had missed it, while digging up the meaning of the name Übel, but now it appeared before him -- an entire filing cabinet drawer marked ÜBEL. He opened it but found it empty. There were other drawers labelled: TREBLINKA. BUCHENWALD. DACHAU. He dove into the first drawer, expecting it to be empty too, but it contained a mess of documents stuffed into it. He went to another cabinet and found more documents. Josef returned to the Übel drawer and stared down at it, puzzled. Just then, the bell above the front door chimed.

Moments later, Saul appeared in the inner doorway wearing purple pants and a paisley button-down shirt. He absently picked up a pen from the desk and began tapping it against the lamp.

"I still can't get used to you in civilian clothes," said Josef, looking up from the Übel drawer.

"You look like hell Josef."

"Coming from you that's a compliment. You look like you just woke up from the 60s." Josef turned his attention back to the drawer: "How's it going at the 'factory'?"

"Fine."

"Working at the Fortress, you must put in crazy hours. Don't answer. I don't want you to have to kill me. But those *Metsada* boys are pretty tough."

"Tougher than those pussies over at *Shin Bet*," Saul retorted, before pointing to the drawer. "What are you looking for, my little half-breed?"

"Some of my parents' files are missing."

"Are you sure?"

"Why would anyone take documents on a tiny little camp? It was barely a blip on the map. Is it possible the police -- I don't know -- grabbed them during the investigation?"

"The door was locked, but I guess anything's possible. In your parents' line of work, they had their enemies."

"How did you know the door was locked?"

"I checked, dummy. I may have retired from the military, but I still have your back." Saul looked around the room. "Let's get out of here. This place gives me the creeps."

"Saul, don't say anything to Asena that I've been coming here, ok?"

"Of course."

"She thinks I've been excavating in the desert."

They headed towards Josef's apartment, where Asena was preparing Shabbat dinner. For almost as long as they had been together, Asena and Josef took time out every Friday evening to prepare a meal that they shared with friends, while Saturdays they would walk along the sun bleached Cardo and then outside the Old City gates. They would wander through the Russian compound and into the neighbourhood of Mea Shearim, where the orthodox Jews congregated. Josef and Asena seemed out of place among such devoutly religious Jews, but he could hear his father's voice speak of the necessity of the ultra-religious, who clung to the ancient practices passed down through history. *If all Jews were like Ben Gurion, God rest his soul, there'd be a Jewish state without Jews. They keep the traditions alive.* His father, of course, never mentioned his role in the 'dissolution of the Jews' by marrying Josef's Christian mother.

Given that both Saul and Asena had strong views, Josef had long avoided bringing them together under one roof. Asena, however, never missed an opportunity to ask why he didn't invite Saul over. He always hedged. That morning, though, she pushed for an answer. Josef bluntly acknowledged that Saul would eat her alive. "I want to see that day come," she said taking up the challenge. "Invite him over tonight. It'll make for lively dinner conversation."

"You're playing the alchemist, Moon, and your experiment is going to blow up in your face."

Josef walked with Saul through the Jewish Quarter. Saul reminded him how new the buildings were compared to every other Quarter in Old Jerusalem. "The Arabs had to destroy everything that belonged to us after the war. It wasn't enough to drive us from our birthright, but they had to raze it, too. You see what they did to Hurva? They destroyed the synagogue to punish us for defending ourselves."

"You sound like my father."

"At least I don't sound like you."

"I should say the same thing, Mr. Liebowitz. I've known terrorists with more compassion."

Saul grinned and slapped Josef on the back -- a little too hard.

"I taste blood," said Josef, smacking his lips.

"So you heard Albert Speer finally died."

"Yeah, last month in London. Natural causes."

Saul couldn't resist: "Sure, natural, if you consider Mossad *natural*."

Just then a woman on the street called out, *Thief!* A young man was running away at full tilt, glancing over his shoulder with hunted eyes. He was coming straight at Josef and Saul. As the man passed, Saul stepped into him and in a single movement snatched his wrist, twisted his arm, and had him on the ground with his knee pressed on the thief's neck.

"Give it up," said Saul, just as the woman arrived. The thief dropped the gold necklace.

Josef was genuinely impressed. "What the hell are they teaching you at the factory?"

"How to get shit done."

As they walked down the hallway, Josef talked excitedly about the take-down. They entered his apartment, but before Josef had a chance to explain, Saul caught sight of Asena's altar in the corner of the room and gave a knowing laugh. "Of course."

"She's a pantheist."

"—But I've never forgotten I'm a Jew," said Asena, as she entered the room.

"None of these religions would want to be lumped together."

"Unlike some people, I appreciate that others have histories and have suffered for it too. And their suffering is as much ours as ours is theirs. That's why I have my own altar, because it embraces all possibilities." Asena smiled. "Now that that's out of the way, let's eat."

Around the table, Asena lit the candles and said a Shabbat prayer. Josef poured wine to the brim, in the not-so-secret hope of pacifying the dinner-time conversation. Together they sat, Asena and Saul at opposite ends of the table. Asena served rice spiced with saffron, lemon chicken with vegetables, and couscous topped with pine nuts. Saul ate with quiet concentration. "Mossad isn't feeding you or what?" queried Josef.

Saul shovelled in a few more mouthfuls of food then pointed his fork at Asena. "So Josef here says you're a pretty smart cookie."

"I'm not sure I know what smart means anymore," she demurred.

"Tell Saul about your latest paper on purity."

"Why are you trying to embarrass me?"

"I want to hear. Really."

"Well, it's just a simple idea about how purity is this goal that pervades so many philosophies. You know, Communists want to be purified of the evil of greed; Capitalists seek to be rid of the impurity of controls -- letting greed and ambition elevate and purify them; Christians are looking to be purified of sin and go straight to paradise in heaven; Buddhists seek the purity of existence so they can reach Nirvana and never have to return to earth again. And the Nazis, of course, sought to cleanse everything they considered impure in order to become gods."

"Cool, isn't it?" Josef boasted.

"If you say so," said Saul.

"The trap, though, is when people think they can achieve a permanent state of purity, and it becomes a pathological obsession. Life is always in flux and to try to freeze humanity in an unchanging state is completely impossible and very damaging to the fabric of human consciousness, which is always emerging."

Saul had already stopped listening and was pointing at Josef: "Remember the time when—"

"You love that story."

Asena perked up. "What's the story?"

"Well, when we were kids there were these boys in the playground who wanted to beat on us."

"He loves the story because according to him, he maintained control of the situation by—"

"Let me tell the story. It's my story."

"It's our story."

"So here were these big kids coming to get us. I did some quick calculations. You know, their numbers versus ours. Our size versus theirs—"

"And so to deter their attack, he attacks me."

"A predictable move by a special forces man in his formative years," Asena added.

"From a logistical standpoint, it makes perfect sense—"

"From a standpoint of friendship, it sucks."

"I strung him up on the fence by his underwear. The big kids had a laugh and walked away."

"And I ran home crying -- and to change my underwear."

Saul could see Asena wasn't amused. "Relax. It was funny."

"I may be a leftie, but I can still laugh."

"Sometimes," quipped Josef.

"I'll take Annie Hall over the abuse of friendship any day."

"Americans," said Saul, under his breath. "They take everything so seriously."

"So where did you grow up, Saul?"

"Here. My parents fled in '33. My father and uncles all fought in the Bund back in Germany. They used to hang outside Nazi rallies and wait for the fascists to come out so they could beat the crap out of them. They rebelled against the image of the Jew as the sickly intellectual. But when Hitler came to power, they knew what was coming. They fought among the Irgun in the War of Independence—"

"Really. I read the accounts of the massacre at *Deir Yassin* by the so-called Liberation Fighters. They raped the women and hacked to death the whole village."

"An isolated incident."

"If that's what you want to believe. It's no secret. The freedom fighter ultimately becomes a terrorist."

Josef closed his eyes.

"You're absolutely right," said Saul, calmly. "That's the nature of power."

"Honestly, when do you suppose it'll ever end? When the Jews kill all the Arabs? Or when the Arabs kill all the Jews?"

"I don't want to lecture you. You're a big girl now—"

"I don't mind you lecturing me. But don't patronize me."

"Josef," he laughed. "She's got bigger balls than you!"

"Never measure someone by the size of their balls," said Asena. "Balls are notoriously easy to break."

Saul pointed his fork at Asena and smiled. "All kidding aside, you just have to open your eyes to see the truth. After '67, we didn't think the Arabs would attack again. We were convinced they'd learned their lesson. *We were too strong to be defeated*. We thought the Arabs knew this, but they went ahead and attacked in '73. And I was there, on the front. Those were grim days, Asena, and I wouldn't wish them on my worst enemies. We pushed back hard, our jets pounding the crap out of Egyptian positions along the Suez. The goddamn Arabs retreated, leaving their dead behind like garbage after a picnic. We never did that. You understand? Every life of ours was sacred. We risked lives just to retrieve our dead."

"Saul has seen things that would make us all cynical," Josef interjected. "You know, I thought he'd been killed. But not only did he come out unscathed, he was decorated for bravery after parachuting in behind enemy lines in the Golan Heights and single-handedly destroying three gunners' nests that had killed a dozen Israelis."

"That's why we can never let our guard down," continued Saul. "Not because we're warmongers; not because we enjoy killing people. We're lucky to have survived to see another Yom Kippur, but we can't let it happen again. The Arabs can't be our friends; they hate us."

"Well, I don't agree. Maybe if you'd watched your home bulldozed, your entire family wiped out by the Israeli military, you'd understand their resentment. If you give people nothing then they have nothing to lose by fighting. Raise their economic standard, and people won't support violence that endangers their way of life."

"You heard about the Palestinian boy in the market today? They found a bomb in his backpack. What kind of twisted society uses an eight-year-old boy for a political cause he can't even comprehend? And let's be clear here, Iraq and Iran have been at war for over a year now. They aren't fighting Christian or Jewish infidels. No, it's Muslim killing Muslim. You see what I'm getting at? These aren't peaceful people. They need their enemies; they need blood to feed their civilization."

Asena's spine stiffened. "It must be nice to paint entire cultures with a single brush stroke. The problem with Israel is that it never should've become a Jewish state. It should've remained open to all persecuted people."

"Perhaps. But if we show we're weak, they'll end up using us like a doormat, and I'd rather die than be someone's doormat. You know, the intellectual lefties are great at talking, raising their fists at demonstrations and chanting some shit about peace at all costs. But they can't compete with the commitment of a dictator or some religious nut. The system has always rewarded the most ruthless, the most brutal. You and Josef may have been able to avoid combat, but I wasn't." Saul leaned back in his chair and drained his glass of wine. "Believe me when I say, you wouldn't want to know the things I know."

Asena turned to Josef accusingly. "Josef, you haven't said a word."

He stood and began clearing the plates. "For once, I want a conversation that isn't an argument. That would be nice."

"That's why he likes to dig for dead things," Saul quipped. "The dead don't talk back."

"That's what you think."

"Politics is an Israeli disease," offered Asena. "We can't live without it. We are addicted to the drama."

"So, Josef, how goes the battle?" asked Saul.

"Are you shit disturbing again?"

"What battle?" Asena asked.

"The battle hunting Nazis."

"I'm not hunting Nazis." Josef returned to the dining room with a bowl of fruit and a plate of sweets. "I'm just doing some research. Who wants coffee?"

"Josef thinks there's a connection between his parents' death and their Nazi hunting escapades."

Seeing Asena's confusion, Saul grinned. "Didn't Josef tell you? He's doing work at his parents' Nazi hunting centre. I'll have a coffee."

"I thought they were antique dealers?"

"They were," said Josef. "I'll get you that coffee."

"And they hunted Nazis."

"Only in their spare time," Josef called back.

"Why didn't you tell me?"

Saul grabbed an orange from the bowl and began peeling it. He sat back and watched with mild amusement, as the conversation travelled back and forth across the room like a game of ping-pong.

"Why are you researching the Holocaust? You're an archaeologist."

"They killed my parents."

"The Nazis?"

"Someone."

"You know, fighting only for the Jews solves nothing," she said. "Justice has to be for everyone. Otherwise, there's no justice at all."

"Tell that to the terrorist who murdered my parents."

"Tell that to the Palestinians killed by Israeli guns," Asena fired back. "Tell that, Josef, to our Palestinian friends. Tell them to their faces that they have less of a right to life and liberty than you."

"Don't moralize now."

"Someone has to."

Saul was deeply amused: "Josef, you have Palestinian friends!? That's hilarious! Well, your Arab friends should be grateful they don't live in Guatemala right now. Talk about a hell hole."

This meant something to Josef, and he stopped dead in his tracks. "But, Saul, you told my parents you didn't know anything about Guatemala. Or is your 'furniture' company now exporting to Central America?"

"You just have to turn on the news, dummy, to see what's going on. People are being murdered every day. That's not a secret." Then he added, "And no, we aren't exporting furniture to Guatemala. We are importing wood from there."

6

ELLEGUA – AT THE
CROSS-ROADS

New Year's Eve celebrations ringing in 1982 were already underway in the Christian Quarter, when Josef heard Hector's voice call from the past like the echo of the muezzin's invocations to prayer: *The visions were born to you on the first of the year. I'd guess you've only seen the tip of the iceberg. You can try to run away, Josef, but I wouldn't suggest it. If you confront the visions, you might find something you weren't intending to uncover. But the sea is vast, and if you wade in too far, you risk drowning.*

During his time in Cuba back in 1979, Josef had done everything in his power to be rid of the visions. He had even undergone an initiation into Palo, a religion with its roots deep in Africa. The shed behind Hector's house in Loma Pequeña housed cauldrons containing human bones. "You see, the body of the Dead lies in the cemetery, but the soul lives in the trees. We invoke the aid of the dead for matters on earth," Hector had explained. That's when he suggested Josef undergo the initiation. "The Dead are very powerful and can protect you from harm. You may think when you dream, you dream alone. But in Cuba, this isn't so. Here, we dream together. We dream together of colour and sound, honouring God, the *orishas*, and the Dead -- the makers of life. Problems aren't solved alone. They're resolved together."

Josef had resisted Hector's call, but his desire to be rid of the ominous visions was more powerful. A few days later, Josef helped Hector prepare for the initiation. From the side of the shed, Hector had brought out a ladder and propped it against a wall, directing Josef to hold it while he climbed up to fetch something from a storage space in the rafters. Hector reached for a giant cauldron. It was only as he brought it out into the light and glimpsed its contents that he lost his balance and nearly let go of the clay vessel.

"What is it?"

"A scorpion nest." He handed the cauldron down, warning Josef to be careful.

"But it's a blessing to be stung by a scorpion."

"These are babies," he had said, grimly. "Far more poisonous than their parents."

Hector cleaned the cauldron of the scorpions but was careful not to kill them. As he explained, scorpions weren't only a symbol of death but transformation and resurrection and so must be honoured in life. He filled the cauldron with water and then retrieved several brown paper bags from the house. From each bag, Hector removed handfuls of leaves. "There are twenty-one herbs, a balance of the sweet with the bitter, the medicinal with the religious," Hector had explained. "The preparation of herbs brings out their *aché* -- their divine power -- and it's your job to crush them together."

Josef rubbed and squeezed the herbs together, as if washing clothes. In time, he became lost in the exercise, no longer aware of Hector, who walked this way and that, disappearing, reappearing, and disappearing again. The earthy aroma of the herbs seemed to be an elixir. He scrubbed the leaves for perhaps an hour until finally, like a sacred sign, the water turned absolutely black. Hector peered over Josef's shoulder and nodded, satisfied.

Long before dawn, Josef had been awoken. Hector, Cecilia, and even Laicy moved purposefully between the house and the shed. Josef leaned against the kitchen counter, sleepily downing a super-charged espresso that Laicy handed him. Then Hector prompted him to go to the bathroom to undress. He stepped into the room illuminated by a single candle and began to take off his clothes. Layer after layer were peeled away.

The man dressed in white, whom he'd witnessed fall under the spell of the *orishas* at the party, walked into the bathroom with a steaming pail of *omiero*, the sacred bath of herbs. He didn't seem at all surprised to see Josef. As he directed him into the shower, Josef reminded him that they had seen each other at the party. "Yemayá was very strong when she came down," he had explained, "and I don't remember a thing."

But I do, Josef had thought, puzzled by the nature of his own visions of the prisoner inside the German death camp.

The man gently poured cups of warm herbal water over Josef's head then scrubbed his scalp, cleansing and purifying it with the twenty-one herbs. In time, Josef had been left to wash the rest of his body, which he did with the mindfulness of a monk. When he was finally ready, he dressed in a white linen shirt and pants and stepped from the bathroom. The man secured a blindfold and directed him outside by the arm. He stumbled around in the darkness like a blind man, sensing he had become separated from the world, without an identity or address, perhaps even outside of time itself. Josef was taken inside the shed in the backyard.

On his knees in the darkness, there was no fear. Worries about the emergence of the visions and the truth still buried beneath so many layers of sediment did not plague him here. Hector gripped his arm firmly and nicked him with a razor. Josef flinched. Hector squeezed the wound, then nicked him again at various points of the body, placing cotton on the wounds to absorb the tiny offerings of blood.

A hand reached out and prompted him to drink *chamba*, a potent concoction of *aguardiente*, hot peppers, garlic, and ginger -- the same elements found in the Palo altar. His blood was being collected to give to the Dead, Laicy had whispered, while he symbolically consumed the altar by drinking *chamba*. Josef was being unified with the Dead.

After a moment or two, the blindfold was removed and shadow gave way to the candlelight of the Palo lair with its cauldrons of bones, iron spikes, and feathers. The room seemed as old and primitive as any pre-historic dwelling. Josef took a certain comfort kneeling in the dirt, satisfying a primordial instinct to stay close to the damp earth. Like any newborn, Hector had said, he needed a name. Josef's birth name was put on paper, wrapped in corn leaf, and braided with a piece of hair taken from his head. With his old name bundled and being held over him, Hector commanded him to say his name.

He responded in a low voice, "Josef Levi."

"It used to be," Hector said. "What's your name?"

Again and again, Hector had commanded Josef to repeat his name until finally he bellowed his name. "Josef Levi!"

Hector informed Josef that he would receive a new name that would remain a secret to protect him from spells cast on his old name. As the dull light of dawn splintered through the cracks in the wooden shed, Hector placed a chicken in Josef's hand and told him to present it to the altar as his offering. Hector, Laicy, and Cecilia sang, filling the old shed with a love and devotion that could almost be touched. Then Hector stepped before the altar holding the chicken and with a swift movement of the blade cut the chicken's throat, letting the blood flow down the knife's edge onto the palero's cauldrons. When the blood offering was complete, Josef was brought from the shadow of the altar and led to the front of the house. They paused for a moment by the door before Cecilia swung it open. The morning sun rose above the tree where he'd first met Hector's father-in-law all those months before. Josef was presented to the sun as a newborn child.

———

Josef and Asena quietly celebrated his birthday with a few of their friends in the back room of a small Arab café in the Old Quarter. They took turns smoking from a *hookah* and sang and played guitar. Josef was in a somber mood, this being his first birthday without his parents. And, he lamented, there were still so many other firsts he would experience without them. From his place on the couch, he studied Asena with a quiet intensity. In these surroundings, Asena seemed most at home. He had never met anyone like her who revered musical instruments with such intensity. They were magical to her, the sounds they produced divine in origin, as if each note was a revelation, a definitive answer to all imaginable questions.

It was late when they stumbled home, exhausted. Then, as Josef settled into bed, the ground heaved with an artillery bombardment. He struggled to push the vision away, begging for it to leave him be. *What do you want from me?* But he was already deep inside the dream and couldn't force the words out.

The rattle of machine gun fire splits the air. He drags the young prisoner down the corridor and out of the Inner Station. Officers shout at the guards as they race from the barracks and fling armloads of documents onto an enormous bonfire. Even as it's all ending, they still stiffen at attention and salute him. He looks at the cuffs of his jacket, revealing the insignia of the German Wehrmacht. *He is an officer, not a prisoner in the camp.* The ground shudders. Artillery shells land beyond the gates. There is no escaping the acrid fumes churned out from the chimneys of the crematoria or the human ash that falls like snow. There is frantic activity in the courtyard, as the camp is dismantled, a slate being wiped clean. In the near distance, emaciated bodies swing from the gallows like marionettes dancing in the flickering fire light. Along the perimeter, motionless prisoners are tangled in the barbed wire. A half-naked figure peers out from behind a building then makes a suicidal dash for the fence. The prisoner is immediately cut down by machine guns from the watchtower. In his final moments, he twists and struggles in the barbed wire, a fish caught in the fisherman's net.

Skeletons with shovels dig a large trench, while prisoners standing at the lip of another grave are lined up and shot by drunk soldiers. The condemned that don't fall into the grave are picked up by other prisoners and dumped into the sea of corpses. Pleading voices can still be heard calling from the grave. The soldiers take turns drinking from a bottle, while they reload. Some fire blindly into the pit in an attempt to silence the undead. A short distance away, a line of prisoners stretch long, awaiting entrance into an underground tunnel. An officer shouts at them to undress quickly and in an orderly fashion to avoid punishment. The world is incomprehensible. The women help the children undress, whispering for them not to cry. From all corners, the shadows hide the faces but can't conceal the groans, which are intermittently drowned out by the sound of machine guns and exploding artillery.

He pulls the young prisoner with the tattoo on her wrist through the courtyard past the guards and officers standing around the bonfire fuelled by their deeds. Some of the officers weep and sing old German folksongs, as if standing around a campfire in their youth. He does not even acknowledge the guards at the gate, as they salute. He drags her out of the camp and across an open field. The pale creature doesn't resist; perhaps she has no strength left. In his other hand, he clutches his diaries. As the rising sun edges above the distant hills, it is suddenly eclipsed by the allied bombers, which fill the sky like deathly crows.

When the bombers are overhead, they drop their devilish weapons. The young prisoner cries when she sees the bombs falling to earth in a giant chain. All around, the fields light up. The ground is pulled from beneath them, but they keep moving, crawling through the fire and debris. But this is not like the Somme or any other battle from the last war. There is no barbed wire or gunners waiting in nests on the other side, but the bombers rule the skies, and they are winning. A furnace blast catapults the pale woman from his clenched hand, but he finds her, still alive and breathing. He hoists her up and continues on through the smoke until a pointed church steeple can be seen in the distance. The village is a sanctuary, untouched by the madness. He tugs her hand and races on toward his fate. As he looks up at the night sky, Asena hovers above him.

"Wake up, *Sukkar*. Wake up."

All the sorrow bottled up sprung free. Asena kissed Josef's tears. Something in her gaze made him feel she already knew what happened in Loma Pequeña and the Sinai Desert. "It's like having a shadow follow me wherever I go," he finally said. "I don't want any part of any war. Do you understand? But they found me."

"Who found you?"

Hector had warned that he'd lose his mind if he didn't confront the visions. Now his prophecy was coming true. If Asena learned that he was having visions of a German officer inside a death camp, she'd dismiss him as an utter lunatic.

"I went to the Sinai to dig alone," he confessed but couldn't bring himself to say more.

"Josef, you need to tell me what's going on. I know you're going through a lot, but you have to let me in."

He closed his eyes and recounted the days and nights spent working at a site in the Sinai hills cradled between two ridges, where he would watch the stars emerge only to vanish below the horizon as they had for the desert nomads ten thousand years ago; and before that for the Homo Sapiens, Erectus, Habilis, Australopithecus Africanus, and, finally, Afarensis.

"But who found you when you were weak?"

"I excavated through layers of earth," he explained. "And in the shadow of a giant cave I sifted through the debris, sometimes finding the remains of the past. One of the first things I found was a sickle and the skeleton of a dog, probably domesticated, from an Amorite encampment, during the time of Abraham. Imagine that. Imagine my sense of privilege finding these treasures. Beneath this upper layer were the remnants from the Bronze age -- weapons, pieces of glass and fragments of clay tablets -- possibly brought by traders from Sumer on their way to Egypt five thousand years ago.

"I found flint tools, blades and scrapers, from the lower and upper Palaeolithic era. I touched these objects, like the pieces of chipped pottery, marvelling at the hands that shaped them thousands of years before. I had a theory about that cave," he told her. "It was a lair for everyone who'd ever passed through the Sinai. From what I'd found, I was quickly assembling evidence of multiple occupations back to the beginning of time."

"The cave of genealogy," Asena whispered.

In the darkness, he told her he felt an eternal sadness for the things he'd never find. The genealogy died where he stopped digging. More layers needed to be unearthed. The endless desert was a constant reminder that the infinite potential of knowledge would forever remain buried. "In the Sinai," he continued, "I came to dread everything unknowable. When night grew around my tent, I'd stay inside. I did anything to keep my mind occupied -- reading, writing, studying -- but I knew it was there, outside the tent, surrounding me. I was afraid something terrible was going to happen."

"I don't want to get all existential on you, but maybe what you were afraid of out there was really fear of what was inside the tent -- you."

"I felt like I was the only living thing left. The endless desert mocked my fears. What I saw was nothingness. It was nothing. I was nothing. Life seemed futile, and I really thought I was going to die from the uncertainty."

"My love, even if we are alone, it doesn't mean the universe is empty and hopeless," Asena declared. "I don't see it as nothingness; I see it as everythingness."

"I'm lost, Asena."

"You're the Jew of scripture -- the Wandering Jew. Without a territory, we carried the nation in our hearts. History became everything, memory the only way to sustain a collective identity. We didn't have a country or a flag, so for millennia our history became our home, our only defendable territory. Before Israel, some travelled in search of something that'd make them whole again, because no matter where they were they didn't feel they truly belonged. But now we're a wandering people with a nation, so some continue to search -- sometimes spiritually, sometimes geographically. There're so many like us, searching the world looking for a spiritual centre to the universe. I think you already know it's not Jerusalem, otherwise you'd never have gone to Cuba. An inner spirit sent you away to learn about a truth that grows wider than any one religion or nation can contain."

Josef found something amusing and managed a smile.

"What is it?"

"I feel like I'm at Yashiva."

"A little Talmud is good for the soul."

For a time, a silence gathered around their bed before Josef described how a stranger appeared one day on the desert horizon. A flock of birds flew above him, and even with the blowing wind, the dust didn't rise behind his footsteps. Josef was convinced he was a mirage and turned to look at the clouds. But when he looked back at the horizon, the visitor had already arrived at the foot of the hill. He continued walking toward him. From the hunch in his back and the way he shuffled his feet, Josef had figured he was old. But what was he doing in the desert all alone? From the robes he was wearing, Josef guessed he was a holy man on a pilgrimage, maybe from Egypt. The ancient wanderer came to a stop just in front of Josef, his face appearing as old as the desert itself.

"He spoke quickly in an ancient Hebrew dialect that didn't make any sense to me," explained Josef. "I gestured I didn't understand. He smiled and rattled on. He pointed toward the clouds then toward the mouth of the cave. There was something forgiving in his eyes, so I remained patient. He pointed again at the cave. I nodded, as if to say I wouldn't go in. He grinned, exposing his toothless gums that appeared moist for a man who'd been walking in the open desert. I offered him water. He smiled gratefully, clasping his hands together to form a cup. I poured water in his hand, which he drank from. I only looked away for a moment, and he was gone. There weren't even any tracks leading up or down the hill. I was confused and turned to face the cave, its dark hollow mouth threatening to swallow anyone who entered. A dozen birds rested above the entrance."

Asena looked at him ever so strangely.

"I know. It sounds crazy." Josef shook his head though couldn't stop himself from speaking. "In all those months at the site, I'd never considered entering the cave. But I was worried the old man was lost, so I went in. Each footstep took me deeper until I was plunged into total darkness. After stumbling around awhile, I gave up searching. Then, just as I was about leave, I was overcome by a strange presence. '*Shalom,*' said a voice. It was the old man. '*Shalom,*' I replied. But he was nowhere to be found. As I backed out through the darkness, something lurking in the shadows startled me. Figures emerged from everywhere, reaching out and touching me. I turned and ran as fast as I could toward the light."

"Then what happened?"

"Nothing. I never went back."

In the morning, Asena moved around the kitchen, a piece of toast in her mouth, one arm in her coat. Josef barely noticed her, lost in photographs from the Holocaust. *The gas chambers of Treblinka. The starving masses at Dachau. The cold stare of an SS officer looking down at a kneeling prisoner.* He was sickened by the revelation that the visions plaguing him were not that of a prisoner but a German officer working in a death camp. When Asena caught sight of what he was reading, her smile faded. "I don't think looking at death all the time is good for you. It'll give you nightmares." She managed to get her other arm through the coat and kissed him, but her lips landed somewhere on his chin. "Happy birthday. Your birthday present is coming!"

The room where his parents had worked for so many years was like a time capsule from 1955. It had remained virtually unchanged since Josef's childhood. The desks. The typewriter. The shelves. The war map on the wall. Josef sat behind his father's desk calling various centres around Israel, Europe, and North America. It was noon when he received a call back from a Nazi hunting centre concerning his request for information on Übel. "Mr. Levi," the voice said, "why would you care about such a small camp?"

"Every life counts."

"There're far bigger fish to fry."

"My parents were hunters—"

"I know who they were. They didn't capture a single war criminal in thirty years."

"Well, there was Kurt Strasser."

"But he swallowed cyanide before the Argentinians cuffed him."

"At least they never gave up," Josef barked, before hanging up.

For weeks, Josef pursued information, but it quickly became apparent why the Übel filing cabinet had been empty. It hadn't been the work of thieves but the work of the Nazis, he concluded. Next to nothing had been preserved from this extermination camp -- no eye-witness accounts, no survivors, no records. The lack of information seemed peculiar for a regime that prided itself on documenting every last order of copper piping and every last massacre.

Josef read about the companies that benefited from the Nazi machine during the war, companies that still existed today. *Degussa* manufactured Zyklon B for the gas showers at Auschwitz. *IG Farbenindustrie* and *Siemens*, among so many others, benefited from the slave labour from the camps. "Everyone is in everyone else's bed," said Saul, when Josef called him in disgust. "America was built on slave labour, and Europe made its fortunes through slavery and the plunder of South America's gold and silver. It may not be right, Josef, but that's how it is."

Josef contacted Beate and Serge Klarsfeld in Paris, who were old friends of his parents. He liked their physical approach to the hunt, confronting the Nazis head on. In 1979, they successfully pressed for the trial of three high ranking SS men guilty of war crimes in France. Until the Klarsfelds had found them, Kurt Lischka, the infamous Gestapo chief, and the others had been living in West Germany as free men. There were thousands more like them who remained at large, hidden in plain sight. Beate encouraged Josef to continue hunting but said in all her years she had never found a scrap of information on Übel or the Nazis who ran the camp. She, too, had to ask why he was so focused on such a small camp.

"Because I think it's linked to my parents' murder," he confessed. "They found something that maybe someone didn't want them to find."

Josef took his task of researching Übel seriously, obsessed with uncovering its hermetically sealed mysteries. Drawing on the patience acquired from years of archaeological excavation, he delved beneath the layers of Holocaust history told by the many voices -- witnesses and executioners, bureaucrats and sadists. He penetrated as deeply into history as the surviving records allowed. The hunt for information on Übel had become a hunt for all things that remained unknown. He searched through the genealogy of horror and the Nazi capacity for cruelty and violence, seeking justice for all those who perished along the road of history. And in the multitude of photographs that documented the Holocaust, he saw his parents among the countless faces. In every child, he saw his sister. He searched for glimmers of a man clenching a bloody dagger but found none.

For months now, his nights had been filled with sleeplessness. Fatalistically, he would lie awake, waiting for the visions, sensing a presence just beyond the darkness of the bed. When they struck, his body trembled, as he drowned in memories that weren't his own. It was all very real, and each time they returned the details became more vivid. What were the origins of the visions and where were they leading him? If Hector had known, he never said. The more he asked the question, the further he seemed from a plausible answer. The only thing certain was that the Holocaust beckoned him in both his visions and his work at the centre so that he could no longer separate himself from it.

It was well past midnight when he dialed the number for a war crimes centre in Tel Aviv. It was run from the home of a Holocaust survivor named Arty Belkin. Josef had been in contact with him several times, and he had told Josef to call anytime, day or night. So he was. When Arty answered, he seemed annoyed. "Do you have any idea what time it is, Josef? Let me give you a clue. It's 2 am."

"Sorry for waking you."

"You didn't wake me."

Josef rested his head in his hand and stared at a photograph of a stony-eyed guard at Treblinka. "I can't sleep," Josef confessed. "The hunt."

"I know. It gets under the skin."

"I'm desperate for information on Übel."

"You might want to reconsider."

"What do you mean?"

"I went there. To Übel."

Josef stood. "You never told me that."

"Five years ago."

"So what did you find?"

"It's a ruin," he said. "Nothing's there."

"There's got to be something."

"I assure you, there's nothing left. Unless you consider field mice something."

———

The bell above the front door to the antique shop chimed. Josef was startled awake at his father's desk. Moments later, Saul appeared in the inner doorway, the morning light washing over the furniture stacked behind him. Saul gave Josef a bear hug that resembled a strangle hold. He sniffed. "You stink. Has Asena already kicked you out? It doesn't take long, does it. Life was definitely easier when we lived in caves and didn't speak."

"Simpler. Not easier," Then Josef remembered his annoyance at Saul's most recent disappearing act. "Where have you been? I've been trying to call you for weeks."

"Away on business." Something on the desk caught Saul's attention. It was a copy of the Tibetan Book of the Dead -- the Bardo Thödol -- that Josef had taken out of the library. Saul picked it up and absently thumped into against his palm. "What the hell, Josef? I know you're only a half-Yid but Christ, Buddhism? Do you believe this reincarnation shit?"

"I don't know."

"I'll tell you what I believe. I believe in life and death. That's it."

"The Tibetans believe that when a person dies, the dead may not realize it has separated from the body. If the soul is enlightened – like yours clearly is -- then it knows the difference between reality and illusion and will end the cycle of re-birth. But most seek a new body."

"Well, that's pretty fucking stupid. Anyway, I didn't come here to talk about this bullshit. Are you still looking for information on Übel?"

"Everyone thinks I'm wasting my time."

"You need to be a lion, Josef."

"Like you, Liebowitz."

"Yeah," he said, smiling. "Now shut up and listen. The camp opened in late '42 and accounts for about 90,000 deaths. Only one prisoner was known to have escaped."

"One?"

"She's never been found. Now I contacted a friend at the Wiesenthal Centre, and she uncovered a name connected to Übel. Erich Hauptmann. There's no record of his death, so he either died in the final battle, changed his name, or fled the country. It's difficult to say which. His wife died a few years back. That's not all. Hauptmann was known to have been a Nazi from as early as 1922." Saul pulled out a photograph of a group of men standing in uniform on the steps of a beer hall. He pointed to a man buried in the middle. "It was taken in Munich. My father and uncles probably kicked his ass at one time," he said, proudly. "Anyway, the picture was taken a few days before the uprising in '23. Hauptmann arrived at Übel in '43. I wish I had more, but that's all I got so far. It's spooky. Übel is a world of its own. No one knows what happened inside, at least no one who's writing the history books. You've got a real story here, Josef, so don't give up."

Josef hugged him. "I can't thank you enough."

"Don't tell anybody who gave you this information," he said, prying Josef off. "You do and I'll have to fucking kill you." He looked around the room, haunted. "Anything more about your parents?"

"They would be glad you're so concerned."

"They treated me like a son."

"From day one, you were a brother to me. As for the investigation, I stopped counting the months. The police still haven't turned up shit. Only that the bomb was small but sophisticated. No motive. Nothing. He's still out there like those goddamn war criminals."

"It hasn't been easy for any of us."

"What bothers me is that I saw him."

"I know."

"I go over it again and again 'til it makes me crazy. Why did they need to deliver that package so early?"

"Package? The police report doesn't mention a package."

"My parents were delivering documents. To a newspaper I think."

"Keep this under your hat for now. Let me look into it."

"If they had just slept in, I wouldn't be an orphan."

"We'll get you answers."

With Saul's departure, Josef fell back in his chair. *Overnight a Haifa bus bound for Akko was hijacked by four Palestinians armed with knives and grenades,* said the voice on the radio. *The all night stand-off ended with the safe release of all passengers and the death of all four terrorists. Details are still emerging from the city of Hama of a massacre by Syrian troops of their own people in February. The government of Hafez al-Assad had ordered the full assault on the city after the Muslim Brotherhood declared the city's liberation. In other news, reports from a remote region in Guatemala continue to trickle out of the massacre of thousands of Mayan Indians by government forces as part of a campaign to destroy the Communist rebel movement there. Military attacks on Mayan refugees have extended over the border into Mexico, where victims have been allegedly tortured, raped, and hacked to death.* Josef could no longer stand it and turned off the radio.

He went home to sleep for a few hours and when he awoke, he found that a package wrapped in worn brown paper had arrived from Cuba. Josef sat before Asena's altar with the box in his lap. He carefully shook the package. It seemed too heavy to be a spirit of the dead and too light to be rum. His fingers hovered over the letter affixed to the box. Then he tore open the envelope.

May 1, 1982

Querrida Josef,

I hope this letter finds you well. People around Loma Pequeña still ask about you. You really should come visit your padrinos, if not to pay your respects to the orishas and the Dead, then at least so we can embrace once again and talk freely.

Laicy asks about you often and expresses her deepest gratitude for involving her in your work. To my great pride, she was crowned with the orisha Ochún.

Things have not changed much in Cuba. I know you like the work Fidel did universalizing schools and health care, but there are no books except propaganda. And from the safety of this sealed letter, if Cuba's system is so wonderful, why does he have to keep us here by force. Shouldn't people want to flock here?

But Josef, I didn't write you to complain that Cuba is a virtual prison. I have something very serious to write to you about. I only hope this letter gets to you in time.

The orishas have told me bad things are happening to you. It's important you listen to your dreams. You must have learned by now that your parents' legacy to you was not their memories of the past. Those visions are yours, a residue from another time. It is not for you to understand how they found you. The Dead have their ways. The important thing is what these visions will reveal. You'll need to be a warrior and a trickster like the orisha Ellegua.

I had a dream a few nights ago, and that's why I'm writing. But it wasn't my dream; it was yours. Something big is approaching. In my dream, I was walking along the beach and heard the ocean roar. Yemayá -- the orisha of the seas -- was very upset with you. You'd forgotten her. But she understood and gave her blessing for you to cross the ocean, which is a good thing. She's telling you it's time to go.

So please listen to me. The time for contemplating is over. You have to act if you're going to survive, and I want you to flourish more than anything else in this world. I would like so much to see you again, just to glimpse that smiling face of yours that has brought me and my family so much happiness.

I hope to God you receive this letter. Please go, but go carefully. Aché para tí.

Con cariño,
Hector

Josef read the letter over again, listening to Hector's deep voice that spoke so clearly. He imagined his finger pensively drawing down the length of his nose, a cigarette held between his lips. With eager hands, he opened the package and immediately placed the gift among the objects of veneration in Asena's altar. Ellegua, the mischievous deity, stood at the crossroads of destiny, the two faces painted on opposite ends of the coconut gazing toward the future and the past. Josef sensed he had arrived at the place Hector once spoke of -- a place of in betweenness, no longer who he was and not yet who he'd become. The events of the past -- the death of his parents, the birth of visions in Cuba, the cave in Sinai, and his work at Liberté hunting for clues to his parents' killer -- no longer seemed unrelated but rather connected in the most startling way.

Just then Josef became aware of Asena's presence standing in the doorway. "You didn't come home last night," she said, accusingly. "Where were you?"

"Alone."

"I booked an appointment for you tonight."

"What kind of appointment?"

"It's your birthday present."

"Better late than never."

She crossed the room and sat with him among the pillows on the floor. That's when she started talking about the Buddha. "Have you ever heard the story of the Buddha and the lotus?"

He shook his head.

"Well, the Buddha raised a lotus in front of his disciples. Everyone struggled to understand the significance -- except for one -- Mahakasyapa, who smiled. The Buddha saw everyone else suffering with the meaning of the gesture. But he knew Mahakasyapa had directly experienced the lotus and the universe contained within it. He'd found enlightenment, which lay beyond the world of words or form. The others weren't prepared for the simple truth. Mahakasyapa was."

"Why are you telling me this?"

"Because you can hear the truth a thousand times, but it's meaningless until you're ready for it. So maybe what you experienced in the cave is like a kung-an, a key to your awakening. But if you don't answer the call, you can take comfort in Freud's words: sometimes a cigar is just a cigar. Maybe the cave is just a cave." She allowed a silence to fall between them before adding, "But I doubt it very much."

7

EMERGENCE

J osef had sensed a shift in the weather all day and felt deeply uneasy as the sun set over the city. From the balcony, Jerusalem appeared in flames, a fiery orange haze clinging to the jagged skyline. The hollow echo of the muezzin's call to prayer rang out over the dusty landscape from loudspeakers, as the last wedge of sun illuminated the dark clouds drawing in over the city. He heard whispers. Faces peered out from the walls and windows of the Old City. He saw the map of wartime Europe, red pins marking the extermination camps. Darkness had come to steal away his last breath, as thunder rumbled in the distance and the first drops of rain were soaked up by the parched stone. His sight blurred as a vision threatened to possess him. He entered the apartment then hurried down the stairs to the street below, escaping toward the appointment Asena had made for him.

He ran north through the Muslim Quarter and fled down a narrow staircase covered in Arabic slogans, under the endless strings of electrical cables and stone archways stained with urine. The steel doors and barred windows of the Old City offered no protection. A lone Arab man made his way home in the dark, prayer mat beneath his arm, a sopping newspaper covering his head from the falling rain. The scent of spices from the street vendors in the deserted market had all but vanished, carried away by the downpour. Josef pressed on. Above, stone balconies rose floor after floor, where clothes left in the rain fluttered like apparitions. A loose shutter, somewhere beyond sight, slammed restlessly in the gusting wind. Then, just as he sensed the presence behind him diminish, a gap appeared between two buildings, revealing the looming night beyond Old Jerusalem's walls. He escaped down an alley and kept running until he arrived at the wooden door Asena had described.

There was no sign on the ancient building, nothing to give away the secret of this place. The only distinguishing feature was the carving of a hand, palm open, etched into the door. It was the hamsa, the hand of Fatima, to deflect evil. He knocked and waited, shivering in his wet clothes. To the south, somewhere in the shadows, stood the Dome of the Rock. Again, he knocked, but there was still no response. He pounded on the door then stared up at the falling rain. The door creaked open. A stout man stood before him with an amused grin and beckoned Josef inside. The proprietor's pale grey eyes followed him across the threshold of the doorway. The front area appeared to be a waiting room or perhaps a departure lounge. Photographs and postcards were taped to a board alongside various foreign currencies. In the far corner, a bookshelf set into the wall was filled with travel books. The air inside was humid and as still as a morgue.

The proprietor was an eccentric looking man and wore a captain's hat with golden laurels wrapped around a black band above the peak. He studied Josef intently from behind his elegant beard. Wearily, Josef extended a hand. The proprietor looked at him conspiratorially. "If you don't mind me asking," he said, "What do you do?"

"I'm an archaeologist."

"This place was built for you," he said, amused. He ushered Josef into a small antechamber. On the walls above a bench were several hooks for his clothes. A colourful mosaic of tiles formed a rainbow path leading to a door. The proprietor's tone was quiet now, and he communicated in near whispers, then merely in gestures. He guided Josef into the inner room. The water-filled tank, with its hoses and gauges, looked like a space capsule and seemed out of place in such an ancient setting. "Have you ever used an isolation chamber?" he asked. Josef shook his head. "It's like a womb. The salt water is the same temperature as the body and will make you weightless. It's sound proof so nothing can disturb you here. In your suspended state, you can go anywhere you like." He smiled sedately then turned to leave the room. "Bon voyage."

Josef stepped back into the antechamber, where he slowly undressed just as he had that Cuban dawn, as he prepared for the initiation into Palo. Hesitantly, he followed the tile rainbow back into the room with the tank. He pictured the chamber and turned off the light, planning how many footsteps he needed to reach the tank. Stepping forward, he counted back: *Seven. Six. Five. Four.* History reversed itself. *Three. Two.* The beginning was impending. His footsteps rang clearly. *One.* He stood frozen on the platform, every muscle aching with uncertainty. He took a deep breath, loosened his feet from their place, and began descending, left foot then right. The right foot was the first to touch the water. He let go and sank into the placental fluid of the isolation chamber.

In the perfect darkness, he felt calm, mindful of his muted breath. A halo of water formed around his face, leaving only his nose, eyes, and mouth above the surface. His ears pulsed with the slow beating of his heart. In this suspended state, he no longer sensed where his body ended and the silent water began. The voice in his head -- the one questioning and judging everything -- slowly grew mute, leaving him in peace.

He saw himself standing before a closed door and heard Hector's voice tell him that all the moments before this had been leading him here. Josef pushed open the door and entered the desert, descending into the parched landscape, walking across the vast stony plains, an ashen landscape that grew white with the unforgiving sun. A lizard basked motionless on a rock. Between the desert canyons, torrents of sand rose on the wind. The sky above shifted as he stumbled through the rocky ravines. For one hundred years, he travelled among the dark ridges beneath a deep blue sky, the pluming white clouds stacked miles high. A dry steady wind blew. Then, as he gazed around, a sea of birds appeared, momentarily eclipsing the sun. He followed them and saw in the near distance a hill rising toward the heavens. Along its edge stood a figure staring at the clouds. As he approached the hillside, Josef became dizzy with recognition. He had inadvertently returned to the wilderness of Sinai, where he had spent so much time digging for the genealogy of humankind at the mouth of the cave. He climbed the hill, shuffling his feet as if he were a small child or a very old man. In all corners, the sky rested on the earth. The cave appeared as a shadow amongst the crags of the canyon wall. It was only now he realized he hadn't escaped the visions but instead walked directly into them. They had disguised themselves to bring him back here. Without hesitating, he walked inside the cave.

He was alone. But not for long. Figures emerged from the shadows. A murmur from behind. He turned and the power of the cave was revealed. There appeared before him a great chain of men. He saw his father, Abraham, speaking to his grandfather, Arthur, near the entrance. Josef held his father tightly, afraid to let go. For a short while father and son were reunited, before Abraham pressed Josef forward. Josef looked back one last time, but his father was already gone. And so he walked down the path of his Fathers. Every father, every son, appeared in the faint light. Arthur was begot by Abner in France in 1880, who in turn was begot by Noah in Poland. As he moved onward, the damp corridor darkened, though he remained unafraid among his kin. Noah chatted with a man he had never met, his father's father, Abraham, who died before he was able to welcome his grandson to the family.

Names repeated themselves every few generations, tying the younger generations to the ones already passed.

And still further on, the ringing of voices, hundreds of years beyond, when Samuel was begot by Gershom in 1494, the first generation to be born on Polish soil. They were nervous and poor when they arrived at the fabled city. Two years of travel after being expelled from Spain had taken its toll, but renouncing their faith to remain in Iberia was too great a demand by the Spanish Monarchy. Gershom was begot by Yosef, 1475, in Salamanca, who was the son of Noah, a doctor specializing in leech therapy. Noah was begot by Izer in 1436. "Were we not delivered from the Pogrom of 1391 in Sevilla? Do we need any more proof that God exists?" said a voice from the darkness. The voices grew louder as Josef penetrated deep into darkness, passing faces as old as Moses Mamoinedes. Time flowed backward effortlessly, until he reached North Africa. Then, as simply as it had begun, his ancestry faded before its completion. Something dark loomed just ahead. Josef stood in the lair, waiting. Then, from the surface of the cave emerged the brick wall of his visions. He could no longer hesitate. He willed the image into focus and suddenly it exploded.

In a dream it was closing -- the diaries in his hand, the indecision, the war, his life. He counts backward to the beginning. Forty-seven. Of those years, he has known innocence for only fifteen. The rest has been stolen from him, by him. How can it be that it is all coming to a close? What has taken twenty years to build is now quickly coming to an end before his very eyes. Artillery shells pound the area surrounding the camp. The massive bonfire fed by the constant stream of camp papers are dwarfed only by the chimneys pluming smoke. Frantic voices from all over camp cry out to one another, "Faster, faster, they're coming!" Heartbroken officers stand before the pyre, singing songs about the glory of Germany. Some cry. They choose not to smell the death caught in the barbed wire or hanging from the gallows. Their sins are buried in mass graves and rise from the chimneys in thick clouds like smoke signals to the gods.

He conceals the sacrificial dagger beneath his uniform and drags the young woman with a number tattooed on her wrist across the courtyard. Certainly, no one will care about the disappearance of one more prisoner. He pushes his way into the Inner Station, shoving guards out of the way, as they carry armloads of documents out to the fire. At the end of the hall, he pushes open a door, sending the prisoner through. He locks the door and leans against it. For a moment he gazes at the telephone. The grey of early morning can't penetrate the blackness of the windowless office. On his knees, he stabs at the wall with a chisel. He digs deep into the stillness of the brick. A shell explodes somewhere overhead, sending a beam caving in. There is movement on the other side of the door. A knock. He looks over at the steel door then toward the woman. For an eternity they don't breathe. Finally, the footsteps recede. She starts to cry. He returns to the desk and studies the SS dagger streaked with blood. With several quick motions, he cleans the blade and places it in the wall. From a dossier, he removes a photograph and draws a black line through it. He tucks three personnel files inside the niche before replacing the freshly mortared bricks. With a sweep of his arm, he sends the gramophone with his favourite Debussy album crashing to the ground.

He pauses to look at a photograph of his wife. He starts a fire in the garbage pail and kisses her image one last time before throwing the photograph in. No-one will defile her image. The flames take hold, corners curling inward, blackening and erasing her. *Goodbye.* He grips the young prisoner by the arm and steers his way through the mob in the hallway, running through the Inner Station and out into the courtyard -- hoping, praying, no one will notice their shadows. Several more shells explode close to the fence, sending guards scurrying for cover. Several prisoners dash toward the open gates in a bid to escape but are shot by guards in the watchtower. They have been given their orders: no evidence must escape the camp.

He clutches his diaries, as they run away past the furnaces and beyond the iron gates. They crash through the meadows heading west, in the opposite direction of the pursuing sun. He has a single wish and that is to be a bird and fly away. But the sky is already eclipsed by planes and soon the fields are on fire. Just ahead, shrouded in trees, a church steeple. They pass the sign for the village *STENEDAL*. When they reach its deserted streets, he knocks on the door of a farmhouse. When no one answers, he stands back and calls up to the second floor in a loud whisper. "Jon. Jon." A young man appears at the door with a bundle of clothes then closes it quickly. The world is slipping away and so too does the young ghostly woman, who escapes down the road.

He runs into the yard with an armload of clothes. Frantically, he tears off his shirt and pulls down his trousers. A noise from behind. He turns. There is no escape. He is surrounded. With hands clasped, he begs the officer, who steps forward from the line of troops, to be merciful. But the German uniform lying in the mud betrays him, and the officer points a condemning finger in his direction. They drag him across the yard, kicking chickens out of the way as they march. In his hand, he still clutches the leather-bound diaries. The soldiers curse him and roughly toss him against the barn before stepping back. He turns to face his executioners, staring out at the guns trained on him. He holds the diaries up as a confession. They think he is saluting Hitler.

And, just like that, the vision faded. Josef found himself staggering around the lair. It was impossible to say how long it was before Asena, from nowhere, appeared. He reached out and Asena touched his hand -- one miraculous touch and the past and present converged so that he knew where he was. Asena stood above and raised him from the waters of the isolation chamber. He felt her concerned eyes watching him, though he continued to stare ahead. It had always been written in the blood of dreams where he must go.

Through the doorway that opened onto the courtyard, the grey morning light filtered through. "The proprietor forgot about you last night," she said, wrapping a towel around him. "I got worried so came looking for you."

Josef couldn't focus on Asena's voice but instead recalled the name Hector had given him after his initiation in Cuba: *Lucero Camina Mundo Busca Sendero Encima Entoto*. It meant, Morningstar World-Walker Searches For The Path On Earth, Hector had explained. It meant Josef had far to go.

Asena looked into Josef's eyes, trying to figure out what he was thinking. But he spoke first. "I'm leaving."

"Where?" Her voice was full of regret.

"Germany."

"Are you trying to draw blood from ghosts?"

"Yeah, maybe I am."

B O O K
T W O
The Hunt

"We must now fear the person who obeys the law more than
the one who breaks it."
DWIGHT MACDONALD - *Modernity and the Holocaust*
By Zygmunt Bauman.

8

THE RETURN

All cultures have their creation myths, Asena once said. The Jews were no exception. They believed God created the earth and then brought light to the darkness, transforming the world into a place teeming with life. Yahweh planted a garden in Eden, away to the east, and there placed the man and woman He had created. They dwelled in the Garden, living in blissful peace, until sin sent them from paradise. The Nazis also had their myths -- about a superhuman Aryan race that lived on the island of Atlantis. They also fell from grace and were forced to live among mortals. That was the purpose of the Third Reich -- to pave a road leading the German people back to paradise, back to the place where they would be God-men. And fifty million people died in pursuit of that dream.

With a backpack weighted on his back, Josef ran down the platform and leapt onboard the train just as it was rolling out of the Munich station. He found an empty cabin and from his satchel retrieved a war map of Germany. He became lost in place names -- Dachau, Metz, Stuttgart, Nürnberg, Dresden. At the bottom right-hand corner of the map, eight kilometres east of the town of Stenedal, awaited Übel. The train sped through the suburbs of Munich and out into the countryside, the Austrian Alps pale against the horizon. Amid the fields and old stone houses, history seethed. It was a history Josef had visited countless times through the dossiers of wartime. That was the only Germany he had ever known, the Germany that overwhelmed Western Europe in a day, the one that inspired French Nazis to steal his parents' freedom and starve his older sister to death at the internment camp Le Vernet.

The clickity-clack of the train echoed loudly, as it plunged into a lightless tunnel. In the darkness, Asena's voice cautioned not to dismiss Adolf Hitler as crazy. To do so, she said, one must dismiss all Germans at the time as being mad and then the lessons taught by history would be lost. Hitler didn't rise to power alone. He was helped by the likes of Himmler, Heydrich, Rommel, Goebbels, Hess, Speer, Rosenberg, Krupp, Göring, and, if Saul was right, Erich Hauptmann. There were so many to blame. Hitler borrowed and built on the ideology of racists like Theodor Fritsch, while others were all too anxious to fulfil his dream, flocking to *him,* crowding the sidewalks to glimpse the saviour as he was driven through the streets, saluting.

Late in the afternoon, Josef crossed an ancient bridge and wandered Stenedal's main street lined with medieval stone buildings in search of a place to stay. The central square was dominated by the ornate Gothic spire of a Roman Catholic Church. An old man armed with a hack saw kneeled on the angled roof behind the pub, cutting off a dead limb. A bird fluttered across the street and landed on a tree behind a farmhouse. Down below, an aged woman sat in a doorway looking out from the shadows, saying nothing to passers-by but a toothless good-day. In all likelihood, most of the old people grew up in the shadow of Übel. What Josef didn't want to hear from them was how they hadn't known of the atrocities happening next door, that they were just following orders, or that the war hadn't happened the way the Allies said it had. *The winner always writes history*, he heard them whisper.

Josef's research into Stenedal had uncovered an impressive history, having been occupied in one form or another since the end of the last Ice Age ten thousand years ago. In the 1300s, it served as an important market for farmers, as well as long distance trade in salt and lumber. All this prosperity ended during the 1600s with the Thirty Years' War, when the plague swept through, littering the cobblestone streets with the dead. But the inhabitants rebuilt the village, re-affirming their roots in the Bavarian soil. With the discovery of thermal pools in the 19th century, Stenedal became a small spa town, hosting the infirmed -- until one day the source of the thermal water simply dried up. It was a bad omen. In 1937, Hitler established a candidate school for SS officers nearby. Over the course of several years Übel was built as a labour camp to supply local factories until it was outfitted with new equipment so that it could fulfill its part in the final solution.

Josef found a downtrodden hostel, a last resort for those passing through. After paying for two nights up front, he climbed the crooked steps to his room, unpacked his things, showered, then tumbled into a short dreamless sleep.

He awoke with a start and through the window saw that daylight had already bled beneath the horizon. The plan was to visit the death camp under cover of darkness, to avoid suspicious eyes. He slung his satchel over his shoulder and walked out of town along the side of the road, accompanied by the sound of the nearby river. Underfoot, the road stretched long into the distance. The trees became silhouettes against the vanishing sky. A dog barked in the distance. Before midnight, he turned off the main road onto a narrow overgrown path. The fields were blackened, burnt by the absence of daylight. Beyond a string of rusty barbed wire loomed Übel. Cracked cement posts lining the perimeter gleamed like broken bones in the moonlight. He ducked beneath the fence and waded through the tall grass toward a cluster of brick buildings.

He stopped at the first structure beyond which stood the ghostly remains of Übel's chimneys. The entrance was boarded up. From his satchel, he removed his chisel and wedged it between the wood plank and the brick, using his weight to force open the sealed entrance. But the board didn't yield. He leaned against the chisel with as much force as he could muster. The plank moaned and finally gave way with an alarming snap. He stood at the threshold of the Inner Station, the silence of the corridor ringing in his ears. Josef imagined Hector beckoning him on and so he entered, broken glass crackling underfoot. With the beam of his flashlight, he attempted to destroy the darkness. Yet, in the depths of the hallway, shadows threatened to overtake him at any moment. He glanced back, mis-stepped, and stumbled to the ground. He clutched his ankle and cursed -- cursed the Inner Station, cursed Übel, cursed the goddamn Nazis for building such a place.

Drawing on the memory of his visions, Josef moved toward the final door on the left and pushed the steel door open. It swung only slightly before meeting an obstruction. He forced his arm through, feeling around in the darkness. He found nothing blocking the way. On his knees, he groped along the ground but still found nothing. He stood and stretched long. Just across the top of the door, a wooden beam blocked the entrance. He pushed it away and swung the door open. He had arrived at the heart of the Inner Station of his visions. A voice of doubt begged not to go any further, warning that his life could never be the same if he stepped inside. He crossed the threshold and allowed the flashlight to sweep over the room. There were the remains of a squatter's fire and a backward swastika spray painted on the wall. Josef turned to face the wall. *Hands and knees.* He stooped down and felt the wall, as if by touch and not sight he'd find what he was searching for. And then, as he ran a finger along the mortar, he felt a peculiar change, more granular. He saw the square segment of slightly discoloured cement. With his tools, he began hammering, at first with hesitant taps and then with forceful blows. A moan from behind. As he turned, he was struck across the head. The flashlight flew free, throwing the room into darkness.

He felt around for the flashlight, grasping the wooden beam that had fallen from the ceiling. Among the rubble, he found the broken pieces of the flashlight and threw them in frustration.

Josef took a deep breath and gathered himself.

In total darkness, he crawled back to the wall. From the floor up, he drew a finger along each line of mortar, until eight lines up he came upon the dents made from the first hammer strokes. He went to work, the noise shattering the silence of the tomb. The hammering sent a cluster of birds into flight up through the hole in the roof. Perhaps the dead themselves were being woken. With each stroke of the steel hammer on the chisel head, his shoulders and arms grew tense. Blood and sweat now ran freely down his face.

After twenty minutes, the final layer of brick gave way, and with it collapsed the barrier between dream and reality. Between past and present. In that instant, Josef saw his parents poring over the stacks of Nazi documents at Liberté then Asena raising him from the salt water of the isolation chamber. Hector puffed on a cigarette and drew a finger pensively along the length of his nose. He was right. He had always been right. The power of the visions was real. In the pitch black, he felt around a sealed chamber in the wall. His hand brushed over papers. Further inside, he touched the point of a long knife. The weight of history pressed down and, in his relief, he bowed his head and laughed. He laughed until tears streamed down his face, until the dull light of early morning seeped through. The room was grey and lifeless; tired beams rested on the cracked and pitted floor. He stacked the bricks in the wall and left the room, moving through the corridor of broken glass toward the light.

Hours had passed in a single moment. When he stumbled outside, the sun peered above the horizon. From his solitary place among the ruins, he sat cross-legged beneath a tree, holding the dagger adorned with the German eagle and double SS bolt on its handle. He ran a finger along the blade and read what was engraved in German: *My honour is my trust*. He pulled out the personnel files of three camp commanders, as well as other documents, including photographs and drawings. A sketch titled *self-portrait* was signed by Erich Hauptmann. How could this Nazi have created such sensitive works? Now other questions came flooding in. Which officer had buried these files and why hadn't he come back to claim them?

With Übel's secrets tightly in hand, Josef made his way back through the tall grass to the road. With each footstep, Übel receded into the distance. The wilderness appeared to close in around the ruins, as if to conceal it forever.

9

GRAVE

When Josef was a child, he used to sit very still and watch his father adjust the big knob on the shortwave radio in the room behind the antique shop. When that failed to bring in a clearer signal, he would adjust the telescoping antenna, moving it an inch this way or two inches that way. The radio would squawk and crackle and voices would call out, bringing news from every corner of the world -- sometimes in Russian, French or Hebrew, sometimes in English, Cantonese or Armenian. When Josef was old enough, his father let him play with the dial, which rolled velvety smooth in his fingers. He could have spun that dial all day, riding up and down the bandwidths -- 2300kHz, 5900kHz, 15550kHz -- those short wave signals reflecting off the ionosphere hundreds of kilometres above him, only to get captured back on earth by the silver antenna on his father's radio like some sort of sonic Venus flytrap. It felt like a sacred process in search of just the right spot for the signal to come through loud and clear. When he would hit the mark, his father would smile and that was enough reward to sustain Josef for days.

He had brought the shortwave to Germany, as if it would somehow allow him to hear his parents wherever he went, keeping him company, their distant voices following the earth's curve, riding a bandwidth that only he could hear. As he sat in his room overlooking Stenedal's main street, the radio reported intensified violence along the Lebanese – Israeli border. The PLO had been launching attacks on Israel from inside Lebanon, while Israel had reportedly bombed a sports stadium in Beirut that it claimed was being used to store ammunition.

From his satchel, Josef retrieved the SS dagger and hid it beneath the mattress. He then pulled out the dossier, its pages swollen and brittle with time. He held each page in his hands like a holy scripture. Some documents were written in the finest penmanship, others by the mechanical tap of a typewriter. The dossiers outlined the distinguished careers of SS officers whose crimes were detailed at great length as reasons for promotion: efficiency and pride in the act of genocide. Photographs of the Nazis of Übel were scattered over the bed along with a sketch of a young man, a boy on the cusp of change, unsure of where he belonged. Josef brought the page closer. It read, *Sketch of Jon Küssel by Erich Hauptmann, Fall 1943.*

He sifted through the files and the black and white photographs of Colonel Erich Hauptmann, Doctor Wolfgang Ziegler, and SS Colonel Hans von Flintz, the camp commandant. Hauptmann was a great big man with broad shoulders,

light eyes, and brown hair. The Nazis recorded everything --
genealogy, height, weight, age, birth parents, favourite colour,
etc. Colonel Hauptmann was 6' 1", 191 pounds. He fought
in both wars and was decorated twice on the Eastern Front.
Married to a nurse, Marta Fromm, in Munich in December
1918. No kids. Josef looked closely at something scribbled in
faded ink. It read: *Marta pregnant!*

Josef turned to the photograph of Dr. Ziegler. His stiff portrait revealed a sinewy and hostile looking man in brass-rimmed
spectacles with a narrow animal face. 5' 5", 125 pounds. His
official title at Übel was *Physician of Garrison Health*, but the title couldn't conceal his duties on the selection platform and the
medical block. *G-wing. Bio-medical experimentation.* The final
photograph was that of SS Colonel Hans von Flintz. 5' 11,"
180 pounds. He had a face not easily forgotten, with a sharp
jaw and vicious eyes. Something struck Josef, and he brought
the photo closer to take a better look. A puzzling line in black
ink had been made across his throat.

After gleaning all he could from the records of these criminals, he collected the Übel files scattered over the bed and
escaped the dank hostel room, driven by the thought that he,
Josef Levi, was rescuing history from itself. He found the only
fax machine in town tucked away at the back of a small shop.
Josef placed a small stack of *Deutsche Marks* on the counter
and told the young clerk he wanted to send a fax himself. The
teen grinned, swiped the money off the counter, walked over
to a magazine rack, and flipped through an adult mag, while
Josef faxed the Übel documents to Saul.

——

Josef walked the streets, approaching people and introducing himself in German. Some, such as the old captain of the Wehrmacht, shooed him away. When he asked an ancient woman perched in her kitchen window about Stenedal's history, she made no apologies for hating the Russians. She pointed east. "The Slavs wanted everything, but we wouldn't give it to them. So we fought pitch-fork in hand, defending the soil. They're bad people, worse than the Jews."

He moved up and down the main street like a fisherman trawling for information on the overlords of Übel. But with each person he approached, he sensed word had spread as to why he was in town -- to needlessly pick at old wounds. He stood at the entrance to the local pub. It was dark and filled with trails of cigarette smoke. One group of young men huddled around a flashing pinball machine. Another shot a game of pool. The town veterans drank pints of foaming beer. Some were boisterous with their bravado and back-slapping. Others clung sullenly to the shadows. When they noticed his presence, they stopped and stared until Josef retreated from the doorway.

For hours, he could get no traction with the locals and, with his frustration mounting, he entered the medieval Gothic church in the main plaza. He sat beneath the high vaulted ceilings and looked around, taking in the ornate interior. The soft light and flickering candles lent themselves to quiet contemplation. And it was in such a moment of quiet that it came to him. He immediately stood and returned to the plaza where he began to plant the seed that he was, in fact, Erich Hauptmann's son in search of the whereabouts of his father. There was a noticeable shift. Though not all of it was positive. While some warmed to his presence, sympathetic to his hunt, others remained hostile. Along the main road through town, Josef approached a woman, perhaps in her seventies. She immediately waved him away like he was contagious. He told her about his father, but the grey-haired woman didn't believe him and wanted proof.

"My mother was a nurse from Munich," he said. "Marta Hauptmann. Her maiden name was Fromm." The elderly woman seemed satisfied and pointed a bony finger toward a sturdy-looking poplar recessed by a farmhouse.

Only as he crossed the road and approached the yard did he recognize the farmhouse where Hauptmann had been confronted by the soldiers in his visions. He rested a hand on the poplar's thick trunk, taking comfort in its rootedness.

A noise forced his attention away from the tree. An old woman sat silently in a chair on the porch. She appeared as old as the land itself. A man in his fifties stood in the doorway, looking on with a hollow expression. But her gaze was inviting, so he sat with her. They talked a while, speaking of the hot weather, the kinds of rainfall that best suited the fields, and the beautiful rolling countryside all around them. Then she said, "You're Hauptmann's son, aren't you."

"Yes," he lied.

"I heard you were in town, asking questions." She paused and almost smiled. "I always wondered when you would come back to look for your father."

Her son appeared uncomfortable and withdrew into the house. The old woman made no such gesture of flight and instead looked at him sympathetically.

"I was a young woman during the war. This was my grandfather's farm. My father planted that tree," she said, pointing to the poplar.

She was about to speak again when Josef removed the black and white photographs of SS Dr. Ziegler and Hans von Flintz. She took them and stared for a long while, before nodding in remembrance. "They came to Stenedal to drink. The doctor kept to himself. He was a nervous man. I always imagined he had a small heart that beat fast even when he was sleeping. Von Flintz--" She shook her head, woefully. "One look in his eyes and you knew he had killed people with his own hands. And he enjoyed it. He took advantage of some of the local girls. But no one could stop him. His SS uniform made him invincible."

"Is he still alive?"

"If he's dead, his soul is burning in hell."

He pulled out the third photograph, the photo of Erich Hauptmann. She looked at the man in uniform and then into Josef's eyes. Something welled up and tears rolled down her weathered cheeks. A finger lingered on the photograph. "Your father," she whispered. "I haven't seen that face since the war."

With a wavering hand, she pointed to the farmhouse on the other side of the tree.

"What is it?" asked Josef.

"You really don't know what happened to him?"

"No."

She sighed heavily. "They shot him. I remember the day so clearly. January...No March 1...No. April. 18, 1945. That's it. April 18, 1945." She dabbed her eyes with an old handkerchief. "He had a young prisoner with him. No one could figure out what he was doing with her. Even today, I still wonder."

"Do you know what happened to her?"

"She escaped," the ancient woman sighed. "We could hear the artillery. We didn't know whose it was or which army was going to pass through next. In those times, everyone's doors were closed to strangers. So when the girl wandered through town, no one helped her. People hid in their houses and watched the girl drag an old chair under the swing near the centre of town. She climbed the chair. Maybe they thought she was going to steal the rope. She looped the rope around her neck and kicked the chair from beneath her. Everyone was too afraid to do anything. Maybe the Russians would come as the villagers were unstringing her and they'd think it was they who'd killed the poor girl. They cut her down after dark. It was only when they were burying her that they found gold and diamonds in her pocket. She had enough to start a new life somewhere far away from any war, but maybe she didn't feel she could go on. No one will ever know just how much she suffered in her short life," the old woman moaned.

"The allies made us walk through the camp. The ovens were still filled with bodies. And the smell in the gas chambers. I will never forget it. The scent of bitter almonds. That was the smell of cyanide used to kill those poor people. We were all crying and looking away, but the soldiers forced us to be witnesses. They even made our children look...my son...he was fourteen. What had Jon to do with the war?—"

"Jon? Jon Küssel?"

"That's my son."

"And my father, what did they do with him?"

"I told you. They shot him, and we buried him right there." She pointed to an unmarked place in the dirt beside the tree.

"He's still there?"

The old woman bowed her head sullenly.

"Do you have a shovel?"

She stared long into the distance. "We want to forget." The clouds embedded in the sky remained perfectly still. She turned to the wooden door and called inside. "Jon, bring me a shovel."

There was a long pause before he peered through the doorway.

"Please," the old woman said again, "a shovel."

He fetched an ancient implement and placed it in Josef's hand. Jon avoided looking at him then disappeared into the house.

Josef quickly found himself in his element, digging up the past. He was up to his knees in dirt when a rough looking man in his twenties stopped at the edge of the trench with a cigarette dangling from his mouth. "You shouldn't be here, *aüslander*."

"Where should I be?"

"Gone."

Josef continued to dig. The young man looked at the sun descending behind the tree in the yard. "Leave before sunset. Or you'll regret it."

"Sounds like a threat."

The young tough hoofed dirt in Josef's face, temporarily blinding him. "It is a threat, *arschloch*!" he said, then flicked his cigarette at him and stormed off.

The sun slowly made its way toward the horizon. Dirt was flying, as Josef frantically dug down into the earth. As the sky was growing pale, the point of his shovel hit something hard. On hands and knees, he scraped away the dirt like a man possessed. Then the trench was thrown into darkness.

A group of young men had circled him. The roughneck kicked dirt over him. "Let's bury the *aüslander* alive." There were grunts of approval. Warily, Josef kept digging. The boys seemed to edge toward him, growing agitated. They kicked more dirt. "This is private property, *du dumme sau*."

"My father was a colonel in the Wehrmacht. He has the right to a proper burial."

But that didn't seem to satisfy their hunger for confrontation. "We don't want you here."

Josef continued digging, hoping the voices and faces would simply vanish, but they didn't.

"Are you deaf?"

Josef stopped abruptly and sat up on his knees. "This isn't your land," he said. "It's theirs." He pointed to Jon Küssel and his mother. "They decide what happens not you."

The old woman's frail body seemed to shrink under the pressing weight as all eyes turned to her. The cluster of restless men grew silent so that the only sound was the crackling branches swaying in the late afternoon breeze. It was impossible to say how long they stood there holding their breath, waiting for her to say something, anything, to break the spell that had been cast over them. Then the old woman nodded before closing her eyes.

Jon looked relieved. "Dig."

There was a gasp and a release of pressure.

"But—"

"Get off our land," Jon shouted.

The group's resolve diminished completely. As they dispersed, the roughneck approached Josef and whispered, threatening. "I don't care if your father was a *fucking* king, you better be gone by morning, *wichser*."

Jon smiled sadly at Josef before retreating onto the porch.

He kneeled above Erich Hauptmann, relieving the dirt from around his bones, uncertain what exactly he was hoping to uncover. Little by little, the German officer was revealed. His frame was curled up in a semi-foetal position in the makeshift grave. There was something eternally sad about witnessing Erich's body, his skull and bones defenceless. From behind, the old woman wept. Then Josef was startled by a discovery. Clutched in Erich Hauptmann's skeletal fingers rested two locked diaries bound in leather with the initials E.H. Josef had found what he hadn't realized he was looking for. He hid the journals in his satchel.

Unsure what to do with Hauptmann's body, he told the old woman that perhaps it was best he remained where he had fallen. She agreed. When Josef had finished re-burying Hauptmann, he placed the shovel on the porch. The old woman sat in her chair as still as death. Josef took up her hand, and she gazed into his eyes. Something dawned on her, and she said it aloud, without hostility: "You aren't Hauptmann's son."

"No," he said. Then he told her the truth about his hunt.

"It was a terrible time for the Jews…For everyone," she moaned, as if pressed from inside. "It's not easy, is it."

"You're a very brave woman," Josef offered.

"I'm afraid it's you who's the courageous one."

Josef saw Jon in the doorway and retrieved something from his satchel. He handed Jon the sketch Erich had drawn of him as a young man. He looked at it in utter amazement and gazed up with a puzzled look that begged to know how he had come to possess the sketch.

"Did you find his diaries?"

Josef nodded.

"Good," continued Jon. "We never opened them. It didn't seem right at the time. But maybe now it is. I hope you find what you're looking for."

Josef laid a hand on Jon's shoulder, which seemed to bring comfort to both of them. Then Jon turned away, looking down at the drawing, beaming.

⸺

The wooden frame moaned as Josef sat down on the edge of the bed. His nervous hands gripped the diaries. He glanced at the old oak door, afraid at any moment the town's people would clamour up the narrow staircase and knock it down on some sort of witch hunt. On the bedside table, Hauptmann's youthful self-portrait looked on with pleading eyes. From beneath the mattress, Josef retrieved the SS dagger. He studied the blade then used it to cut the leather strap of the diary. With the delicacy of a surgeon, he expectantly opened the diary that had remained pressed closed by the earth for the last thirty-seven years. He flipped the diary open to the first brittle page. His eyes darted around with incomprehension. He flipped to the next page and then the next. In reckless desperation, he took hold of the second diary and cut the clasp in one violent motion.

"It can't be," he cried so loudly that he thought all of Stenedal had awoken. Just as there was no way to breathe life into the dead, there was no magic to revive Hauptmann's words, to bring the ink back that had drained from the pages. Only four words had survived the ravages of time: *The Barber of Berlin.*

His gaze came to a rest on the self-portrait of Hauptmann. His eyes, so life-like, drew Josef inward. He grabbed the sketch, holding it inches from his face. He whispered to the drawing over and over again like a prayer. "You buried the files, you rat bastard. You wanted me to know! So tell me, goddamn it. Tell me what you want me to know!" That was when the charcoal face began to move so that he could see behind the powder black impression, so that he was looking at a mirror in which he was reflected. His head pounded, and he could feel himself being moved by the waves swelling up from the past. His whispers grew louder as he was carried along passageways where distant voices echoed, until the confusion suddenly ended. He passed through the final doorway and his sight became as clear as the stranger's thoughts passing through his head.

Erich sketches himself using a small mirror he keeps tucked in his vest pocket. His eyes are wide and curious, his mouth straight and serious. In the near distance, beyond his easel, a boy fishes from a giant rock in the river. The rise and fall of the humming crickets and the deep fragrant smell of grass reminds him that the long summer days are drawing to a close. The warm mid-afternoon light sparkles off the surface of the river and makes the boy on the rock look like an angel.

"I never want summer to end," the angel says, reading his mind.

"Hey Julius. You know what my grandpa says?"

The angel shrugs.

"If you wish for something hard enough, it'll come true." He looks at himself in the mirror. *One day I will be famous. A famous painter and my work will hang in important galleries everywhere!* He smiles proudly. When he looks up again, Julius whips his line out into the river and drags it through the water. His line begins moving on its own. He pulls and meets the resistance. His face tense, Julius no longer appears like an angel. He grimaces and jerks on the fishing rod, struggling against the will of the fish that wrestles with the line.

"Jeez!"

The fish disappears beneath the surface and continues to fight the hook.

"Watch your line, Julius. Don't let it snap. You have to tire him out."

Julius remains focused, biting his lip. Erich grabs the net from the bank of the river while Julius yanks on the line.

"Not so hard, Julius! Not so hard!"

The fish resists but grows weak. Julius draws the line out and triumphantly swings the fish into the awaiting net. "Your grandpa's right Erich!" says Julius. "What you wish for does come true!"

Julius strips to his underpants and jumps off the rock into the water.

Erich quickly follows him into the river. "Wait for me!"

As the sun sets, they walk down the dirt road. Julius carries his fishing rod over his shoulder -- his prize dangling heavily off the back, while Erich struggles to carry all his painting supplies, including the easel. "Grandpa wants me to go to art school in Vienna," Erich tells him. "But Father wants me to join the army. He says it's only a matter of time before we go to war."

Julius continues to walk but says nothing. One of Erich's paint brushes drops in the dirt but Julius doesn't help. Erich leans over to pick it up, conscious that Julius is getting away from him.

"Not to fight would be wrong," Julius finally says.

"Of course, I love my country." As Erich reaches for the brush, he sees a stray kitten in the bushes. He extends an inviting hand. The kitten pounces over to him.

"It won't be long," says Julius. "They're already bombing Tripoli."

"Where's Tripoli?"

"Spain," Julius says, authoritatively.

"If it happens, I hope we're old enough to fight."

"We'll go anyway."

Julius looks over at Erich petting the kitten. "Cats are stupid."

Erich doesn't think so and tucks the kitten into his pocket.

Julius keeps on walking in the falling light. Erich races to catch up.

—————

Not a single tree stands as far as the eye can see. The land is as barren as any desert. It is a rolling wasteland of mud, snaking trenches, and artillery craters. The mud is deep and soldiers rescue each other from its clutches when they can. Others are left entombed in the caved-in bunkers and fox holes. Coils of barbed wire go on and on for miles with shell cases and soldiers scattered over the battle field. The countless bodies draped in thick oily mud look like bronze statues or the frozen stone people of Pompeii. Wooden crosses are everywhere. The remains of a bi-plane with French markings lie splayed in the mud, its pilot slumped over and being plucked apart by scavenging birds.

Erich peers out over no-man's-land. He is many miles and many weeks away from the Munich railway station when a band had played. There were people milling around, some crying and waving handkerchiefs to faces in the departing trains, while Julius and Erich sat against the wall waiting to leave. Julius had convinced him to enlist right away. Otherwise they risked missing out on the excitement of the Front lines. Erich had only finished his first year of art school. Julius promised the war would be finished by Christmas and that he would only miss a few months of class.

The music on the Munich platform made Erich feel important so that his chest puffed with pride. More soldiers loaded onto the train. *For the glory of Germany!* shouted one of the men. Everyone on the platform raised their fists and shouted, *For the Glory of Germany!* It was only as the train pulled out that he thought of his mother's tears. She had touched his cheek and said, *What a beautiful boy. Come home soon.* He wanted to cry on the train so badly, but he was surrounded by men. He and Julius were too young to enlist but they let them join anyway. The cabin was jammed, full of sweaty men smoking and drinking and playing cards, shouting at each other. *No, you played that card! You can't take it back. That's my money!* Greedy hands swept winnings into a hat or a boot or whatever would contain the riches. They laughed easily, as if they were going off for a holiday in the countryside. *It's a just war*, his father had said, *to save Germany's honour.*

He's still staring out at no-man's-land when Julius comes up beside him, a cigarette between his lips. "Don't worry so much. The frogs can't get you here." He passes Erich a cigarette and pulls him down to the bottom of the trench. With his arm slung over his shoulder, they stand before a group of older men casually sprawled out, smoking and talking about women. A young soldier holds a picture of a naked woman and looks ready to explode with excitement.

"Fritz. Run along and do your business," one of the soldiers suggests, making a stroking motion with his fist.

The young soldier appears to think this a good idea and runs off.

"Hey Fritz. Don't get your head blown off!"

He waves, acknowledging their words.

"The little one, that is!"

The men have a laugh. A scrappy looking soldier with blond tuffs of hair sits on his elbows. Nearby, Jacob Zimmer, a soldier in his thirties, smiles at Erich and indicates he should put the cigarette in his mouth. Jacob lights it as Erich clenches the cigarette between his teeth.

"You have to inhale," the blond soldier says impatiently.

Nervous, Erich inhales too deeply. His throat and chest burn so badly that he doubles over and retches on the blond soldier's boots. Everyone laughs -- even Julius.

"What the hell are you doing—" the blond soldier shouts, reeling backward.

"What does it look like?" A soldier imitates Erich's retching.

"Leave him be," Jacob says. "He's becoming a man." He removes a flask from his coat, raises it in a toast to the enemy lines and hands it to Erich. "It's Armagnac. A gift from our French brothers!"

As he takes a drink, the whiz of an incoming shell grows louder. The soldiers' eyes light up in recognition. "Ah shit," the blond soldier says. A gust of hot wind becomes fire. Large metal fragments come walloping through the air, slicing through everything in their path. The earth slides and sends Erich off his feet and face first into the mud. A wall of smoke and debris consumes the trench, and he has to fight hard to breathe.

Some slowly begin to move. Jacob coughs and rolls over. Erich is still gasping, trying to draw air into his burning lungs. Julius is nowhere to be seen. An officer runs out of a bunker waving his pistol. "*Charge* you lazy bastards or I'll shoot you dead!"

Julius immediately resurrects from the mud, grabs his rifle, and scrambles up and out the trench. Erich searches for his weapon. Beside the head of the blond soldier, whose body lies in the near distance, he finds a working carbine and runs out of the trench. "Wait," he cries to Julius.

As the earth shakes and clouds of black smoke drift overhead, he runs head long into the madness screaming. His eyes are filled with the screaming, his mind numb. He sees a soldier at 50 yards, as he emerges through the smoke. There is no fear. Only rage. Erich is running and yelling, closing the distance quickly. 30 yards. 20 yards. 10 yards. Then he is upon him. Erich's eyes are wide open. He can't blink. He pokes his bayonet clean through. The other soldier's eyes look sad and horrified. He is a kid like Erich but a Frog or a Limy, a Scot, a Canadian or whatever. It doesn't matter because he is dying and Erich is the one who has done this to him.

No time to think. He charges on like a maniac through the smoke. Another soldier staggers from the haze and Erich spears him too. He goes wild like some sort of animal. Bombs are blowing off, but it makes no difference. He is going to run to the end of the world and throw himself over the edge.

When Erich and the others regroup in the enemy's trench, his compatriots pat his back proudly. He is covered in foreign blood. Jacob Zimmer grits his teeth in agony and elation. "You did what you had to do," he says.

Fritz approaches muddy and petting a kitten.

Jacob isn't amused. "Look what the cat dragged in."

"He disappears with a naked picture of a woman," says another soldier. "He returns with a pussycat."

Fritz holds up the cat proudly. Erich manages a smile. Fritz sees this and says, "I'll let you pet him, if you promise not to eat him."

"I promise."

The sound of sporadic gunfire can be heard from down the trench, as mortally-wounded French soldiers are put to rest. Pop. Pop. Pop. Julius is already at the bottom of the trench leaning against the wall, chest heaving and smiling. Jacob pulls out a cigarette and offers Erich one. "This time, don't inhale so hard."

For months now, the front has not moved, but like winter remains frozen. Waves of soldiers continue to push over top ridges and out of fox holes, spat out by the earth like retched seeds, advancing a hundred yards, occupying trenches abandoned by the French. But victory is always short-lived, and they are repelled by a furious barrage of artillery followed by a counter-attack. With all the lives paid, they should have won the war ten times already. The trenches are filled with the dead. Erich is forced to crawl back and forth over the frozen bodies all day long. Some of the faces are familiar. But no tears can be spared in a place where life and death are so intimately entwined. He remembers watching Fritz hysterical after discovering someone had eaten his cat. Erich had felt sad, but it was a distant feeling, and he couldn't help but resent Fritz for being so weak. Even news of the death of his grandfather couldn't draw tears from Erich.

Exhaustion creeps through the trench. Soldiers sleep anywhere at any time -- among dead comrades, while eating, even during firefights. Like zombies, they charge across the fields, a muddy twisted chessboard of the living and dead. Here they grapple with strangers, smelling their stench, staring them in the eyes before stealing their last breath with a bullet, a knife, or a bayonet to the guts. But no amount of blood ends the nightmare and that is a big problem.

In war, it's always the poor who pay the highest price. Erich's grandfather tells him from the grave. *We've conquered everything but conquered nothing, because the final frontier is the soul where a man finds love for everything.* The beloved old man describes the prehistoric paintings of *Les Eyzies* and the riches of Aladdin's cave. He reads from *Arabian Nights*, telling Erich a story every night. He jokes that he does this just as Scheherazade had to keep her husband Schahriah curious enough not to kill her. If Erich dies, so too will the memory of his grandfather. *The alchemists who sought to transform base metals into gold were looking to purify their souls.* His grandfather tells him he is an alchemist searching for the purity of love.

Julius and Erich sit at the bottom of the trench shivering. Julius looks strange, brutalized. His eyes hold a demented light. At Julius' insistence, Erich slits open an envelope and unfolds the letter addressed to his friend. Rats run through the trenches, feeding on the dead. Some of the soldiers swat them with their helmets then spear them to cook over small crackling fires. Julius twitches nervously. *"Dear Julius, all is well at home. We will miss you at Christmas,"* he reads from the letter.

Jacob Zimmer passes them with a smile, holding the pulpy remains of a rat by its tail. "Lunch is served."

It's too cold to smile, so cold Erich has to stop reading just to catch his breath. Julius starts to pull off his boot. "Don't do that!" Erich yells. "You'll never get your boots back on." But then Julius raises his trousers. A horrible stench pushes Erich backward. His toes are black like rotting death, his foot deep purple, and his ankle green and yellow all the way to his knee. Erich grips his arm, shouting in his ear that he has gangrene. "You can die from that. You need a doctor." But Julius pleads for him to finish reading the letter. The gangrene has ruined his brain. Erich resists, but it is futile. He reads from the letter, speaking slowly so that Julius can savour his mother's words. Peace fills his eyes and he smiles like he is sitting in his living room again, like nothing can touch him where he sits. "*You are now an uncle. Your sister, Berta, is now the proud mother of an 8 pound boy.*" Julius jumps for joy. There is the fast approaching whine of incoming artillery. Julius, a silent angel, smiles with an unlucky halo hanging above his head. A flash of colour ignites, emanating from a single point behind him, closing in and swallowing him. There is a giant metallic roar and then everything turns black and silent.

10

ONWARD

In the wee hours of the morning, Josef removed the desk and chair braced against the door and slipped out of the hostel. He moved through the shadows of Stenedal's medieval streets to the train station. The platform was empty but for a kiosk attended by a railway official sleeping behind the glass window. The arrivals/departures board indicated the departure of a train at 06:30 bound for *Munich/Nürnberg/Hof/Berlin*. A clock on the wall, with a glowing face like the moon, read: 06:24. Josef didn't know where he was going except that he had to escape Stenedal in a hurry. He had found the Übel files, yes, but they'd been buried for nearly 40 years and certainly wouldn't provide any information that could lead to the war criminals' present whereabouts. And if none of these Nazis could be found, why would they have gone after Josef's parents in Israel? Josef spotted a payphone on the platform and dialed through to Israel.

"We invaded Lebanon," Saul said matter-of-factly, when he answered. "They really have to learn not to fuck with us."

"I think it's more complicated than that."

"If you want to be a doormat, be my guest. Anyway, I received your fax."

"And?"

"And…as far as Colonel Von Flintz – I didn't find any information. Ditto for Erich--"

"Hauptmann is dead."

"How did you come up with that little factoid?"

"A little birdie told me."

"By the way, he has a son."

"I know."

"Did you know he's alive and living in the U.S.?"

"No shit," Josef said, taken aback.

"It looks like he doesn't want anything to do with his German ancestry. As American as handguns and apple pie. And you're going to love this."

"What?"

"Ziegler."

The sound of a train approached.

"What about him?"

"He's at Werl Prison, in North Rhine-Westphalia."

"Holy crap. I guess he wasn't a big enough fish to land himself in Spandau."

"Hey, only seven lucky Nazis got to stay there. Ziegler is being housed with a bunch of Nazi grunts and common criminals at Werl. He's awaiting trial for crimes committed at Auschwitz."

"The doctor also worked at Auschwitz?"

"Nah, I don't think so. They'll probably have to free him when they figure that out."

The train appeared like a phantom around the bend.

"Your man is being held under the name Wolfgang Eitorf. Do you want me to call ahead?"

"No, I got this one."

"I have your back, if you need anything."

"I need to know," Josef hedged. "Where are you getting your information?"

"I may have left the military, but I still have intelligence guys that owe me favours. And, anyway, I want you to learn the truth."

"According to you."

The train came to a squealing halt, but no one stepped on or off.

"Make sure to hunt downwind," said Saul. "So they don't pick up your scent."

"I'm not sure what that's supposed to mean."

"It means don't be obvious. Don't be Josef Levi, son of Nazi hunters, looking for his parents' killer."

Josef hung up and ran for the train.

———

The Werl train terminus was an old house with a series of built-on additions. Nearby, Josef checked into a rundown hotel located above a series of shops. In the lobby, long term residents and penniless backpackers chain-smoked and watched a TV bolted to the wall. No one was smiling. They didn't appear to be the type of visitors arriving on a pilgrimage to see the three hundred year old statue of the Virgin Mary at the *Wallfahrtsbasilika*.

Upstairs, he laid out a new business suit and briefcase purchased during his stopover in Berlin. The room was musty and smelled of boiled potatoes. Old stained curtains hung lopsided from a thin rusted rod. He pulled back the bed cover to reveal the dirty blood-splotched sheets. *Bed bugs, great*. When he called down to the front desk, he was told clean sheets cost extra.

Josef moved toward the grimy window. He glimpsed his reflection though found himself leaning against a farm house, a dozen rifles aimed at his chest. He protested that this wasn't his fate; it was the fate of Erich Hauptmann. He walked into the bathroom and turned on the shower. It sputtered and moaned, before rust coloured water spewed from the faucet. He began taking off his clothes. When the water ran clear, he stepped into the basin, washing his face and body, scrubbing his hair, allowing the steaming water to purify him.

When he stepped from the shower, he studied himself in the mirror above the sink, taking in the details of his face. The two faces of Ellegua -- the trickster -- appeared. The *orisha* of destiny looked toward the future and the past, toward the living and the dead, Hector had told him. He lathered his face and shaved, one stroke at a time. Carefully, he drew the razor down from the edge of his sideburns.

Using the mirror, Josef focused on the intention of each movement and gesture. He jutted his chin forward more authoritatively. Next, he opened his mouth wide, stretching it, and then allowed it to fall closed unhappily. A serious man, without a trace of humour. He bowed his head toward the sink and splashed water into his face, rinsing away the last spots of shaving cream, before looking back into the mirror. He stared at himself, mouth serious, chin up, eyes fixed so they revealed nothing. He flashed an arrogant smile and, with a measured gate, walked into the adjoining room and dressed in his new suit.

———

In the lobby, Josef bought a pack of cigarettes off one of the long term residents of the hostel, paying him double. This led to a cascade of demands to buy cigarettes from the others, too. Josef escaped unscathed. After a few minutes on foot, he hailed down a cab.

"46 Langenwiedenweg."

"Werl prison it is," the driver said with a laugh. His smile faded when Josef looked at him grimly.

Josef saw glimpses of the 4th United States Army Field Artillery detachment stationed in town. American jeeps bumped around the streets, while soldiers could be seen relaxing near the green steeples of the basilica. And as he passed the store fronts along the boulevard, he imagined Germany in the 1930s and the slogans written in paint across Jewish businesses. *Kauf nicht bei Juden!* Don't buy from Jews! *Ausländer raus!* Foreigners out! *Jude verecke!* Die, Jew!

The taxi driver seemed nervous and his words stalled as they came out of his mouth. "Are you some kind of lawyer?"

Josef nodded.

"Can I ask what you're doing at Werl?"

"No."

The driver pressed on the gas and sped up. He glanced back with his ever-shifting eyes. "There's a lot of war criminals at Werl, but there's even more walking around free, you know. I'm sure I've even given them rides. You can't tell who they are. I won't give rides to skin heads. Then again I don't pick up Turks or Africans either." He drove on, still talking and stumbling over his words, complaining about immigration and the rising cost of living before skidding to a halt.

Armed with his briefcase, Josef followed the signs to the visitor's counter at the prison. He placed his briefcase down authoritatively and allowed the clasps to spring open noisily. An official put down his newspaper and approached.

"I'm here to see Wolfgang Eitorf."

"Identification."

Josef slid his passport over the counter, stuck out his chin, and continued to stare at the officer. The tight-lipped officer flipped through the passport methodically, stopping and scrutinizing each page. Josef pointed to his watch but the officer continued to view the passport.

"I'm his lawyer."

"A Jew?"

Finally, he slid the document back over the counter. He gazed down at a giant ledger, scanning a long list of handwritten names. His eyes narrowed and again he began at the top of the page, moving down line by line. "No," he finally said.

"What do you mean by no?"

"No is no."

"Insightful. Who's your superior?"

A female officer looked up from her desk. "What seems to be the trouble?"

"He says he has an appointment; he's not in the book. Rules are rules—"

"It's your adherence to rules that got you people into trouble in the first place."

"We've already paid for the sin of losing."

"Your sin was obeying a madman."

The female officer scribbled something in the ledger. "What did you say your name was sir?"

"Josef Levi."

She pointed down the hall to a large steel door. Josef bowed and walked toward it. The soldierly looking guard marched by his side, directing Josef through the doorway and down a narrow corridor. Silent figures moved restlessly or sat perfectly still in their cages. The cells were bare, stripped of civility, with an open toilet and an old wooden desk bolted down. The walls were yellow, the beds steel and comfortless. At the end of the hallway, the guard turned and faced a cell. "Number 2115," he stated. The prisoner looked up sadly from his stool. "You have a visitor. A lawyer from Israel."

The guard turned to face Josef. "You have fifteen minutes," he said, before walking away.

For a moment, Josef fidgeted with the chair bolted down outside the iron bars. Then he took a deep breath and looked up. From behind the bars, the doctor appeared small and insignificant. He was as withered as an ancient grape, his face grey and unshaven. There was little evidence of the zealous Nazi doctor. Only a destitute shell of a man worn down by flight, isolation, and the two years of court proceedings.

The prisoner's penetrating blue eyes followed Josef as he sat and opened his briefcase. Dr. Ziegler wrung his hands.

Josef withdrew the pack of cigarettes. The old Nazi's eyes widened then narrowed.

"We're not allowed to smo-smoke in our cells," Ziegler stuttered.

"Go ahead," Josef commanded.

Ziegler stood and approached. Through the bars, he took a cigarette. Josef lit it, and he inhaled deeply, closing his eyes, as he exhaled. The doctor gave a nervous smile. His shoulder twitched then his mouth. He paced back and forth. "Why wasn't I told—"

"Operation T-4."

"I shouldn't be here. I'm a family man, not a criminal. I've never broken the law."

"Operation T-4."

He gazed up at the ceiling and then shook his head. "I can't recall."

"I'll ask you again."

"What does it have to do with my case?"

"Leave the questions to me," said Josef, raising his voice. "Is the term familiar to you?"

Ziegler hung his head but kept his eyes fixed on him. "Should it?"

"Of course."

"That's a lie. I was never at Auschwitz."

"I know."

Ziegler stopped, startled and then empowered by the strength and clarity of the pronouncement. Josef pulled out the ancient black and white photograph from the dossier and flashed it through the bars. "Dr. Ziegler, you were at Übel."

With a gasp, the doctor fell back on the bed and clutched his chest.

"Calm down. I'm the only one with the file."

Ziegler tried to hold his chin up though was unable.

"You are a Nazi—"

"I wa-was a Nazi." Then he added, "In another life."

"You can say what you like." Josef brushed the creases from the sleeve of his suit jacket with measured sweeps then looked toward Ziegler.

"It was war. Bad things happen. We were the victims of *his* diabolical plan."

"You don't need to make excuses for me. I'm not the one judging you." Josef pointed up. "That's who judges you -- and the gentleman you will be present before in a court of law."

"It isn't just God or the courts that judge me," he said, pointing a finger to his chest. "I judge myself." He looked into his hands, ringing them sadly. "We had no choice. We were following orders." He raised his hands as if to display them. "My hands were the instrument of the Reich."

Josef paced outside the bars. "You were a doctor -- you were supposed to care for the sick and dying, not kill them."

"It was our war -- the doctors. We had a duty to place the health of the nation above the health of individuals. Operation T-4. I know of it. The world was no place for the sick and crippled and wa-we aided them on their journey out of this cruel existence."

"It was murder."

"We shouldered that responsibility alone, we doctors, to cu-cure Germany. I stayed up late at nu-night afraid, convinced biological pollutants were ruining the country." Ziegler indicated he wanted another cigarette. Josef passed one through the bars and lit it. Ziegler gave him a trembling smile and inhaled deeply.

"You didn't actually believe this?"

"Fool! For one second, think about the times we lived in! Biological determinism. Darwin. Do you remember that from your text bu-books? In my time, it wasn't theory. It was fact. Strength was inherent in biology and weaker genetics could only lead to further social degradation. I believed we could take that knowledge from nature and use it to fulfill our destiny as a people."

"But how could you actually believe in the perfectibility of humankind?"

"You can't be so blind to what's going on. These theories are still alive. They've ju-just changed names. Scientists are still trying to improve upon na-nature, upon our genetics, to replicate genes that make us smarter, create clones. Find the gene for aggression and concentrate it to build the perfect soldiers that don't feel fear or pain. Now what if these scientists were motivated by altruism and wanted to carve away a gene that makes us violent. Would we still be men without aggression? Imagine a world without violence and the only cost was one gene. Would YOU be willing to pay that price -- for a world without war?"

"Of course," responded Josef.

"But what's left of a man without his aggression? Would we give up trying to survive or st-stop looking for love?"

"Are you trying to tell me this kind of thing could happen again? The quest to build the perfect civilization with perfect citizens?"

Dr. Ziegler didn't stutter. "It already is."

The click of approaching footsteps rang down the hallway. "Wrap it up," the guard called out.

"Dr. Ziegler, what do you know about Liberté centre?"

"I don't even know what it is."

"Abraham Levi?"

"Never heard that name before."

"The documents from Übel will remain safe with me. But I need information about the other officers."

"Like how dramatically the war changed our lives?" He shook his head contemptuously. "A name change perhaps." Ziegler looked at Josef conspiratorially. "Last names only. No-no one ever likes to chu-change their first name. *It's too unnatural.* After the war, it was business as usual. The architects kept building, the doctors kept healing." Ziegler smiled ironically. "The barbers kept cutting."

"Where's the Barber of Berlin now?" Josef nearly choked on his own words.

Ziegler gave a reluctant laugh. "Guatemala City."

He lifted his shirt and pointed to a faded blue marking of the twin SS lightning bolts in his arm pit. He whispered just loud enough for Josef to hear. "The Ju-Jews weren't the only ones tattooed. The SS were so thorough. We never thought it would end. I tried everything to scrub it off."

"And Hauptmann? Tell me about Erich Hauptmann."

"He-he was killed."

"What did he do at Übel?"

A spark of life entered Ziegler and his bent back straightened slightly. "Why would you want to know about a dead man?"

"I need—"

Ziegler backed away from the bars. "I've already said too much."

"You haven't said enough. What do you know about Erich Hauptmann?"

Dr. Ziegler gained more strength, fixing his gaze on Josef.

"That's it," the officer called out, as he stepped into view.

A smile of comprehension crossed Ziegler's face, and Josef knew he had lost him.

Josef pushed up close to the bars, clasping them. "I have the Übel files."

Ziegler smiled and looked around his cell, arms opened toward the room. "And what? What else can you people take from me?"

In the near distance, the officer looked over with mild concern. Ziegler moved close to Josef so that he was blocked from the guard's view. He suddenly looked panic-stricken, shocked, as if something unexplainable was happening to him from the inside. He looked like he was having a seizure -- his face red, his veins and eyes popping. "Guard!" screamed Ziegler. He broke from his place, clenching his throat.

The officer ran toward Ziegler, who was doubled over.

"This man! He's an assassin! He tried to strangle me."

"He's lying."

The officer grabbed Josef and pushed him up against the bars, twisting his arm painfully behind his back. "Now you've done it," he whispered into Josef's ear.

Prisoners in other cells hung off the bars looking amused as the man in the new suit was being dragged down the corridor. "You're going to take the word of some Nazi nut bar?"

"Shut your Jew-hole!" The guard pushed Josef into an empty cell and slammed the door behind him.

11

THE PRISONER

Josef sat on the prison bed, his back pressed against the cold wall. He thought of Ziegler and how the doctors had tried to cure a sick nation. Medicine built the metaphors for Nazi Germany -- political medicine, political nutrition. Racial degeneration was caused by reproduction of the weak and sick. A strict program of race hygiene was necessary to purify the land. The therapy was simple: cleanse the society of all impurities. The final solution. He stood and peered out between the bars of his cell, trying to get a view down the dreary prison corridor, hoping to catch the attention of a sympathetic prison guard who could straighten out this mess. In the near distance, Ziegler stared across the corridor at him. Other lonely eyes gazed, too, while one lunatic hung off the bars of his cell like a chimpanzee. "You're one of us! You're one of us!" he shouted. A long trail of spittle ran down his chin.

Hours passed like a dripping tap until the lights were shut off, leaving Josef alone with his fears. *Everyone born on New Year's day is born with a gift,* he heard Hector declare. Josef took a deep breath and held it, uncertain how to descend into the visions. He lay perfectly still and then exhaled, allowing his lungs to empty completely. He stared deep into the emptiness, utterly present in the moment, feeling himself move beyond the physical container of his body and the walls of the cell. In his mind's eye, a long dark tunnel appeared. He was approaching what sounded like a crowd in the distance. His breath remained steady, the pulse of his heart filling his head like the tick-tock of a metronome. Still he saw nothing. He was almost convinced he hadn't entered a vision, until Erich Hauptmann's voice, his thoughts, spoke to him from the darkness.

It is so dark inside this tomb. A heaviness presses on his face. He is not alone, though. There are voices from every direction. Squeaking wheels roll by and recede into oblivion. *Where am I? To what kind of hell have I been sent?* He hears light footsteps approaching that could only belong to a woman. There is low breathing by his side now and he asks, "Am I dead?"

She makes a sound and he almost hears her smile. "No, you're not dead." Her voice sounds so sweet that he feels his throat swell and his face squints as he fights off tears. He has not heard a woman's voice in years. To keep the voice by his side, he asks what time it is. She tells him it's 2:00.

"In the morning?"

"Afternoon."

"Why are the curtains drawn?" He hears so many voices. It's hard to distinguish their misery from his own. "Where am I?"

"Mr. Hauptmann, you're in Munich."

He has a sinking feeling in the pit of his stomach. "Why can't I see?" He brings his hands up to his face and feels the thick skin of gauze wrapped around his eyes. He feels sick. The world is movement and vibration, memories and agonizing groans from other beds. He tells her to leave him alone but she does not go away.

"What did you do before the war?"

"I am -- I was -- a painter."

"Tell me about your paintings."

He imagines Julius fishing off a rock in the river, the glow of falling light on a Viennese archway, and the twilight colours that showered his grandfather as he painted him sitting on the porch. His mind focuses on the warmth of her breath and then he asks again, "Why can't I see?"

He tries to visualize her lips from the darkness. "You were blinded in an explosion." Her warm hand comes to a rest against his arm. She begins to stroke it.

It's so dark in here, but the hand resting on his chest brings red and yellow to the blackness. "Don't leave me," he begs, when he feels her getting ready to move.

"I'm sorry Erich but the ward is very busy."

In a moment of desperation, he confesses, "I like classical music."

When he again travels up through the darkened tunnels of sleep toward the waking surface, he hears Chopin's Nocturne crackle on a gramophone by his bedside. A hand strokes the hair cropping out from above the bandages. The hand is unmistakable. He already knows its size and softness.

"Thank you," he says to the thin air, and she lets out a gentle laugh.

She says nothing but touches his cheek with the back of her hand.

"What's your name?"

"Marta."

"Marta," he repeats. "You're beautiful."

He reaches out and, to his surprise, she doesn't resist when he places her hand on his chest so that she can feel the beating of his heart.

In his waking hours, he conjures up images of his paintings, naive expressions of beauty, drawings of a world that will never be the same. He hears sounds from outside -- the clang of a church bell, the sound of the breeze rushing through the branches of a tree. Marta is talking to someone, then he hears the long contented purr of a cat. Erich calls out, stumbling over his words, asking for the cat. In the next moment, Erich feels something small and warm sitting on his chest. She purrs and kneads his chest. Erich is bursting and petting the creature.

"She just arrived on our windowsill this morning," Marta informs him. "Perhaps she came looking for you."

"What colour is she?"

"A tabby," she smiles.

Beneath his bandages, he safely cries.

"If you treat everyone as gently as that cat," says Marta, "then you are what my mother would call a *keeper*."

In time, Marta comes to occupy all his thoughts and, in every corner of his future, he sees her. Her voice is like a colour palette that he paints with. He draws her face a thousand times, imagining her eyes, her hair, the arc of her brows. He tries holding his breath during the times she is not by his side, though he takes comfort in the tabby, who finds her way to his chest every day. When Marta is making her rounds and finally hovers over him, Erich clings to her. She has to explain that there are others who need her, perhaps more than him. Then she laughs and says she is the one who has to compete with a stray cat. Still, he waits for her to touch him, even if only to shave his face.

He hears Marta's footsteps and asks if it is day or night. Day, she tells him. "Congratulations," she says.

"Why?"

"The war is over."

He cannot help it. His body shakes. He is telling himself to calm down, that it will be all right, that the war is over, to forget about it. But it is impossible. He cannot forget any of it. Someone else approaches. Marta places her hands on his shoulders and guides him to a seated position. A man's hand holds his face and he can feel pulling and the sound of scissors cutting through cloth as they cut away his gauze mask.

A brilliant haze forces his eyes shut. Marta is talking, a rainbow of colour filling the fog. He opens his eyes a crack. Water streams from them. He opens them wider.

"Can you see anything?" the doctor asks.

Shadows and vague figures move about. The sting in his eyes is the most beautiful pain ever. Marta holds his hand then cleans the fluid from his eyes. In a few anxious minutes, his sight begins to clear. Marta is the first person he gazes upon, a halo hanging above her head. Beyond her, dozens of beds with amputees and faceless people moan. The doctor and Marta clap in celebration of his reborn sight. A weight presses down on his head. He sees the flash that stole his sight and stole Julius from this earth.

"I want to see a mirror."

Marta takes him by the arm past the other wounded toward a mirror at the other end of the room. His face, he imagines, is disfigured beyond a doubt. When he looks up at the mirror, the face he has always known appears but older and more worried looking. He turns to Marta and kisses her on the mouth. She backs away and says he shouldn't do that because other people might see. Her words drive a jagged wedge right through his chest and all his joy drains away.

It is late at night. Erich tosses and turns, unable to sleep because of the doubts plaguing him about Marta's feelings for him. Clicking footsteps approach. He sees her. She leans close and smoothes out his pillow, her beautiful round face only inches from his. Then, in the darkness, she looks both ways and presses her lips to his. It is so wet and warm that it fills his body with sensation.

"You're being released tomorrow."

"Where will I go?"

"Home."

"I don't have one. You're all I have, the only one I love, and Christmas is coming."

She hedges.

"I'm scared for Germany, Marta. I'm scared for all of us... You...You said if I treat everyone as well as that cat...that I'm a keeper...And I do and I am."

She laughs and holds his hand. "Then you can live with me. We'll get married."

———

Outside dead people haunt the streets of Munich, legless and walking on knuckles, stopping only to beg. He watches former warriors dressed in rags sweep the streets and stagger drunkenly without direction. Faces around them are hard, harder than any stone. Do they not realize what they sacrificed? Or do they only see in them defeat? Where is Germany's pride? Rummaging through the garbage for something to eat.

As he stands at the window, the stray tabby lounges beside him in the grey afternoon light. There is the sound of a key in the door. Marta is home but he cannot move from his place. She stands before him, still wearing her nurse's gown. Her long black hair is tied in a bun beneath her pillbox hat, her shoulders slumped.

He opens his mouth and says something, anything, "You look terrible."

She starts to cry. "I can't do this on my own any more. Do you hear me? I can't. You've got to help support us. Maybe your friend Jacob Zimmer can help you find a job."

Erich is a statue, watching her from a distance. Then her words creep up on him, and he feels a terrible rumble of anger. He becomes a storm, crashing through the apartment knocking over everything in his path. The cat bolts and escapes under the bed. Erich tries to calm himself but it's impossible. He takes Marta's vase and pitches it against the far wall. The sound of crashing glass does nothing to loosen the knot strangling him. So to stop himself from doing something horrible to Marta, he makes for the door and slams it behind.

In the drizzling rain, he wanders the streets, startled by the rumble of the horse-drawn street cars. A woman with her children sifts through the garbage, handing them scraps to eat. A decorated man in uniform, his pant legs pinned neatly where his legs used to be, holds out a tin can for charity. The sound of artillery thunders in Erich's ears and he can see bodies strewn in the streets. Armless. Headless. Gutted. So much blood from the war has been worthlessly drained away. And for what? Humiliation? His bleak surroundings are dizzying. In these miraculous days of new born sight, he casts his eyes down so he does not have to see.

Two men tumble out of a pub, beating each other. One man grapples the other and throws him to the ground, stomping on him. The man on the ground grows unconscious. Erich backs away down an alley and hides in the shadows. Something already moves in the darkness. He hesitates then draws closer. For a moment, he sees two lovers pressed against the wall kissing and he almost manages a smile. But he sharpens his focus and immediately grows tense. A man is beating a woman, punching her as she lies slouched on the wet ground like a rag doll.

The man with the giant scar across his forehead looks out from the shadow and sees him. He yells to beat it. Erich recoils but does not move. The scarred man makes a motion toward him with a raised fist and, like a coward, he backs out of the alley, helpless to aid the woman. When he reaches the open street, the police are dragging a man away from the body in the road, beating on the accused with their night sticks. They seem uninterested, perhaps satisfying an old habit. The arrested man makes no effort to fight off the blows, as if the pain reminds him he is still alive.

———

A clang and Josef woke up surrounded by prison walls.

The guard unlocked the gate but wouldn't meet eyes with him. Behind him stood a narrow figure of a man in a suit, who bowed his head. "My most sincere apologies."

"Just make sure the Ziegler file gets into the right hands," said Josef, as he straightened his crinkled jacket.

As the prison official escorted him out, he said, "It looks like someone up top was looking out for you."

"What do you mean?"

"The brass in Israel," he said matter-of-factly. "The one who had my boss pissing his pants and scrambling for the key."

Then it came to him.

"Saul Liebowitz?" uttered Josef.

"That's the one."

12

ACROSS ANOTHER SHORE

The human traffic moved so briskly through the Berlin airport that it appeared like a photograph where movement was blurred and captured in streaks. Clusters of families staggered through the terminal carrying suitcases, while a man in a suit burst through the mobs, racing for his flight at the departing gate. Police brandishing machine guns waded through the crowds on the look-out for suspicious characters and unattended luggage.

Through the panels of glass running the length of the building, the morning sun flooded in, casting boxes of light framed by shadows. Josef approached a bank of telephones and dialed a long chain of numbers. As he waited, he turned to face the crowded corridor. Amid the countless faces that streamed by, he saw Cecelia with puffed cheeks spraying him with rum. *Aché para ti*. In the distance, an airplane thundered upward and disappeared into the low ceiling of clouds. Yemayá, Hector had written, was giving her blessing to cross the oceans.

"I miss you, Asena," he stammered, when she finally answered the phone.

"Where are you?"

"I don't know where to begin—"

"Begin by starting."

"I went to Übel," he confessed. "I found documents buried there. Names. Photographs. I know you think I'm crazy—"

"You told me no one had found anything?"

"They weren't archaeologists."

Things have changed here," she said, her tone dark.

"What do you mean?"

"Haven't you been watching the news? We invaded Lebanon. We've become the bad guys. Even Naseer and Daoud are nervous to meet. They're afraid of the Jews and they're afraid of what other Palestinians might do if they find out they're consorting with the enemy." She sighed into the phone. "Come home."

"I can't drop everything. Not yet."

"I need you here."

"Moon, if this was your search, you wouldn't give up looking, even if I begged you. Not in a million years. Just as you know I can't."

"You're trying to slay your parents' demons. But that kind of guilt can't be erased."

"You think I'm going to fail, don't you?"

"I didn't say that. But sometimes things just *don't* work out."

The cobblestone streets of Old Jerusalem came back into view. The Shadow carefully left the package on the doorstep. An orange fell and the Shadow picked it up, popping it playfully off his elbow. His mother and father opened the door, surprised to see the package. The Shadow started to run. Josef raced toward his parents. But it was too late and they were swallowed by the flame.

"When will your search end, Josef?"

"Real people were murdered at Übel. Even the dead have a right to justice. Someone has to be their voice. Someone has to tell their story."

"It's not just about storytelling. You have revenge running in your veins," she said.

What followed was a long and painful silence.

"I hate disappointing you."

She sighed. "Thanks for the painted coconut."

"Ellegua belongs in your altar."

"Who is he?"

"A trickster."

"Lies are a form of violence against the truth. I'm not asking you to walk on water or breathe life into the dead, but I need to be able to trust you. This is your life, Josef. This isn't a dress rehearsal. What you do matters."

"I need to go to Guatemala."

"It's a dangerous place. There's a civil war."

"I know."

"Is Saul helping you?" she asked, accusingly.

"I think he's Mossad," he breathed.

"You really think so?"

"Well, he definitely doesn't sell furniture. He pulled some strings here that I can't explain."

"How far down the rabbit hole do you think this spy shit will take you?"

Josef couldn't answer.

"Believe me, I know a few people who got tied up in that world. Then they got tired of the cloak and dagger crap, the gratuitous assassinations, the plots and counter-plots. They got out but not before a piece of their soul was left on the floor. You never get that back."

"I'm in Saul's world right now. I need his help."

"Be careful Josef."

"Whatever Saul's up to, I'm totally loyal to him."

"But is he loyal to you? Go to Guatemala," she huffed. "Hunt for your Nazi. But remember, I can't live with a murderer." And with that, Asena hung up.

The plane jerked into motion and taxied to the end of the runway. It turned. Then the cabin rattled and was filled with sound, the runway accelerating past his window. As the nose of the plane rose from the ground, Josef closed his eyes and breathed slowly, clearing his mind of all questions -- about how Hauptmann had found him in his dreams or the prisoner who had escaped from him only to hang herself. Then everything grew black and he found himself walking down

Hauptmann's past along a darkened corridor into an open beer hall.

Like a place of worship, the room is filled with hundreds of people and dozens of red and black flags. Most gathered have scars -- gouged eyes, missing limbs, lacerated flesh -- though the deepest wounds remain invisible to the naked eye. Cigarette smoke clings like a veil of incense. It has been such a long journey to get here even though the hall is just across the river from his apartment. A great big jovial man named Hermann Kessel had found Erich wandering the streets and convinced him to come here.

Erich is jittery and light-headed. The air is charged with a euphoric hum that raises the entire hall above the glum dank streets of Munich. He looks around the smoke-filled room and sees everyone gazing toward the man at the podium. Their eyes are wide open, as if for the first time they are hearing what they have always known in their hearts to be true. And he is hearing it too and cannot close his eyes to it, either. The man at the podium decries Germany's suffering from the war. The audience shouts and applauds wildly. Erich is captivated by his sincerity and emotion, encouraged by those around him. And as he listens, a miracle is taking place. The soldier at the front of the room speaks aloud the thoughts in his head. "The feeling of disgrace you carry inside you. Cast it off. It doesn't belong to you! It belongs to those who stabbed the army in the back! Germany has been plagued by confusion and turmoil brought about by the Communists, the cultural parasites, and the industrialists. These things are assaulting our ancient Germanic ways, building factories where there used to be farms. We live in dangerous times," he shouts, "and we must defend ourselves. But these affronts must not stand in the way of Eden, which is rooted in German blood and German soil. German nationhood can be sacrificed for nothing; everything can be sacrificed for our nation! It's up to us to fight! Man creates his destiny and the strongest man rules! Who is the strongest? We are. It's our right to build our dreams and those not willing to fight don't deserve to live! Nature crowns those who master others." He pauses to allow the frenzied crowd to shout and applaud. It's hypnotic.

Erich stares at the floor, shaking in disbelief at his good fortune. He rubs his unshaven face and smiles at the ground then looks up, staring at the man speaking, his black oily hair slicked smooth across his forehead, his fisted hand slamming the lectern. Then it dawns on him that maybe he is right, that this monumental betrayal cost him his pride. It stripped him of his soldierly dignity so that he could do nothing to stop Goliath from beating the woman in the alleyway that rainy night.

"Germany is the greatest nation in the world," the man at the podium continues, "and we must protect it from the internationalists, who are willing to sacrifice it for profit. While we eat and sleep in the streets, profiteers are still exploiting us, working us to the bone until we have nothing, until we are nothing." Everyone applauds so loudly that Erich feels disoriented with a kind of vertigo.

"The age of reason has betrayed us!" he says, after a formidable pause. "Now we must be ruled by our emotion -- to bring us from the depths of despair." He raises his hand and salutes. The crowd in turn salutes him, arms raised in unison, saluting over and over again until Erich's feet rise from the floor and his sight blurs. *There is nothing left to look back on.* There is only shame behind him. He breathes in and exhales then lets himself go completely, saluting and crying out his name. The figure at the front of the room stands stiffly surveying the crowd with approval.

———

It's cold where he stands in the doorway on *Rosenheimer Strasse* within sight of the Ludwig Bridge, where the police have gathered. He can see his breath like some kind of dragon. A hand rests on his pistol strapped to his waist and he feels the cold weight of his rifle pressed against the length of his back. Erich has already said it a thousand times: he is prepared to die for Germany's liberation from the internationalists. Platoons of SA soldiers run back and forth through the streets, spying or guarding key installations. They are warriors once again.

"The march on Berlin has begun," a voice shouts. The police seem only now to awake to the arrival of the revolution and scramble into position. They form a human chain to block the way over the bridge. At the very front of the procession, coming from the direction of the Bürgerbäukeller, Swastika and Bund Oberland flags flap; the glorious leaders of the revolution follow. As the flag carriers pass, the Führer confers with Rosenberg and Ludendorff as they walk. Behind them, a column of several thousand armed troops march, followed by trucks filled with storm troopers. Among the faces, Erich spots Hermann Kessel in his black rubber coat, a steel helmet framing his pudgy face.

"This is an illegal march," a policeman shouts. "Stop or we will fire." Police guns are trained on them and theirs are trained on the police. A group of SA break from the column and beat the police with the butts of their rifles, clearing the way for the advance of the revolutionary army into downtown Munich.

Erich runs from the doorway and jumps into the procession, crossing over the Ludwig Bridge. He feels at one with the armed column, at one with the Nazi revolution, as they move through the streets to the click of marching feet. His chest cocks with pride, as more and more people line the streets shouting support and waving flags as they pass. When Erich arrives at the *Marienplatz*, it's still snowing and the balconies teem with swastikas and imperial banners. People shout and sing *Deutschland über Alles*. The noise from the excited crowd is deafening. More bystanders join the revolutionaries, marching beside the column.

The loud whipping crack of a pistol shot. For a single moment, silence sweeps over their numbers. Then several bursts of gunfire tear through the silence and the column breaks apart completely, rifles un-slung, barrels aimed and firing in a monumental blaze. Right before Erich's eyes, the leaders fall in a hail of bullets. He drops to the ground, thinking he has been struck, hiding behind a small pile of wounded soldiers. He touches the blood on his coat and realizes it is not his.

Erich looks up to see Hermann Kessel clutching his groin, blood flowing between his fingers. Kessel winces in pain like a piglet being slaughtered. He looks down in shock, before falling to the ground.

Panic sweeps over the bloody scene and some from the ranks of the SA flee. "Help me," Kessel says, closing his eyes against the pain.

"Yes," says Erich. He slithers away between the living and the dead, before rising to his feet and running away.

"Coward!" Kessel shouts after him.

"Long live the revolution!" cries Erich, as he escapes the chaos.

13

GUATEMALA CITY

The lobby of the Conquistador Hotel was brightly lit. Men in dark suits reclined on sofas outside the lounge, while a lady strutted across the lobby with two poodles on silver leashes. It was a surreal introduction to a country that the news reported was in the midst of a civil war. Everything about the hotel was clean and sanitized but for the view from his room. Guatemala City appeared gritty and hostile. Josef unpacked the shortwave radio then removed the SS dagger wrapped in cloth, studying its details -- the German eagle and double SS lightning bolt on its black handle and the words *My honour is my trust* engraved on the glistening blade. He placed it under the mattress and fell back on the bed, allowing the tide of exhaustion to wash over him.

Night fell early in Guatemala. Josef rose from a troubled sleep and ventured into the darkened streets, despite a stern warning from the doorman that it wasn't safe after dark. But only the homeless were there, laid out on flattened cardboard boxes. Just off *Ruta 5*, he peered between the iron bars of a window and saw a quiet *cantina* illuminated by a single Coleman lamp hanging from the ceiling. The place was empty but for a barman and a young girl. He entered and found himself a table in the corner of the room where shadows gathered.

"*Cerveza?*" the young man asked, as he approached the wooden table with names and dates carved into it.

"*Algo más fuerte?*"

He brought a bottle of corn liquor to the table. "*Fuego*," he said. "Where did you learn Spanish?"

"Cuba."

"*Un revolucionario.*" He smiled widely. "We need a revolution here." But something stopped him from speaking further. "*Pues, habla muy bien,*" he said quickly, before leaving the table.

The walls were empty but for a poster of an American woman with blond hair groping a beer bottle clutched closely to her breasts. The Mayan man silently cleaned the counter with a rag, while his daughter stared curiously at Josef. Her smile was contagious. He waved to her then turned away, self-conscious of the liquor bottle and his solitary presence before it. He poured a little alcohol from the bottle onto the floor. "*Aché,*" he murmured, in salutation to the *orishas*.

The bartender seemed to recognize the gesture and smiled. "Even gods get thirsty."

A stranger, maybe in his mid-twenties, walked in off the street and ordered a bottle of corn liquor from the counter. As he passed Josef's table, he commented in an unsmiling manner, "If you stare at the poster any longer you'll go blind."

"Care to join me? We can go blind together."

"I'm not much for blonds, but the company is tempting." The young man studied Josef rather grimly then sat down across from him. He introduced himself as Dimitri and pointed to the cluster of enormous moths dancing and smacking suicidally into the gas lantern. "That's us," he said.

"Perhaps. After a few more drinks."

"Guatemala is an open flame. It's the wild west."

"What do you know about it?"

"Too much," he said and picked up the bottle. He glanced toward Josef bitterly before taking a drink and nearly emptied the bottle. Then he added to the silence, "And not as much as I should." He placed the bottle down roughly and nodded his head woefully. "When did you get here?"

"I just arrived."

"Take a week or two -- you'll discover the dark side, the death squads and disappearances. The people are so friendly, you'd never know there's a civil war."

"So what are you doing here?"

"I wanted to ask you the same thing." The tension in Dimitri's posture broke. "We created the Third World, you know? I can't live a normal life in the States knowing what's going on here. Knowing that while some of us are trying to help, my government is training the army how to massacre villagers. And the Guatemalan military is savage. It doesn't waste bullets on women and children. They're smashed against walls, choked, bayoneted." He wobbled in his chair, as he looked cautiously around the room. The bar remained empty.

"You ever hear about the CIA bombings in the fifties?"

"No."

"In '54, those *cabrones* bombed Guatemala City. What for, you ask? I'll tell you. Because they didn't want anyone telling them what to do. The United Fruit Company owned half the country and the president at the time, a dude named Arbenz, proposed they hand over the land they weren't using to the landless peasants...Now this makes my blood boil. United Fruit had always claimed the land was only worth a million dollars, which obviously meant they paid less tax. So Arbenz proposed to compensate them with the one million dollars they said the land was worth. Then the company turned around and demanded they receive the sixteen million dollars that the land was really worth. Ah, but you claimed the land was only worth a million dollars when you had to pay tax on it!" said Dimitri, slamming the table. "Arbenz politely told them to go fuck themselves. To this, the American government, my government -- *for the people by the people*, goddamn it! -- responded with a small band of terrorists and the bombs began to drop from CIA planes."

Josef couldn't speak, his head heavy with drink.

"You can't begin to understand the politics of Central America," continued Dimitri, "without considering land. It has always been a problem, with a handful of the most powerful controlling all the best land, leaving only the scraps for the poor subsistence farmers. In North America and Europe, we think slavery ended a hundred and fifty years ago and that somehow, in the meantime, everything has been equalized. But in reality, almost nothing has changed, because the racism and oppression against the indigenous remains the same -- as does the poverty, poor education, and health. And I'm not just talking about Guatemala. This history has repeated itself throughout Latin America."

"So does the U.S. still have their hands in the pie?"

"Fucking right they do! The CIA has been paying officials in G-2."

"G-2? Sounds like a rock band."

"Only the most powerful military intelligence organization in Guatemala. They have safe houses everywhere and orchestrate the big civilian massacres. This country is ripe for something larger and more terrible to happen." Dimitri reclined in his seat then sprung forward menacingly. "The truth is out there. It's waiting to be discovered. Sometimes the truth can be found on the front page of the newspaper. It's just most people can't see it for what it is. Guatemala seems unimportant to the world so almost anything goes."

"It's late," Josef said, overwhelmed. "I think I'm going to go back to my room. Let me buy your drinks."

Dimitri grinned. "The Peace Corp is lousy pay." As he got up to leave, his face darkened. He clutched Josef's shirt sleeve, pulling him close, as if to whisper something. But then, resigned to silence, he let go and stood.

On the sidewalk out in front of the *cantina*, the American looped his finger lazily in the air. "History always repeats itself." He waved good-bye and staggered down the middle of the darkened street.

——

The sun is setting, its warm light falling over the Munich shrine for the martyrs of the *putsch* of 1923. Erich stands among his comrades, receiving a medal in honour of his historic actions that day. It is also a day marking the importance of self-sacrifice. Sixteen brave souls died that day, their blood drenching the righteous flags of the march. Their blood is holy water and Erich is touched with the flag so that he will be blessed for all times.

When Erich walks into the apartment, Marta is there. She looks upset and is listening to the radio. He proudly marches around in front of her so she can see his glistening medal.

Marta slaps his face. "You fool. They took away Jacob Zimmer."

"Who did?"

"Who do you think? Your National Socialists."

"Calm down. I'll go see Herr Kessel."

"And tell him what? To release Jacob? That he isn't like the others? That he's one of the good Jews?"

He can say nothing to appease her.

"And what about the others?"

"At the very worst, they'll be resettled in Poland or Madagascar."

"We aren't talking about *they*. We're talking about people we know. And if you think that's the very worst that can happen to them -- that they'll be shipped off to God knows where -- then you really are a fool."

He picks up the phone and begins dialing. "You'll see. Everything will be fine."

———

Erich is escorted into the austere office at the *Bendlerstrasse* in Berlin. Herr Kessel remains seated behind his desk looking uninterested. Erich stands arrow straight and fingers the medal on his uniform. "Herr Kessel, it appears a Jew named Jacob Zimmer has been mistakenly arrested."

"I can assure you, it wasn't us. And if he has been taken away, it's because he's a communist."

"Jacob is a veteran of the First War. He was my captain at the Somme."

"Traitors are everywhere. The communists are sucking dry the blood of our country."

"You don't understand. Jacob is good man. He's a German officer of the highest order—"

"How dare you! There's no such thing as a German Jew! You can't be a German if you're a Jew. It's a biological impossibility."

"You must help me—"

"I need do nothing at all."

Erich takes a deep breath to quiet his trembling voice. "Herr Kessel, in my thirteen years of service to the party, I've given everything and asked for nothing in return. Jacob Zimmer must go free."

Kessel frowns and seems about to dismiss him when he takes notice of the medal on his uniform. "So you've been with us from the beginning."

"Yes."

"Maybe I can help you." Kessel takes several heavy steps and approaches him, a warm smile appearing on his chubby face. He looks up from the medal and meets eyes with Erich. His smile fades and he takes a step back. "I know you."

"Yes, Herr Kessel."

"Now I remember." He says, as recognition sweeps across his face. "You left me for dead."

"It wasn't me," Erich stutters, but it's too late.

Kessel tears the medal off his uniform. "I should have you shot!"

"I've always been loyal."

"A loyal coward! Join the Wehrmacht, you filthy bastard. Get out of my sight!"

———

Morning arrived like a fierce hangover. Josef awoke with the late morning sun pouring in through the bay window, his clothes smelling old and stale. He stumbled toward the window and saw a city in full motion. Lumbering buses, side-walk vendors, and women dressed in traditional Maya garb crossing the road. Then it all came back to him. Guatemala City. *The Barber of Berlin.* SS colonel Hans von Flintz, commandant of Übel. If von Flintz was here, he had probably changed his name -- last name only, according to Ziegler. *It's too unnatural.* That's when he heard Asena's voice remind him *never to underestimate the obvious.* He was compelled by a crazy notion and pulled out a phone book to look up all the barbers in the city.

———

Josef left the hotel and headed south along *avenida* 6, past the seventeenth century churches and monuments to the crowded dusty streets of *avenida Bolívar.* His senses were dull and, at first, he was overwhelmed by the chaos, the relentless pushing of humanity, the black clouds of soot spewed from passing buses. In time, though, this feeling passed and what he had seen as a single overwhelming blur began to divide so that he could now see individual forms -- the woman making tortillas at her stand, the multitude of vendors selling every-thing, including single cigarettes from containers and Coca Cola in plastic bags.

Along the avenue, set against the rows of colonial build-ings, young boys and old men kneeled before their shoe stools with their kits of oils and rags, polishing the shoes of bored looking men. One boy worked frantically on the shoes of a man dressed in a linen suit, the boy snapping his cloth loudly on the end stroke, as if to summon the attention of the patron to his commitment to shine above the others. Half-starved dogs ran wild among the booths scavenging for food. Across the way, a boy dashed into the street where a bus waited at a red light. On the tips of his toes, he reached into the window with a bag of mango slices. A hand emerged, pinched the mangoes, and dropped coins into the boy's outstretched hand.

Mayan women were dressed in woven clothes of vibrant reds, purples, and greens. Even the poorest people seemed to possess a most astounding dignity. As Josef moved on, shielding his eyes from the dust churned up by a crowded bus speeding by, he settled into a comfortable pace. Men and women hauled enormous baskets filled with live poultry in and out of buses, across streets, over to stoops, where they placed the baskets down and waited for connecting buses to other outlying regions, perhaps to the jungle region of El Petén or Panajachel on Lake Atitlán.

Set against a row of colonial buildings, the sign had been painted in the colour of dried blood. Josef stood there, head craned, mouth agape. The sign read: THE BARBER OF BERLIN. *After the war, it was business as usual*, Ziegler had said. *The architects kept building, the doctors kept healing. The barbers kept cutting.* It was as if von Flintz was scared of nothing -- or perhaps he wanted to be found.

A bell chimed as Josef pushed open the door. Three older men were huddled by a magazine rack near the front window. The centre of attention was unmistakeably the *commandant* of Übel, SS colonel Hans von Flintz. Josef coached himself to remain calm. The old Nazi patted down his white oiled hair and tucked his hands into the pockets of a wool vest. By all appearances, Hans von Flintz was no longer the man he was during his wartime days, but he was unmistakeably well preserved. He possessed a distinct sense of confidence and stood arrow straight with the posture of a man half his age. Josef was so lost in thought, he remained unaware he was staring until the old men look at him suspiciously. Josef pointed to the row of barbers' chairs facing a long mirror.

"Not today," said von Flintz.

"We're closed," growled a well-groomed but undernourished looking man. His wet eyes kept watch of Josef.

"Today," said von Flintz, emboldened by his comrades' amusement, "I choose not to work." There was a titter, then all out laughter.

Josef flipped over the CLOSED sign on the window and made to leave.

Von Flintz allowed the tiniest smirk to pass over his lips.

"Come on, Hans. Leave the boy alone," said a drawn-looking man, before turning to Josef. "We're just taking the piss out of you." He introduced himself as Max. "But you can call me Maxie."

"Nice meeting you, Maxie."

Reinhard, the man with reptilian eyes, reluctantly barked his name.

Josef managed a smile as Hans directed him to a chair and tied a bib around him. The old Nazi donned a white surgeon's smock and pulled out the straight razor. There was a scar across his neck that appeared in none of the Übel photos. The small clique of men talked amongst themselves about Josef in German. He tried to look relaxed but focused his attention on their conversation. Reinhard whispered something to Max, but Josef couldn't make any of it out.

"*I don't believe in mystics*," Max replied, in a low voice.

"Still, maybe it's a sign."

"Shuuuuuuuuush!" Max responded like a child, looking over his shoulder at Hans.

"Don't cut him Doc," said Reinhard, as he pointed to the scar on Hans' throat.

Hans laughed and raised the blade. His hand shook terribly. Everyone laughed. The hand stopped shaking and Hans slapped Josef's back. "Hans Gründer at your service," he said, before carefully laying out his instruments on a cloth. He moved close and examined Josef's face critically. "How do you shave? Disposable razor, am I right?"

Josef nodded.

"I knew it. Your face is a disaster. Don't use that rubbish again. You might as well shave with a pencil sharpener, my boy. Leave it to the experts." He pointed a thumb proudly to his chest. "We know what's best for you. We've been doing it for thousands of years!"

"The Barber is the most noble profession," Reinhard piped in.

"Shut up." Von Flintz scowled then turned back to Josef. "Some say it's a poor man's job." He grinned and pulled out a wad of money. "I say otherwise."

"And you should see where he lives," said Reinhard.

"But that's not why I do it. We've always played an historic role in the civilizing of mankind."

"I'm sure," Josef responded in German.

"You speak German?"

Reinhard and Max exchanged a nervous glance.

"Where did you learn?"

"My mother."

Reinhard approached the mirror and combed his hair, though kept a watchful eye fixed on Josef.

"As you can see, his vanity has outlived the beauty of his youth," said von Flintz. "He has both admiration and contempt for the young, don't you? Yes, you do." He turned back to Josef. "What's your name?"

"Josef."

"Josef what?"

"Josef…Gould."

"You're Israeli, no?"

Josef's mouth dried up completely.

"I can tell from your accent," said von Flintz. For a moment, he looked at Josef with something approaching familiarity. He rested a hand on his shoulder. As he prepared a hot towel, Hans said, "You can learn a lot from men like Reinhard. Not because they're teachers. No. But their lives are lessons. What you'll learn about men like Reinhard is that they're cowards."

"I'm not a coward."

"In their youth, they were brave -- they took bold steps into the unknown -- but now with old age creeping up, their hair receding, their memory faltering, the only thing left is their vanity. And they have nothing left to be vain about! What's up ahead, Reinhard? Can you see? Your dreaded grim reaper pounding on the door! Until weaklings like Reinhard embrace their fate, I will continue to call them cowards." He paused an instant. "Being from Israel, Josef, you must have served in the military like everyone else."

Josef nodded.

"You're lucky you're here and not in Lebanon right now. Those poor people. Haven't they been through enough already? Apparently, they're calling up more reserves."

"I heard."

"So what are you doing in our neck of the woods?"

"Business."

"Business? Well that could pretty well be anything."

"He doesn't say much, does he?" said Reinhard.

Josef addressed Reinhard directly: "Just because we have mouths, doesn't mean we should always use them."

Hans chuckled, amused. "Well said."

When the old Nazi had finished shaving Josef's face, he stopped and held him by the shoulders.

Max put down his magazine, scratched his pale arm, and looked at Josef. "He looks a lot like him, doesn't he?"

"Yes, he does."

Josef rose from the barber chair and placed several Quetzal notes on the counter, including a sizeable tip. He stepped toward the door then stopped, as an idea came to him. He doubled back to Hans von Flintz, as he cleaned his instruments and whispered: "You're being investigated by a special prosecutions tribunal in Israel. So watch out."

"How thoughtful of you," he grinned. "Are you also looking for old soldiers before they kick off?"

"And perhaps sell them some guns along the way."

"A few of your compatriots have already been by. I've got nothing to hide. I've been in Latin America since before the war."

"Clearly, another case of mistaken identity."

As Josef turned to leave, Hans grabbed his arm. "How long are you here, my boy?"

"A while."

"Well, come back soon." Hans von Flintz pointed to the money on the counter. "And thanks for the tip."

14

INROADS

Josef stood at his hotel room window and watched the grey clouds roll up and over the outlying mountains. He plucked at his neck, deep in thought. *What were the barbershop Nazis up to? Why weren't they in hiding? How could he be certain they were behind his parents' murder? And why would they have done it unless they knew they were about to get caught?* His thoughts turned to the visions. He wondered what else they could reveal, given Hauptmann's diaries had been erased by time.

Then it came to him.

He had to marvel how he hadn't thought of it earlier. From his packsack, he retrieved one of the diaries and opened it. *If he wanted to know what was written on those damn pages then why not will it?* He focused on the empty page, patiently breathing. Big breath in. Long exhale out. *No mind*, he could hear Asena say. Then, just as his thoughts began to dissolve, Josef saw Hauptmann's hand as if it were his own, writing in the diary, revealing the words that so long had been erased from its pages.

MAY 15, 1938

I was recalled from leave. Damn it! Marta and I spent a wonderful few days on the beach in Alba. We sipped champagne and lounged on a blanket. Marta wore a sun hat, her pale skin burning in the hot Italian sun. Each time I came back from swimming, Marta would kiss the salt off my shoulder. I think Napoleon came to this island to live out his days in exile. Who could imagine a more beautiful place to be imprisoned? Times like these must be embraced, because they are fleeting. Peace is fleeting. The world is always at war.

The day before I was called back to base, Marta and I were on the beach when she asked me to draw something. I decided to draw her. She wrapped her arms around her knees with a little girl smile, and I went to work sketching like I used to at art school in Vienna. I drew the details of Marta that I love so much -- her clear eyes, her button-like nose, the thin line of her lips. Two Germans approached. The handsome one wanted me to draw him so he could send it to his girlfriend. Marta offered them some champagne. One of them was from Hamburg, the other Munich. The handsome one had his blood type and the twin lightning bolts of the SS tattooed on the underside of his left arm. I could not help myself and told him I took part in the *Putsch* in '23. He did not believe me. I did my best not to show my anger. I had dedicated thirteen years to the party and in a single moment -- standing before Herr Kessel -- the dream was over. I did what Kessel suggested in his rage and re-joined the Wehrmacht. After all, there was no certainty that I could make a living as an artist and I needed a steady job to prove to Marta that I could support her. Of course, Marta has her ways. She said she would have preferred being married to a poor artist than a soldier possessing all the riches in the world. She never fails to remind me that the National Socialists made Jacob Zimmer vanish without a trace.

When I had finished drawing the SS man, embellishing the sketch with several heroic details not actually present in his person, he did not even thank me. I asked him where he was serving. He told me they were posted in Spain and that it was a disaster for the loyalists. According to him, the Bolsheviks are rounding up and shooting their own. The devilish wolves eat their young, he said, and soon the communist Spaniards would be kissing German feet, thanking us for saving them from those Russian bastards. But Marta stepped out of line when she said, *A pox on all of them, including the goddamn Nazis.* I apologized on her behalf, but the two officers looked unimpressed. She told me not to apologize for her, that she knew what she was saying. I was embarrassed and shaking with anger, and so I smacked her clear across the face. The SS men seemed satisfied with my gesture.

SEPTEMBER 19, 1939

The invasion of western Poland is complete. The opposition consisted of poorly organized formations. We are stationed in a peaceful village near Kalisz. Nobody wants trouble, and we are mostly bored. Eating well, too! According to rumour, the Bolsheviks have taken over eastern Poland. I would not trust them to honour a truce!

APRIL 2, 1940
Up at 5am. The sound of frantic mortar and machine gun fire a few miles away. We have to stay vigilant with the rise of partisan activities. They are using the forests for cover. They know this countryside better than we do. Just last week an entire *kompanie* of infantry was wiped out in an ambush. Cowardly tactics!

NOVEMBER 23, 1940
Dawn again. Partisans hit and run on our camp. Tricky bastards. Went out to survey the damage. Lost seven men. A bloody mess. We caught several partisans wounded in battle. We did not make their end very pleasant, which helped satisfy the men's thirst for revenge. Seeing things that I never thought I would have to witness again. I do not know where this war is going, but I have to believe we will achieve something that we were not able to in the first one.

JUNE 24, 1941
It has started! We have begun to liberate Poland from the Russians! Our *kompanie* is moving east. With the Luftwaffe's superiority, we can advance quickly, smoking out the enemy

hiding in the forests and blow up their bridges. Our plan is to make their lives hell! Good start!

AUGUST 9, 1941

On the move at dawn. Battalion has split off. We are to re-group in a week. If all goes well, the incursion into Russia will be a peaceful re-occupation of lands that have always belonged to the Germans.

AUGUST 14, 1941

We entered the town of Lentsky today, a column of men one hundred and fifty strong. No casualties for two days! Even after an all-day march, the men remained steady on their feet. A brown haze clings to the eastern skies, perhaps a sign of things to come. Unfortunately, news from the bloody front provides us with little comfort. We marched hungry and proud through the centre of town, giving notice that the victorious Wehrmacht had arrived in the name of German *Lebensraum*. My commanding officer is Captain Spiegel. He sniffs incessantly, mile after mile of the march, so that if one is not looking, it sounds like he is amused and is laughing. The town remained quiet, with the exception of a ragged dog that barked and raced toward our column. It was a silly looking thing, with long tangled hair, large floppy ears and a harmless set of teeth. Just the same, a soldier took a moment to reach for it, maybe to pet it. When he could not catch hold, he withdrew his pistol and shot the shoddy-looking creature. It was a senseless thing to do.

AUGUST 15, 1941

Stuck in Lentsky until we get orders from command. We have set up camp in the last house on the street. Captain Spiegel suspected Jews lived there, because it was the nicest house in town; only the blood-sucking Jew would have the nerve to wipe his neighbours' nose in it. My Captain was about to barge in when a well groomed man with a narrow aristocratic face and thick spectacles opened the door. He said he was a school teacher and that his family had all gone to visit relatives in Luninec. Captain Spiegel informed him we were taking over the house. The crazy Slav actually challenged the order. Had he failed to notice the street filled with soldiers carrying machine guns, grenades and flame-throwers?

My Captain pushed past the ignorant man, and I followed right behind. The man pleaded for us not to touch anything, his short footsteps trying to keep up. At the top of the staircase, an ornate cross hung on the wall. I suspected my Captain had been mistaken when he said the teacher was a Jew.

Eventually, Captain Spiegel found what he was looking for in the master bedroom. He pushed his fat fingers through the mess of jewelry inside several ornate boxes sitting on a dresser. It was strange that in the middle of this war, with death ever present and no certainty of life, one would seek to enrich oneself. My Captain saw a wedding picture of the teacher in front of a church and addressed the Jewish question. The aristocrat made the mistake of answering back disdainfully about the lower nature of the Jew. My Captain was none too pleased and warned about being spoken to like that. The Slav still did not understand, so the captain drew his pistol and whipped it against the side of the teacher's face. I was stunned by his stupidity -- how he could be so oblivious to his fate should he continue to be so ill-mannered toward Captain Spiegel? The captain began placing the jewelry into a draw-string pouch.

The teacher protested once more, his face bloody, his broken glasses sitting lopsided on his face. My Captain reached for the teacher's face, pulling off his broken spectacles and crushed them underfoot. The aristocrat called him a bastard to which My Captain sniffed so that it sounded like he was laughing. The teacher actually smiled, perhaps thinking the captain had discovered a sense of humour. The teacher was still on all fours when Captain Spiegel squeezed the trigger, sending aristocratic brains everywhere. Under his breath, Captain Spiegel muttered something about the callous disrespect shown by the goddamn Slavs.

AUGUST 16, 1941

Tragedy has struck! A sleepless night, after a memorable evening with comrades listening to music on the aristocrat's gramophone. The upstairs had been taken over by the enlisted men, and it did not take long for the first of them to uncover a large store of food. An almost deafening roar followed when Private Huber discovered the wine cellar down below.

Throughout the evening, we drank and smoked and laughed above the sound of the records being played on the gramophone, pulling apart links of spicy sausage and eating them on hunks of fresh bread. My Captain told the story of the belligerent teacher over and over again, and with each hour that passed and with each empty wine bottle discarded, our laughter became more riotous. But with each telling, Captain Spiegel became increasingly delirious with rage, foaming at the mouth and waving his arms like a windmill. He said something like, *How can you expect children to grow up like human beings, if their teachers show no reverence for power? These Slavs are no better than apes if they cannot figure out that the master rules.* Drunken laughter filled the room, followed by a "here-here" and a clink of glasses. *His disrespect toward me was inexcusable. I should go up there and shoot him again.* Then he turned to me. His face was swollen and tired, his breath reeking of sausage and fermented grapes. He told me there was another ring upstairs that he wanted and that if any of those thieves up there stole it, he would have the whole *kompanie* shot.

Later, my Captain led us in song. It was wonderful, and I felt I was part of something very important. Then a voice from upstairs cried "Fire." I thought it was a prank and I was very angry. But then I smelled smoke and heard the trample of footsteps rushing down the wooden staircase. I called for everyone to grab their guns, that it could be an ambush. Captain Spiegel was the first to run from the room. He bravely headed up the staircase, staggering and pushing his way past the line of descending soldiers. When he neared the top of the stairs, he cried something about the diamond ring. When we all made it out to the empty street, someone directed our attention to the second floor window. Above, a figure danced around. Flames were tearing off my Captain, as he appeared to be chasing something around the room. He moved to the window and instantly set the curtains on fire. He was shrieking a most unfathomable screech so that all one hundred and fifty members of 2nd *Kompanie* remained absolutely silent.

AUGUST 17, 1941

Entered a Jew's home today. I will admit, the experience has shaken me. After the terrible loss of my Captain, I have taken command of the *kompanie* until we rejoin our battalion. Despite the flames shooting from the aristocrat's house, no one in the village offered a bucket of water to douse the flames. Maybe they were afraid of us. Or perhaps they have always despised the teacher's wealth and so gleefully watched it burn up. My first command was that there would be no more drinking in the *kompanie*. One fire and one captain was more than enough for one night. I decided we would camp out at a house on the edge of town, far from the reach of the teacher's smouldering house. When I arrived on the porch with Private Huber and 2nd Lieutenant Wolf, I saw a mezuzah fixed to the doorframe and knew immediately that Jews lived there. I knocked and a very old man opened the door and greeted us in German. I warned him that Russia was Germany now and that advertizing he was a Jew would get him killed. I cannot remember what he said next, but I offered to remove the mezuzah from his doorframe. He kindly refused and looked out at the road and asked if the whole German army was there. I laughed. It was only a single *kompanie*. He grinned. The Jews have a peculiar sense of humour. I remembered that from my days with Jacob Zimmer in the trenches.

The old Jew introduced us to his granddaughters, Beth and Hannah, then invited us to stay overnight. Wolf called him a dirty Jew and spat on him. The Jew smiled and said he could not apologize for what he was. I sent Wolf away on some duty or other. The Jew stood there with his two granddaughters and asked me if I had any children. His question caused me considerable pain, given the distance between me and Marta and the war that was keeping us apart. I decided not to trouble the Jew and ordered our men to setup camp in a nearby field. Before leaving, I asked him why they had not run away. He said the history of the Jews had always been one of flight and that had not always saved them. So he decided to stay and fight the best way he knew how. I asked him how. He said, *With love.*

AUGUST 20, 1941

Doubt has found me. I have been unable to eat since Lentsky. Sleep comes in fits and starts, and I have no desire to speak. One of the last orders I gave was for 2nd *Kompanie* to strike camp and march east to regroup with our battalion. Before departing, I went back to the old Jew's house and warned him he should leave, that I could not protect him. He actually said, *protect us against what*? I did not answer. I knew he knew, but the Jew wanted me to say it.

I was standing in the dirt street with my men, when the first lorries filled with the Order Police arrived and began rounding up the Jews. Private Huber looked over at me, anxious. We marched out of town and for most of the morning we moved across the terrible landscape. Along the roadside, awful things happened. Three SS men circled an Hassidic Jew, laughing as they cut off his side curls. An old bearded Jew was on his knees begging to several officers. One of the officers unzipped his pants and pissed on him. When I looked back at Private Huber, he was staring down at the ground, his face wrinkled with despair. I do not think he saw the Jews on the outskirts of another Russian town being forced to sing and dance around the tombstones at gun point before being shot. And I pray to God he did not hear the mother holding her young daughter, begging the *Ordnungspolizei* to kill them first -- to spare them suffering -- before the others.

15

THE BARBER OF BERLIN

In what seemed to be an echo from a past life, Josef recalled how Hector had once referred to the emergence of Josef's visions as *dar a luz*, which in Spanish meant "to give to light." It was the same term used for women giving birth. Certainly Josef was still not at peace with the visions, but he accepted that they had directed him to the hidden documents in the wall at Übel, as one would reluctantly accept the aid of an enemy if one's life absolutely depended on it. The visions were a light shining on the past that had been buried for decades. Without them, the terrible life of Erich Hauptmann would have been erased forever.

The phone rang.

Josef looked over at the phone from his place on the bed. It rang again, urgently. He picked it up on the forth ring.

"*¿Quien es?*"

"Do you realize you've done what your parents never did?"

"Saul?"

"You actually caught yourself a Nazi. Mind you, nabbing Ziegler in jail was like going hunting in a zoo." Saul's tone seemed light with relief. "And Hans, well, it looks like he has been hiding in plain sight."

"Saul, how did you pull off my prison release in Germany? Wait. And how the hell did you know I found Hans?"

There was silence on the other end of the line.

"Really, Saul, how long are those tentacles of yours?"

"They can never be long enough."

Josef was disturbed. "How did you find me?"

"I spy on the spies, hunt the hunters," said Saul, unable to contain his hubris. "I can trace the movement of a dung beetle in Sri Lanka if I want. I just don't choose to collect that kind of information. I keep track of my own."

"So do you have *sayanim* running around spying for you, is that it?"

"There's a lot of misinformation about informants. And we spread it around on purpose. Officially, no one volunteers to assist us. And, really, we can't rely on the small Jewish population in Guatemala to help. But money and blackmail are always good motivators for gathering intel."

Josef sank back into his pillow and confessed, "I told the old Nazi my name was Josef *Gould*."

Saul erupted in laughter.

"I don't know anything about this shit. I'm an archaeologist."

"My little half-breed, the ability to lie well is a fucking virtue. Lying is deception; deception is the key to infiltration. And that," he said proudly, "leads to death."

"Death?"

"Do I have to spell it out? Assassination, Josef. You have to get close to kill your enemies."

"My German wasn't good enough to go undercover."

"They would've figured it out in a second, anyway. SS men aren't dumb. There's a reason so many have never been caught."

"I thought that was because of a global conspiracy against the Jews."

"That too."

"Maybe I'll just tell him what I'm doing in Guatemala. *I'm here to put your Nazi ass behind bars.* SS probably appreciate honesty."

"No, they don't."

"Saul, I'm seriously out of my depth here."

"You gotta move quick, J."

"But if I act too fast, something valuable might get lost."

"You think he's hiding something?"

"I think he's hiding a lot."

"So what did you tell him?"

"That I could sell him guns."

"OK, that's not bad. So listen up. You're an arms dealer and you're working for Galil Armaments. They just built a plant in Copán. I'll let them know you're working with them for the next few months. Arms dealers sell their souls the day they sign their first contract," Saul said, bluntly. "They sell land mines painted pretty colours to attract children, who pick them up and get their hands blown to pieces. Not killed. Maimed. So they'll always be a drain on the economy. You understand what I'm getting at here? The nature of the business requires a morally neutral person -- a sale is a sale -- and von Flintz will know this. Remember, hunters don't just track prey. And a warrior isn't a warrior until he's painted in the blood of his first kill."

"Goddamn you, Liebowitz."

"If you're OK with people wiping their feet on you, be my fucking guest. But I suggest you play it cool, Mr. Gould. But not too cool."

———

The bell above the door chimed as Josef entered the barbershop, and for a moment he thought of entering his parents' shop in Old Jerusalem. Perhaps Hans had owned the shop in Guatemala for as long as his parents had their antique shop and, like them, had used the shop as a front for something more serious. Hans wore his smock and stood behind a distinguished looking man in a business suit. As Hans cut his hair, they discussed the importance of cleanliness. Max and Reinhard flipped through magazines, talking about soccer and who'd likely win the *Bundasliga*. Max was looking jaundiced and that wasn't lost on Reinhard.

"I think you're turning Chinese," remarked Reinhard, his eyes watering.

"At least I don't start crying every time the wind blows," Max fired back. When he saw Josef, his face lit up. "Welcome back, my friend."

"Hi Maxie."

"Are you girls going steady now?"

"Jealousy is most unbecoming," said Hans. "Don't pay Reinhard any mind, my boy. He woke up in a foul mood. Sit. I'll be with you in a few minutes." As he went back to trimming the man's hair, he said, "It's a very unhealthy place. The hygiene is awful and something needs to be done about it. There's no respect for life. Just look at the way they treat their dogs. It's a mess. Believe me, I want to see an end to the civil war. I want peace in my old age, a place of rest."

"Yes," the other man said with a sigh, "something must be done to bring peace."

When the distinguished gentleman took his leave, Hans directed Josef to the chair. Right away, he began talking in a friendly manner, as if he was just another patron and not someone who had delivered a warning of being hunted by the Israelis. He wrapped a hot towel over his face, and Josef had to do everything in his power not to tear it off. In time, however, the heat became tolerable and then downright pleasurable. For an instant, he was Erich Hauptmann lying in a hospital bed with the weight of his bandages covering his sightless eyes.

Hans peeled back the towel and began to lather his face with a soft brush. Then he leaned in close to Josef's ear and directed his attention to Reinhard, who was reading comics. "He loves reading the funnies. There's something wonderful about the naivety of women and children. Give them food. Some clothes. A roof. Perhaps some comic strips. That's all.

They never demand profound answers to life's questions. But coming from a man of his former stature," he said, "there's nothing more pathetic."

The colonel continued to lather Josef's face, approaching the task with ritual care. "Do you know when the practice of shaving began?"

"Here we go again," said Reinhard.

"If you prefer, you can go home and sit by yourself doing what you do here -- *nada!*"

Reinhard scratched his pink nose nervously, while Hans continued to remove excess foam using the back side of the straight razor. "The history of shaving begins a million years ago with the Neanderthal--"

"Neanderthal lived about 100,000 years ago," said Josef, politely correcting him.

"We have a Paleolithic archaeologist in our midst!"

"I was an archaeologist in my past life."

"So at the time the Neanderthal walked the earth, they began modifying their bodies -- pulling out their hair, painting themselves. They used shells to pinch and pull the hair out." Hans gently ran the straight razor down Josef's cheeks. "30,000 years ago, our ancestors used flint to cut their hair. The genealogy is fascinating. Would you like me to continue? Of course you do! Now in 3000 BC razors were developed. Copper razors were used in India and Egypt. The Egyptians shaved their beards and heads. Do you know why? I'll tell you. To prevent the enemy from grasping the soldiers by the hair. You'll probably find this fascinating. Men of unshaven societies were known as barbarians -- the bearded." Hans looked down at Josef, holding the straight razor in front of his face.

"Incredible."

"It is incredible, and it isn't just the Egyptians who were civilized. Some years later, the people of the north, *what some would call Aryans*," he added, "also shaved. They had razors with their own leather carrying cases. The mythic battles of the Nordic peoples were etched into those blades. I actually have an extensive collection at home. One day I'll show them to you. Higher societies always had short hair. It was a sign of their advanced state."

"Like the Buddhists."

"Precisely."

Josef looked up at von Flintz's heap of white hair. "Why do you have long hair?"

"At my age, if you still have hair, you should flaunt it."

Hans cleaned the last flecks of soap from Josef's face with a towel. "Alexander the Great brought the Egyptian practice to Greece. He was said to have been obsessed with cleanliness. Before going into battle, he would always shave. There are many virtues of shaving. The face needs to be -- trained -- yes trained to take a straight razor. You -- Josef -- should come back every few days. It will help."

For a moment, Hans regarded Josef thoughtfully. "You said you are doing business down here. What kind of business?"

"Arms."

"An Israeli arms dealer?" he said, looking with mock surprise. "How original."

"Hans, you could use his connections," Reinhard piped in.

He gave Reinhard a sharp look then smoothed his white hair with a hand. "Josef and I are having an adult conversation. Now, where was I?" he said to himself. "Yes, now I found it. Who's your biggest client?"

"South Africa."

"May I ask what you sell them?"

"Small arms. Surface to air missiles. Surveillance equipment."

"So you're keeping Apartheid alive and well!"

"I provide a service."

"That a boy, keep your hands clean. Though one day you may have to take a stand."

"I do every day."

"What stand is that?"

"Myself."

"So I don't imagine you're Mossad then," probed Hans. "You're not in Guatemala developing your networks, handling assets, etcetera etcetera."

"You seem to know."

"No tradecraft -- you know, tailing, coding and decoding of messages? How are you at handling radio detection equipment?"

"I don't use the stuff; I just sell it."

"I heard something fascinating recently. Did you know they interview more than a thousand Jews for just fifteen spots in one of their Mossad training classes? There's a reason they've been so ruthlessly successful. But I'll tell you this, Josef: if you're an Israeli spy, never get caught in Israeli underwear while in enemy territory," he said, amused. "It's a dead giveaway. I think a few agents have been strung up for this little oversight."

"I'll keep that in mind," said Josef. "By the way, I am wearing Israeli underwear."

"Just keep it clean," smiled Hans, "and everything will be alright." Then the old Nazi turned his attention to Josef's family. "So you were born in Israel, I imagine."

"My father was a French Jew."

Reinhard let out a burst of nervous laughter. Max seemed dumb-struck by his candidness. But Hans, his eyes didn't waver.

"My mother was a German from Bavaria. They met at a red cross camp. Her village was bombed to pieces and she lost all her brothers and sisters. She never recovered from the war."

Hans grimaced but managed a smile. "We're the survivors. We must honour that. And we must appreciate that in life, there is pain. Why do you think I still cut hair? Do I need the money?" he asked, turning to his comrades.

"You?" Reinhard broke into a fit of laughter.

"I can cut and shave with my eyes closed. It's second nature, really, and there's a certain freedom about that. Being a barber reminds me of simpler times." He pointed his straight razor at the others. "And, of course, where would these sad fools go if I was to close shop? They need me. And perhaps I need them a little too."

"Are you friends from the war?"

Von Flintz smiled. "What do you take us for -- a bunch of Nazis? Do you want to see my immigration papers or would that still not be enough proof for you?" Hans tossed the towel down.

"It's true," Reinhard said. "Hans arrived here long before the rest of us. I even saw a Guatemalan newspaper clipping about him from the 1930s. 'The Barber from Berlin,' it was called. Wasn't it, Hans?"

Hans nodded gravely.

"Christ, he's been here longer than most of the Indians."

Desperate to escape the cloud that had descended over the room, Josef handed Hans money. The old Nazi waved it away. Josef was forced to retreat to the door. Max appeared to be fighting himself then broke from his place and quickly followed Josef out the door. "Wait up. I've got to run to the bakery for my wife."

As they stepped outside, Reinhard called after them, "But you aren't even married."

On the front steps, Max stopped him. "You shouldn't have done that."

"I'm sorry."

"Why are you bringing the war up? We lived it."

"I live it every day Maxie."

The old German looked at him curiously. "Let's walk."

16

STALINGRAD

JULY 25, 1942.

All quiet the past few days. No casualties among our numbers. Still, I feel anxious. My chest is tight, as if something heavy is pressed against me. We have been advancing at a steady pace though got stuck in a traffic jam when several panzer army groups converged on the same roads. What a disaster! We were forced to camp out for nearly a week. There are rumours that we are to take Stalingrad. I hope to God the war ends soon. This is a country of terrible extremes. In the summer, the sun beats down on our heads, and the winter freezes our fingers and toes off. I say, let the Russians keep this hellhole so we can go home to our families! Since Lentsky, I have come to see myself as a prisoner of this war. I am not free. If I tried to walk away, I would be shot.

AUGUST 23, 1942

Roused from sleep by the sound of hundreds of planes flying overhead. We are still miles away from the Volga River, but we could hear the murderous sound of thunder and feel the earth shake. Stalingrad burst into flames and lit up the night skies. I cannot imagine anyone surviving that inferno. God have mercy on all of us.

AUGUST 26, 1942

Cannot sleep. Days of continuous Luftwaffe bombardment. Stalingrad blazing like nothing I have ever seen before. I am certain not a single living thing -- no rat, let alone human -- could survive such a tempest of flame.

AUGUST 30, 1942

Arrived today just a few hundred meters from the west bank of the Volga. More lorries arriving by the minute. Soldiers are already stumbling drunk and celebrating among the smouldering ruins of Stalingrad. There is a sense of relief here, and the men are playing mouth organs and singing and dancing in the rubble. They have earned the right to celebrate. They have risked their necks to smash their way through the lines of the Red Army. One has to imagine that Stalingrad is not the goal but rather a doorway to the ports along the Caspian Sea. In the distance, I see civilians picking through the ruins of the city. Major Eberhard points out that it is a testament to the Russian devils and their unwillingness to die. He is the type of commander who is fond of saying things like, *Our accomplishments will be forever recorded in the books of history* or *We are living in glorious times*, even as the whiff of rotting corpses is carried on the breeze. A bitter-sweet victory.

SEPTEMBER 2, 1942

I am worried about Private Huber. He is dressed in a shred-
ded uniform and could easily be mistaken for one of those
homeless Russians caught out by the air raids. He is not well
and his mind is unsound. Can anyone blame him? Huber is
the only original member left of our *kompanie* -- the rest were
killed in suicidal counter-attacks by the Russians along the
front last winter. We kept shooting, line after Russian line
dropping, but they continued on in droves until our positions
were overrun. The Russians never seemed to mind the cold.
They did not even seem to mind dying. How can you win
against such an enemy?

SEPTEMBER 3, 1942

Haunted by events that took place more than a year ago.
How many realms of hell have I passed through since
Lentsky, yet my mind still takes me back there. The fiery death of Captain Spiegel in the upstairs window is
as distant and meaningless as all the other deaths I have
witnessed. Yet the old Jew with his granddaughters still
remains buried inside me like a painful thorn. I am convinced he wanted me to witness his humanity and, despite
my resistance, he succeeded in his wish. I am burdened by
the memory of the Order Police gathering the village Jews
by a giant pit dug by Russian prisoners. The old man and
his grandchildren were among them. The commander of
the police battalion gave the call and I was powerless to
stop what happened next.

The machine guns were raised. The old man and his grand-daughters stood defiantly, as if their pride would act as some kind of shield against the bullets. I wanted them to run or resist but they did nothing. For a single moment frozen for-ever in memory, the elderly man looked right at me, his blue eyes staring out across the pit of death. As he turned back to face the guns, he smiled -- as if he understood why I needed to witness this terrible moment. In the next instant, several bullets struck him in the chest so that his pale flesh crumpled and he dropped lifelessly into the pit. His granddaughters remained standing with open eyes when they were shot, their worried faces twisting in agony for only a second before tum-bling into the mass grave of the dead and dying.

SEPTEMBER 4, 1942

While on patrol, we arrived at a scene of terrible carnage af-ter Ivan had dropped a grenade into the midst of some cel-ebrating enlisted men. Blew them to rags. A few survivors with missing limbs howled like wounded dogs. I asked Major Eberhard if we should try to rescue them, despite the presence of Russian guns in nearby buildings. He said that if those goddamn enlisted men were not dead by nightfall, he would personally kill them himself. And I believed him.

SEPTEMBER 11, 1942

Sleep still very disturbed. I lie awake, eyes open. My mind races. I hate my life and wish I could crawl out of my body and escape this place. Clearly, the endless war is getting to me. The Russians scurry like rats through the ruined city, pre-paring to do battle. As Private Huber pointed out, they have nothing left to lose so will probably fight to the last man. Very bad news for those of us who want this war to be over.

SEPTEMBER 21, 1942

Early morning. Patrolling and hunting down the last pockets of resistance held up in the ruins of Stalingrad. We ambushed a unit of women combatants. Several men from our platoon hesitated and that cost us four lives. We finally dispatched those poor devils after a heavy firefight. My god, every time we think we have killed the last Russian, more arrive from across the Volga. This *rattenkrieg* is endless. How do you win a war without a frontline? I am afraid of the answer.

SEPTEMBER 25, 1942

We did three patrols today. Trying to secure this mess. The smell of rotting corpses cannot be escaped. Tens of thousands of dead pinned under the rubble. Dogs feast on exposed flesh. Watched Stukas dive-bomb Russian boats trying to bring more soldiers over. We were caught out by a sniper positioned on the third floor of a half-destroyed building. It was quite a scene. A cluster of Panzer tanks then stalled before a 12-foot mountain of rubble. The last tank began lobbing shells at the building. Maybe he saw what we did not. The long barrel of an anti-tank gun pointing out of a bullet-peppered window. The anti-tank gun lit up and scored a direct hit on the thin side of the tank's armour. The top lid of the burning tank burst open but the helmeted head peeking out was instantly shot off.

SEPTEMBER 26, 1942

Out on another clearing mission. The air is heavy with death. As the battle for the ruins of Stalingrad continues, I am told our supply lines are being sabotaged by partisans to the west, and that is why we are running short of food and ammunition. Stalin has left us no gift parcels of food to eat. And if he did, I would not touch it. He most certainly would have poisoned it! Despite the hardships, I have not been able to bring myself to tell Marta that I am a prisoner of my own army. Instead I write to her from the "sunny shores" of Italy, where boredom is our biggest enemy.

SEPTEMBER 29, 1942

I am sick from this war. Private Huber was killed today, the only person left that I cared about in this damn place. But not by enemy fire. He was shot by Major Eberhard. We were fighting for the remains of a nursery, where a sniper had been picking us off like geese all day. In the same firefight, Private Stürmer was shot through the mouth. Huber had been grazed by the same bullet but was more concerned with Stürmer, who had collapsed and was convulsing on the floor. I cannot remember what happened next. Private Shulef tossed a stick grenade toward the Russians and Ivan caught it and threw it back, striking Shulef in the face before exploding. Major Eberhard was furious with the loss of life, and when the Russian sniper was finally shot and gravely wounded, the major moved to shoot him. Huber intervened to save the enemy under the *Geneva Convention*. Eberhard said there was no convention here and ordered Huber to shoot the Bolshevik. *An order is an order*. But he still refused, so Eberhard shot Huber through the heart. Just like that. I pulled my pistol on the major but the Russians sent him to Hades first. One of the Russians screamed something like, *If you want Stalingrad, you will have to take us all to hell!*

We are there already.

17

A KEY

A small part of Josef still remained among the ruins of Stalingrad. The scourge of war had never seemed more complete or futile than the battle for the Russian city. Millions died fighting in the rubble, a constantly changing labyrinth of debris and decaying corpses. The goal -- to cleanse and purify the city of the enemy. Victory couldn't be measured by daily successes, the taking of a room, because perhaps the floor or even the entire building wouldn't exist the following day. Nor could victory be declared based on the sheer number of dead on both sides. Victory could only be measured by the final outcome -- whether the Russians would be defeated and disembowelled in the ruins of their once proud city, or the will of the Germans would finally snap, the last of their living chased out, carrying with them the peppered remains of their ruined souls.

A few days had already passed since Josef had left the barbershop with Max, wandering the streets where kids rummaged through piles of trash -- competing with the scavenging dogs.

Some of the children took turns sniffing glue from a paper bag, looking momentarily dazed as if they'd just been hit by a numbing fist. And while this scene unfolded, a slick black Mercedes Benz slowly rotated on the showroom floor of the dealership across the street. Max was clearly not at peace with the world as it was. Finally, when they were a long way away from the barbershop, Josef had said, "Promise not to repeat what I'm about to say."

"My word is my honour."

Empowered by the two faces of the trickster, Ellegua, Josef had told him about his mother who suffered terribly under the allied bombardments and his mother's brother who had fought and died for Germany. Max nodded thoughtfully, the mechanical wheels of his mind processing and absorbing his words. With painstaking detail, Josef painted a picture of a sad and isolated childhood in Israel, where he belonged nowhere and to no-one, not even his parents. No one understood or even tried to understand how his Jewish father could have married a German *Frau*; and they blamed Josef, as if their union was his fault. It was history that brought his mother and father together, Josef told Max, but that was all they shared. That and fate. And Josef? He was just a painful reminder of their shattered lives, a failed attempt at reconciling the past and future.

When he had finished reconstructing his past, an archaeology of lies, Max was clearly moved. "There is too much pain in the world, Josef. Listen, it's probably best you don't come back to the shop for a few days. Just until things cool down. It'll all blow over, you'll see."

Josef had taken heed of Max's advice to stay away from the barbershop for several days. During that time, he hired a private car to take him to the Israeli arms plant in Cobán to meet with senior staff Saul had contacted, knowing that the old Nazi would likely have someone tailing him. He walked briskly, moving with purpose, until he arrived outside the barbershop set unapologetically amidst the shoe shine boys and squalor of the city. When he entered, the bell above the door didn't ring. He entered unnoticed. The old Nazis were in the middle of a heated exchange. Hans stood at the centre, silently holding court.

"What's he doing here?" Reinhard demanded. "He's spying on us, that's what!"

"If he wanted to spy on us, why would he tell us he's Israeli?" Max said. He looked ill, his skin yellow.

"He's an arms dealer, they're notoriously unscrupulous -- and not to be trusted, especially Israeli ones. If you pay them enough they'll screw their own mother!"

"He's hiding nothing."

"You shouldn't trust him, Hans. He'll betray you."

"You don't even know him!" Max protested.

"He's a Jew," Reinhard said.

"He's not a Jew! He's a half-Jew from his father's side. That means he's not really a Jew."

"Ha! Now Max is quoting Jewish law! A Jew's a Jew, no matter how you look at it."

"It does make a difference," implored Max, who looked exhausted from the argument. "His loyalties are split. He has German blood running in his veins."

"Maybe he's the one from the vision, Hans." Reinhard looked almost frightened with his pronouncement.

Hans regarded Reinhard, considering the weight of his words. "Every time he walks in that fucking door, I shiver."

"They have the same eyes, don't they?"

Hans nodded mournfully.

Josef clanged the bell above the door and took a step into the room. A conspicuous silence fell over the room. "You told me I should come back in a few days -- *to train my face with the straight razor.*"

Hans silently directed Josef to a chair and wrapped a bib around his neck. The long painful silence continued and he could see Max was trying hard to bring him into the circle. "We were talking about our glory days," said Max.

"You can't talk about the past with someone who wasn't there. Especially a Jew," Reinhard said, boldly.

"But his uncle was Wehrmacht," Max said, almost desperately.

Josef stared accusingly at Max.

"Sure. He wasn't an SS man but that doesn't mean he wasn't committed."

"How do you know this?" Hans asked.

"They're dating," said Reinhard.

Josef shook his head. "You promised not to breathe a word."

Hans regarded him in silence. "It's OK," he finally said. "Your secret is safe with us." He patted his shoulder then laid a steaming towel on his face.

"You know my father was a barber, too," Hans said, when he finally removed the towel. The old Nazi examined his face. "Yes, you're ready for the blade." He brought out his soap cup and mixed its contents with the soft brush. "This isn't any regular store-bought shaving cream, Josef. My father taught me how to make it when I was a young boy. I've never shared the secret ingredients with anyone and I don't intend to start now. Nothing personal. Let's just say it's an ancient recipe passed down through more generations than can be counted." As he began applying the cream to Josef's face, he recounted more stories of the history of shaving. "Hundreds of years before the birth of Christ, the fashion for men in India was a tidy beard with all the rest of their body hair removed. And twenty-three hundred years ago, a Greek named *Publicus Ticinius Maenas* brought professional barbers from Sicily to Rome and there started Rome's long relationship with the blade. Shaving among Romans became a ritual for the entry into manhood—"

"A rite of passage."

"There was a barbershop on every corner. The free man was required to be clean-shaven. Of course, the slave wasn't permitted to shave and had to have a beard." The old Nazi raised his straight razor for Josef to see. "A product of 18th century England. Sheffield, to be precise." He moved in close with the razor, starting at his side burns and carefully drawing the blade down his cheek. His precision and intensity were admirable. "You see, Josef, these events aren't unrelated. They unfold in a way that can be known, that is leading somewhere. And I think I know where it's going."

"Tell him," Max said, excitedly.

Hans paused, considering if Josef was worthy of his knowledge. "The civilizing of mankind."

"I'm impressed."

"You see, we continue to evolve -- not just culturally, but physically. Someday, we won't need to shave."

"Then you'll be out of a job."

"Clever, Josef. Very clever." Hans moved close to inspect every inch of his face like an officer inspecting his troops. Then he moved close to his ear. "Your friend, the one who leads the special prosecutions tribunal in Israel—"

"He's not my friend."

"Friend or foe," he sighed. "Why did you come here to tell me what you told me?"

"It doesn't matter. It won't change anything."

Hans persisted, shaving but pressing his face so close that Josef could feel his breath on his skin. "I need to know why you're doing this, because I want to trust you."

"You shouldn't trust me."

"Still."

"It's personal."

"How so."

"I want to ensure his job at the tribunal fails."

"What are you talking about over there?" Reinhard piped in.

"I can't tell you more, because if this ever comes out, it's me they'll hang." Then Josef added, "He found out you're in Guatemala and knows you own the shop. When he learned I was coming to Guatemala on business, he asked me to look you up -- to be his eyes. But after I met you, I told him you were nowhere to be found, that some Guatemalans took over the shop and weren't sure when or if you'd be back. He thinks you may have fled to Costa Rica."

Hans studied Josef, trying to decide whether to believe him totally or not at all. He smoothed down his white head of hair. "Well," he finally said. "It's all very remarkable considering I've been living in Latin America since before the war -- unless you believe a man can be in two places at once! In which case, you probably also believe in re-incarnation, which would either make you a Buddhist or a lunatic."

Max put on his coat and bid everyone farewell.

"Man, you need to eat," Hans called out after him. "You've lost a stone since last week!" Then he turned back to Josef. "I'll be honest with you. I've known about the investigation for quite some time now, but I have no time for their games. They want to play cat and mouse, but I'm no mouse. I'm a man of my word, a man of action. When they find me, I'll be more than glad to cooperate with them however I can. I have nothing to hide."

"I believe you," Josef said quietly.

With that, von Flintz grew more self-assured. He carefully cleaned Josef's face with a towel. "You've been sent from the heavens, you know that? So what do you want from me?"

"I'm not sure what you're asking."

"Everybody wants something."

"A clean shave."

"Jokes can't steer me from the truth. Tell me why you're here."

"To learn."

Hans searched his eyes for answers. He pointed to his chest. "From me?"

Josef nodded.

"So you know then."

"Yes."

"After we finish up, we'll go for dinner."

When Hans shut off the shop lights, he pushed Reinhard with his wet eyes out onto the street like a stray dog. A limousine was waiting. "You take that Jew to dinner and not me?" Reinhard scoffed bitterly before scampering off into the shadows. The driver opened the door with rehearsed formality and whisked them inside. While they drove through the beaten streets of Guatemala City, Hans spoke affectionately of his dog, a creature of apparent incorruptible loyalty.

They arrived at a restaurant in a posh district somewhere in the heart of the city. The maître d' led them through the dining room crowded with Guatemala's elites to a large private room at the back. Most of the guests had already arrived and were seated around a large table set for twenty. They appeared to be waiting for Hans. The maître d' fussed over him, seating Hans at the head of the table before retreating into the kitchen to yell at the staff. Several brawny and humourless-looking men located themselves at various points of the mirrored room, keeping a watchful eye on the entrance. Hans looked different now, no longer the wool-vest clad old man from the barbershop. He commanded the attention of what appeared to be people of influence. It became clear to Josef that von Flintz didn't just have a past -- but a future as well. He spotted Max from across the table and walked the length of the room to greet him.

"This is just beginning for you, Josef. Me, I'm getting old for this game."

"Come on, Maxie. You're still firing on all pistons."

"Believe me," Max insisted, directing his attention to the guests at the table. "They're all afraid of my old age like it's something contagious. As if it's my fault for falling into a trap that they can somehow avoid by taking the right steps. But there are no magic potions, no fountain of youth, no perfection in mankind. This is our fate, no matter if we believe in God, science, or money." He motioned for Josef to sit beside him. "I still can't believe Hans invited you. Perhaps he wants to introduce you to some new business contacts. There's plenty of money here and plenty of need for your kind of business."

"Is this a regular gathering?"

"Every few months. Like minds." Max paused. "And I think Hans does it to keep tabs on everyone."

"So who pays for all this?" Josef asked.

"Probably the Guatemalan treasury. But Hans doesn't share those kinds of details with me. Not anymore."

The room suddenly erupted with boisterous laughter. Hans had said something amusing at the far end of the table. Josef joined in the gaiety and smiled toward Hans, who didn't seem to notice him now.

"There are some amazing people here tonight," whispered Max. "That man sitting two seats up from Hans on the right. He always stays close to Hans' side. His name is Philipe Manchoni. He blew up a train station in Italy, killing fifteen people—" Max lowered his voice, leaning in even closer to Josef's ear. "Forever the magician, he escaped to Bolivia to help start a revolution. Luis Posada Carriles, sitting beside Philipe, is Cuban. But not the communist kind. He was educated in demolition and guerrilla warfare by the CIA. He was trained here, in Guatemala, for the Bay of Pigs but never made it to the beach and was then thrown in jail for bombing a Cuban airliner. He escaped from a Venezuelan prison and has been working in Nicaragua to fight the communists."

Max winked at Josef warmly before directing his attention elsewhere. "The two men on either side of Hans are Guatemalans, G-2 honchos."

"Where did Hans get that scar across his neck?"

"Not sure."

"Do you think it's safe for the movement to be out in the open?"

"There is no movement," he said. "Anyway, you could goose step down *avenida Reforma* singing *Deutschland über Alles* and not even raise eye-brows." He corrected himself in present company. "Not that you would want to, but you could." Max regarded Josef for a moment. "I probably shouldn't tell you this, but Hans is clairvoyant. He predicts things."

"Like?"

"That the Falkland Islands would fall to the British last month."

"I thought you didn't believe in mystics?"

"I don't. But just because I don't believe it, doesn't mean it's not true."

Josef fell silent, listening to the rising voices at the other end of the table. An American and an Argentinean general were competing for Hans' attention. "The Russians say they have no interest in Latin America," said the American.

Hans grew agitated. "Those Russian bastards are liars! They say one thing but do another. They massacred tens of thousands of Polish officers then blamed us! They have no interest in the truth!"

"So Max," said Josef, leaning close. "How did you find yourself in Guatemala?"

Max sat on the question a long moment then said: "Rarely in life do we end up where we expect. I let the wind blow me here."

Josef was about to press Max further about Hans and the presence of the international military men in Guatemala, but he decided to back off the fishing expedition. It was something Saul had once said about the art of the chase. *Get too aggressive with the lure, and you scare away the fish.*

Josef studied Max's jaundiced skin and shrinking frame. "I'm worried about you," he said, resting a hand on his shoulder. "Maybe you should see a doctor."

"I appreciate your concern but I don't want to trouble anyone."

Josef became transfixed by a strange Canadian with pale skin and no eye-brows. "Hans hates that lump of dough," offered Max.

"Why does he keep him around?"

"He must have some use for him but for what I don't know. Hans doesn't like dead weight."

"And Reinhard?"

Max grinned. "An exception to the rule."

"Maybe he needs a dog to kick around."

"I know you're joking, Josef, but don't say that to Hans. He is obsessed with dogs."

Josef was surveying the room and trying to grasp how the whole scene fit together. "Maxie, how much further does his reach extend?"

"Beyond this room?"

"Yeah."

"All the way to the top. Generals. Prime ministers. Presidents."

The Canadian addressed Hans loudly for all to hear: "So what are your plans?"

"This isn't the time or fucking place," Hans fired back. Then his voice calmed and his eyes narrowed. "We have the medicine to heal a sick nation. And if you doubt my words, remember the Spanish Embassy."

"The Spanish Embassy?"

"Two years ago, the Bolshevik peasants occupied the Spanish Embassy right here in Guatemala City -- they wanted land that didn't belong to them -- so the army stormed the embassy and blew the whole place up, killing dozens. And guess what Spain did?"

"What?"

"Nothing. They complained then packed up and left." Hans raised his glass. "I want to propose a toast. It's only a matter of time before I reveal my life's work."

Josef leaned anxiously toward Max. "What's the plan?"

From the corner of his mouth he whispered, "There is no plan." But before Josef could press him further, Max turned back to Hans and raised his glass.

———

In the darkness of his hotel room, Josef allowed the waves of his visions to wash over him. His hand ached from clenching the pen so tightly. A candle burned, illuminating the office interior in a warm fire glow. There was so much he wanted to say, but he was afraid. Then his pen dipped to the page, and he saw the ink, as dark as oil, soak into the paper.

August 23, 1943

Dearest Marta,

It is impossible to express how happy I was to see you again, even if it was only for a few precious days. Everything about you was exactly how I remembered. I am sorry I had lied to you. Your forgiveness means the world to me. I wanted to protect you from the truth and brutality of Stalingrad. But you were right, I was only protecting myself.

How is the hospital? I worry about you every waking hour, as I learn from the radio that the enemy continues to bomb German cities. Savages!

As for my fate, how strange it is to no longer struggle for the most basic level of survival. In the winter months of the Russian campaign, I could not remember what warmth felt like, bundled up in the same stinking uniform for months, my body rigid with cold. I became gripped with fear at the insanity that had taken hold of Julius as death crept up his leg in the trenches.

When the doctor told me that my injuries from Stalingrad were not permanent but that I was not fit to return to the Front, I cried with joy though also in sadness for the brave men I had left behind. You cannot begin to understand the guilt I feel, having survived when so many of those left in my care perished. They were my responsibility and I let them die.

But my terrible fate is not yet done. I have been made colonel and assigned to assist with the arrival of POWs to the camp Übel, an honour I was told for my valiant work in battle. I was introduced to SS Dr. Ziegler and SS Colonel von Flintz, a barber from Berlin. I cannot say more.

Your Husband, Erich

18

ON THE INSIDE

Josef waited for a bus alongside a dozen or so Guatemalans on *avenida* 7. In time, a hand-me-down school bus from the United States with the name of the school still written in faded letters on its side came to a skidding halt halfway up the sidewalk, nearly killing all of those waiting for the bus. The driver allowed only just enough time for them to board before throwing the bus into gear. Josef gripped the railing tightly as the bus lurched forward and then gathered speed around a corner, narrowly missing an Indian woman carrying a load of firewood on her head.

There was something exciting being packed in with locals and their large sacks of rice and home-made poultry cages with squawking chickens and hens. The light inside was dim and grey but remained alive with the colour of a bustling humanity. Josef managed to find himself a spot by the window near the back of the bus and squeezed himself into the seat meant for children. Three Mayan women skinnied themselves in beside him. It was an uncomfortable fit, but he couldn't help but smile as he stared out at the landscape speeding by the window. The bus spewed black clouds of diesel as it careened through the narrow streets of Guatemala City like a runaway train.

For weeks now Josef had made himself look busy, doing what he imagined an arms dealer would do -- expensive dinners, visits to arms plants, cocktails -- in the event that von Flintz or the Guatemalan intelligence service was tracking him. On the days that he appeared at the barbershop, he worked to uncover clues to the murder of his parents. Still, he only ever gleaned bits of information about Hans von Flintz from Max, who could never keep a secret in his moments of excitement. While Max shared examples of Hans' "clairvoyance," he never gave away the nature of his plans for the future, which loomed larger in Josef's mind by the day.

As Josef looked around the bus interior, his eyes came to a rest on the driver and the icons surrounding him -- the image of the Last Supper impregnated into the clear plastic bulb on the end of the gear stick and the wildly swinging wooden cross and rosary beads hanging from the sun visor. Along the edge of the windshield were stickers of every kind: a blue hand making a peace sign; the profile of a playboy bunny; the Guatemalan flag; and a 3-D sticker of Mary, whose eyes opened and closed as Josef moved from side to side.

The bus penetrated *Zona* 10 and 15, and, at full speed, crossed a spanning bridge beneath which people lived in tin and cardboard shacks. Smoke rose from open pit fires along the narrow walkways below. In a moment, the bus entered a wealthy district, which appeared untouched by the squalor of the nearby ghetto. The homes were large, containing vast open spaces behind the safety of high stone walls. Josef was still looking out the window when the bus screeched to a stop and everyone filed off.

Josef approached the driver and pointed to the mansions perched up on the outlying hills. The dark moustached driver assured Josef in Spanish that no buses passed that way. "If you can afford to live up there, you have your own driver." Then he made a move toward the gear stick, signalling that unless he removed himself immediately, Josef would be enjoying the ride back downtown.

Josef made his way on foot up the steep curving road ahead. Over his shoulder, Guatemala City quickly fell away below. Beneath a billboard for luxury homes at the side of the road, a homeless man slept. He continued on until the estate von Flintz had described came into view. It appeared as a fortress of glass and stucco with shards of broken glass lining the top of the wall and video cameras tirelessly panning the perimeter. A Guatemalan security guard stood by the front gate, cleaning his finger nails with a set of keys.

For a moment, Josef stood beneath a giant tree and summoned all his strength. He thought about justice for his mother and father. Overhead, primordial birds circled, waiting. It seemed a bad idea to be here; though instead of retreating, Josef stepped from beneath the tree and rang the bell fixed to the gate. The security guard gave him the once over and went back to cleaning his nails.

Hans emerged from the glass house and approached the gate, walking with his chest thrust out, his white button-down shirt draped open to the navel. He squinted and raised his hand to shield his eyes from the sun. "You made it!" He beamed, as he opened the gate. "Thanks for coming on such short notice. We have a great deal to discuss."

Josef followed Hans down the stone walkway, passing semi-tropical plants that drooped under their own weight. Von Flintz opened the door and allowed Josef to enter before walking him through a hallway to a room set up like a museum with glass cases under which various razors were displayed. After a tedious explanation of each, Josef found himself genuinely enthused by the sight of a photograph hanging on the wall of Tikal surrounded by forest.

"I've always wanted to go," said Josef.

"Well, my boy, perhaps one day I will take you. The Mayan empire has always fascinated me. They created a society that was a monument to greatness, which transcended their own time."

"Mud huts don't stand the test of millennia."

"Indeed, they don't. Have you ever wondered about the nature of knowledge, Josef? Like how it is that the Maya of the past could've had knowledge of astronomy, science, advanced techniques for building, and yet the Maya of today can't even spell their own names? They have to use an ink pad and fingerprints to sign official documents. How was that knowledge lost?" Von Flintz wagged a finger at the picture of Tikal. "They say a giant war finally brought an end to the empire. But I don't believe it."

"Why not?"

"Because Tikal would've looked like a graveyard."

"I once read a brilliant study looking for links between the Arawak and Maya."

"That's stupid," Hans rebuked. "There's no connection at all. The Cubans have always been communists!".

The colonel delivered Josef to the elevated patio behind the house. Guatemala City spread across the valley floor. Immediately below the veranda stood a satellite dish abutted to a bungalow and a large swimming pool that was presently being cleaned by a young Guatemalan.

A young Mayan woman served tea and as she poured Hans a cup, he grinned and patted her. Von Flintz turned back to Josef and smiled. "Women have always been attracted to men who know what they want." He laughed. "I have the same command of dogs. You know, I would take the companionship of a dog over most people." As he said this, the sound of light footsteps approached up the patio stairs. A white Alsatian appeared, tongue out, tail wagging.

"Come over here," Hans said, affectionately. The dog moved to von Flintz's side. "You're such a beautiful girl. Such an obedient and loving creature, aren't you Blondi? I would never let anything happen to you." Hans looked up at Josef with deep concern. "It's inhumane the way they treat dogs down here. I'm sure it sounds crazy to you, but I'm thinking of starting an animal rights organization." He looked up at Josef and immediately grew uneasy. "Why are you staring at me like that?"

"I was just thinking how fit you look."

Hans rolled up his sleeve, flexed his muscles, and ordered Josef to feel his bicep.

Josef used two fingers as callipers around his meagre arm. "Very impressive."

"Not bad for a gentleman HALF my age!"

Blondi walked over to Josef and began licking his hand, then nudged him to pat her head.

"She likes you. That's remarkable. She doesn't like anyone but me. This is a very good sign," he nodded to himself. "Let's have a real drink," he said in a burst of enthusiasm and snapped his fingers. The servant appeared with a tray of wines and liquors, which she placed on the table to the left of Hans. His face turned red but he forced a smile. "Darling Maria, how many times do I have to tell you? I'm right handed so I don't want to cross my arms every time I take a drink." She bowed and brought the tray around to the other side.

"There really isn't a more intelligent and loyal dog than the Alsatian. They've been bred to perfection." Von Flintz raised his glass in a toast and then took a drink. "Yes, the perfect race of dogs. Thanks to Captain Max von Stephanitz. He had a vision to breed a super-herding dog that would be smart, physically tough, noble and beautiful. Stephanitz began selecting dogs to breed, working towards his ideal. His patience ultimately paid off. We weren't the only ones who understand Stephanitz's genius. The world wanted our perfected canine, and soon the German Shepherd was exported all over the world for her brilliance and savvy."

Hans looked momentarily emotional as he gazed down on his dog. "Blondi saved me after my wife died. I was a wreck and felt I couldn't go on. But Blondi was a beacon and showed me life was still worth living."

"You were married."

"Of course. No man is complete without a woman."

"I'm sorry about your wife."

"It was ten years ago now. She smoked two packs of cigarettes a day, and I warned her she was killing herself. And, sure enough, I was right."

"How long were you married?"

"Thirty-five years. She was a good wife, quiet and neat. You know, it was her idea to open the barbershop as a diversion for me. She knew how hard it was for me to leave Germany before the war, especially because we didn't have any kids. You see, she was barren. It had been suggested that I take another wife -- after all, what greater service could a German do but to have children? But I would have none of that. Then a miracle occurred and she bore me a son, here in Guatemala." He looked away from Josef, as if his sight caused him pain.

"What is it?"

"I'm sure Max already told you, but you remind me a great deal of him."

"Is he here?"

"He died two years ago in a hand-gliding accident in Mexico."

"So much tragedy."

"Yes, too much. I don't want to talk about him right now." Then he added, "My son loved danger -- his father's son. Is it not true that times of peace and happiness leave men wanting? We need danger, sometimes even war, to satisfy our cravings for dominion, to advance ourselves as a species, to write new chapters in our history books. Without conflict, without war, the pages remain empty -- and then what are we left with?"

"Nothing."

"Precisely, Josef. Precisely." Hans smiled from across the table. Several volcanoes rose almost imperceptibly in the distance, and Josef stared at them a long while.

"It's beautiful up here, isn't it?"

Josef nodded.

"And your mother's brother? The one who died fighting. Who was he?"

"A man like you or me," said Josef, sitting back. "But a soldier and an officer."

"Where did he fight?"

"The Somme—"

"A veteran of both wars?"

"He fought in all of them. The Somme. Verdún. Stalingrad."

"Then he's more German than all of us," he said, satisfied.

"I never knew what kind of man he was. My mother was the only one of her family that survived the allied invasion."

"Max told me she died recently."

"My parents were killed by a Palestinian bomb."

"Barbarians. You've had some terrible luck, my boy. But you know, these things happen in war. And Israel has been at war from the very beginning, whether you acknowledge it or not. It has been war punctuated by peace. Not the other way around." Seeing something in Josef's face, Hans spoke. "Don't worry Josef. Your past is safe with me. Now," he said, changing his tone. "I didn't invite you here just to exchange family histories. Though, I consider it a worthy topic. I need to know if you can acquire some rather rare materials for me. I'm willing to pay you handsomely. But this is unofficial business. No paper trail."

"I can arrange that."

"I need to know that I can trust you."

"Of course."

"Actions not words. You're going to have to prove it to me." Hans stood abruptly. His expression shifted and he looked full of regret. "What I'm about to do really pains me." In the next instant two burly Guatemalans emerged from inside and grappled Josef to the floor. As he fought them, he glimpsed the pool boy conspicuously look away. Josef threw his weight against the Guatemalans, but they overpowered him and tossed a black sack over his head.

"Calm down, Josef. This isn't personal. I'm doing this for your own sake."

Josef continued to thrash, as the Guatemalans hustled him inside a car and drove off. Soon Josef grew exhausted from the struggle, and in the darkness, he felt like he was suffocating. *Good and fucked*, that's how Saul would have described Josef's situation. Josef let the weight of his head fall forward in surrender. There would be no more plans to make with Asena. No more walks along the cobblestone streets of Old Jerusalem. No more talk of children. He began to tremble. But just as he was about to become completely undone, a voice within commanded he take control. He forced himself to straighten up and breathe deeply, and soon a calm returned.

From the darkness, Hans began to talk almost philosophically. "Sometimes you must die to be reborn. You see, there is mystery in everything and sometimes we're forced to take a leap of faith. If you want to see the light, you must follow me into the darkness."

The vehicle slowed, stopping and starting intermittently. Horns blared and people shouted. Then the car came to a jerking halt. The sound of the electric window winding down, an exchange of words, and the thunder of a very large steel door being opened. They drove on. From inside the black hood, Josef heard what sounded to be the call-response of military drills.

"Stop here," von Flintz said curtly. "Bring him into the room."

The car door opened. There was the hollering of a drill-sergeant and the clatter of marching boots. By the arm, Josef was pulled with surprising gentleness from the car and led up several steps followed by the creak of a metal door on its rusted hinges. Josef was led through to an enclosed space where voices and footsteps echoed. Someone was screaming, while someone else moaned; he wanted to let his weight sink him to the floor. He took several more steps before the hood was pulled from his head. The room smelled of decay. There were several lockers and a bench where three olive skin men were changing. Hans turned to his enforcers and told them to bring the prisoner to his room. He rubbed the scar on his neck and removed his jacket, replacing it with a lab coat.

"Where are we?"

"You're on the inside, my boy."

"What is this place?"

"G-2," he said, as he carefully buttoned his coat. "My apologies for your treatment. It's a safety precaution. Really, it's for your own good, in case you're captured, you can't give away valuable secrets." He patted down his white head of hair and led Josef down a long hallway.

They arrived in a room, dark but for a spike of dreary light that cut through the open door. Stains, in giant slashing strokes, smeared the length of the far stone wall. From another door, von Flintz's henchmen emerged, holding a man with a sack drawn over his head. They dragged him to a table and tightened leather straps around his ankles, wrists and neck. Hans donned a pair of surgical gloves then flipped a switch, flooding the room with light. Hans fidgeted around with some instruments on a wooden counter. "I like to call it the table of truth." There were dozens of tools created to induce suffering. Some, like the straight razor, were sharp and meant to cut and pierce. Others were blunt and designed to crush. *What kind of men invent such instruments?* The answer stood in front of Josef.

Hans removed a tiny device from his coat. "This is a technique the Japanese invented." He brought the steel cup with the screw close to Josef's face. "You put the testicles in and tighten it until you get the answers. The Korean mercenaries fighting with the Americans in Vietnam carried these things around in their pockets. Very handy." He pulled another spring loaded device from his pocket. "A gift from the CIA. I've collected a lot over the years," he added, merrily. From the desk he picked up a metal ball with S curve razors. "This one may be familiar. An Israeli design."

"Why are you doing this?"

"Because I can."

He drew the sack off the captive's head. As Hans fiddled with his tools, Josef stole a glance at the prisoner but quickly looked away to escape the man's pleading eyes.

A small box with a crank and two long wires with metal clips hung from the wall. Hans excused the guards from the room and attached one clip to the man's ear and the other to his scrotum. "You know, a man can get used to anything, including pain," he reflected aloud. "That's why you have to switch it up. Give the generator a few whirls, will you."

Josef looked to the door.

"Rotate the crank."

Josef hesitated then made several feeble attempts at winding it. The man moaned only slightly. In a moment, Hans pushed him aside and took hold of the crank, spinning it vigorously until the prisoner thrashed in agony, his body stiffening with the strain.

"*Yo no sé nada!*" the prisoner pleaded.

"You're a goddamn Bolshevik!"

"*Por Favor. Tengo trés hijos.*"

"You and your bleeding heart. What kind of man are you, anyway?"

"Perhaps you have the wrong person," Josef suggested.

"A man is defined in the fire," said von Flintz, gritting his teeth. "That's why war is so compelling. It's the only true test. How can we ever know who we are, what we're made of, if we don't test ourselves? We can only achieve the impossible when all lines of retreat have been destroyed. Go forward or die. Pain teaches us about our limits. This is what I believe. I have committed myself -- with all my being -- to this belief. And what about you?"

Josef remained silent.

"Every man must stand for something," he said, impatiently. "If he doesn't, he's not a man at all but a *fucking* parasite." Hans went to work on the prisoner like a surgeon, careful to inflict the most pain. It all happened in snap shots. Finger nails. Pliers. Blood as thick as ink. Eye lids. Razor. Shin bone. Hammer. Josef's palms dripped sweat and he could no longer see clearly.

"Why have you brought me here?" begged Josef.

"Because we both want something from each other. This is the only way we can assure each other against betrayal. I trust you, Josef, so don't interpret my actions in a negative light."

The prisoner made a fist and his eyes squeezed shut to escape the pain. Josef looked over to the table of tools and wondered what it would take to kill Hans. The old Nazi seemed oblivious to his intentions and hovered over the bloodied body. As he worked away with calculated malice, he began confessing, "You know I sometimes think I could be happy retiring to the quiet of a farm, living out the rest of my days with Blondi. But when I began my life's work fifty years ago, I realized I was dedicating my life to something fantastic, something I could be proud of." He directed Josef's attention to the bloody walls and the table of tools. "I made all of this, this sanctuary of justice. With my own hands I made this." Hans bit his lip in an effort to stem tears of pride.

The prisoner was crying, betraying his exhaustion and mortal fear.

"Enough," Hans shouted, before plunging a spike into the prisoner's thigh. The prisoner's scream echoed up and down the corridors of the G-2 complex.

Josef grew light-headed and felt that at any moment he might collapse. Hans von Flintz stood in the fog of Josef's vision. Repeating like a broken record in Josef's head was a phrase he had read from the ancient Mayan text *Popol Vuh*: *They began to fulfill the destiny which was concealed in the marrow of their bones.* Something inside Josef broke, releasing a profound flood of grief. He moved to the table of tools and picked up the straight razor. Asena's voice whispered that he had gone too far and that if he took the next step, nothing could save him from the abyss. In this world that von Flintz had brought him to, there was no ambiguity or lies. The Nazi concealed nothing of his own darkness that perhaps he saw as the light of virtue. Violence was truth and Josef was dead while Erich Hauptmann lived.

His palms slick, the razor was slipping from his grasp. Certainly, Josef knew he would be killed before escaping this place. He counted backward from three, his body tense in anticipation of his next swift action. *Two.* Hans shamelessly wiped the blood dripping from his gloves and raised a Polaroid camera. *One.* "Smile," he commanded. The flash temporarily blinded Josef.

"Now we have a bond that links us together until death. And I have pictures to prove it. I imagine your wife, Asena, would love to see them. You standing by one of her beloved leftie activists." Hans laughed at Josef's disbelief.

"So you know who my parents were."

"Josef, what do you take me for? An idiot? I know exactly who they were and what you are doing here."

Josef shook with rage. Was he really standing before his parents' killer? The old Nazi seemed to lose interest in his victim and walked Josef back to the change room, where he removed his white overcoat and washed his hands. "Join me at my estate the day after tomorrow. 7pm. There's a lot to discuss. We have to move ahead quickly. What I need from you, I need soon."

Josef couldn't speak.

"Oh, I almost forgot," said the old Nazi, as he patted Josef on the back and directed him to the door. "Don't be alarmed but we have to put the hood back on before we escort you out. What goes on in here must not escape these walls. And this isn't to protect ourselves but to protect the world, because it's not ready for the truth."

BOOK THREE

THE FINAL SOLUTION

Many new tyrants have kept in their drawer Adolf Hitler's
Mein Kampf: with a few changes perhaps, and the substitu-
tion of a few names, it can still come in handy.
PRIMO LEVI -*The Drowned and the Saved*

19

ENTERING THE GATES

A fierce wind blew through Guatemala City. A man walked briskly toward Josef, a black umbrella gripped in hand. As he neared, the umbrella snapped back like the broken wings of a crow. It seemed an ominous sign. Josef darted inside the lobby of the Conquistador Hotel, where the faces of the rich seemed distorted like masks. Josef made no effort to conceal the prisoner's blood that stained his shirt. *He must have been robbed,* someone gasped. He rode up the elevator with three patrons, whose masks were flushed red. *The country is just so quaint,* said one. *So colourful! And everyone smiles! I've always believed the less you have the happier you are!*

Josef stepped off the elevator and walked stiffly down the corridor, as if at any moment his rigid joints might break off. A hip. A knee. A shoulder. An elbow. Body parts fell behind him in a cascade. The walls closed in, whispering loudly about his complicity inside the torture chamber alongside the monster who, in all likelihood, was his parents' killer. *Breathe.* He fixed his gaze on the door to his room. Beads of sweat rolled down his forehead.

He was trying to tell his heart to slow down but it wouldn't. His anxiety rose as he tried unsuccessfully to push the key inside the narrow hole. He used two hands to steady the shaking, pressing his head against the door to focus. Then, like a knife entering flesh, the key slid in and he entered his well-polished room with its perfect view of Guatemala City's squalor. The shortwave radio reported the latest news of Israel's invasion of Lebanon.

He locked the door and leaned against it, as if his weight could hold back the floodtide of grief that was already upon him. He tried to release everything bottled up, pounding the door until his fists hurt, crying and screaming. But the noise couldn't release the pain. He ran into the bathroom and crammed his fingers down his throat.

Josef sat on the cold tile floor shivering, the room as black as spilled ink. But the floor couldn't cool what Hector once called a "hot head." He was out of balance. He knocked his head against the toilet, trying to make himself bleed to relieve the pressure. That was when he staggered into the bedroom and took hold of the SS dagger hidden under the mattress. He pressed the knife against his skin, imagining it to be Hans. Perhaps with the sharp edge he could also carve away Erich Hauptmann, if he could just figure out where he was hiding. In the darkness, he lay down exhausted. He shivered and sunk into the bed, his head so warm it soaked the pillow. He lay in the stifling darkness, certain he'd die all alone so far from Asena.

From the shadows, the radio played. "*The latest report from Amnesty International documents that hundreds of human rights violations have taken place in Israel in the past twelve months.*

Amnesty figures state that....." For a moment everything was clear to him. The Jewish covenant sanctioned the exile of the Palestinians. Perhaps Hans and G-2 had a covenant here in Guatemala. Who was to say? Who was to say what God thought or wished or who He chose to forsake? In a sudden flash, Josef reached into the darkness and hurled his father's radio across the room. Like a mirror containing a thousand lies, the radio smashed against the far wall, splintering and raining plastic and metal over the room. "Forgive me," he cried to the broken radio. But his parents didn't respond.

Josef lay back in bed, quaking as a vision closed in. But it wasn't a vision of Erich Hauptmann or the war. He saw the desert shimmer in the afternoon heat. Boulders torn loose by the quick and sudden desert rains were scattered over the moonscape. His mouth was as dry as the Sinai, his lips cracked and bleeding. He grew blind until a shadow was cast over him. Josef gazed up to see he had returned to the place he'd discovered in the Sinai. Without hesitation, Josef entered the cave, knowing that he must continue his journey back in time. If he could reveal his origins, maybe he could find the source of his faith.

He passed quickly into darkness. Voices spoke. There were conversations -- son to father, father to son -- through the ages. He moved forward and found his father again. Then beyond, past faces now familiar, down the city streets of Granada and Andalusia into the Talmudic academies of Spain. The cities were controlled by the Islamic caliphs. Abraham told him Jews had autonomy of law unless a Muslim was involved. Christians also lived peacefully under the leadership of the caliphs. Then Josef crossed over the Mediterranean by boat and wind. There were so many names and faces yet to meet, so many stories yet to be told.

Josef continued back to 636 AD at the time Arab Muslims invaded Palestine. A movement was born in 610 AD when Mohammed was struck by a vision. It was 468 AD and the Sassanids were burning the synagogues of Babylonia. There was a lot of crying and fear. Josef's brothers, sisters, fathers and mothers sat in a circle talking beneath the desert stars.

From behind, Josef was startled to hear his father's voice. He must have followed him inside the cave. He was telling Josef something, trying to explain what had happened all those years ago -- before he was born -- at the internment camp in France. A group of internees had been selected to go to the deportation camp of Drancy the following day and he was one of them. "Terrified of being separated from your mother," his father explained, "my friend Cristophe Noire helped me pull out three gold filled molars. In the morning, during the head count, I approached an officer. My face had ballooned with the infection. I knew I looked hideous so I forced him to look into my eyes. And in his hand, I placed the three gold filling. I begged and clenched the officer's hand but he roughly pushed me back to the line of internees. I wept, blind with grief. But then I saw the officer direct the steward to strike a line from the list of names. Another name would replace mine on that train to Auschwitz. It was Cristophe Noire.

"Imagine such a fate? Imagine my guilt? Not only had I killed my friend, but I was the reason your mother was in the camp in the first place. She had sacrificed so much needlessly. Do you realize the enormity of her sacrifice? She didn't belong at the camp with the rest of us Jews and politicos. She was a Catholic from a good family protected by the Vichy government, but she chose to stay with me.

"When Cristophe was taken away -- he smiled at me. He didn't resent me. You see, Josef, he wasn't married and was willing to sacrifice himself if it meant Monique and I could stay together with your sister. *God rest her soul.* I never forgave myself for the death of Cristophe or your sister. Never. Every single file I worked on at Liberté, I did with them burning like a fire in my heart. Every time I look at you, I see Cristophe's sacrifice, his gift."

The echo of his father's voice grew distant, while shadows pressed in on all sides. Josef saw the tools of *truth* laid out neatly on the table and Hans' meticulous use of them. He forced these thoughts away and began calling out to Erich Hauptmann by name. Maybe he could learn something from him about Hans von Flintz and maybe about himself, too. Josef willed Erich Hauptmann's visions into being and quickly heard Erich's voice in his head. The selection platform came into view.

It's dark when he arrives and hundreds of lights cast an otherworldly glow over the courtyard. SS guards patrol the grounds with German Shepherds. Several search lights sweep over the barracks and the factory's chimneys. There are guard towers every 30 yards where men sit in their nests smoking cigarettes and staring out coolly into the night. Several bodies swing from gallows. Others are tangled in the coils of barbed wire around the camp perimeter. The prisoners must have known it was impossible to escape but they tried anyway, preferring to die than to live inside the camp.

Several cattle cars filled with half-naked beings are unloaded as the gates close behind him. SS colonel Hans von Flintz stands beside a Red Cross truck and looks sympathetically toward the disembarking crowd, "You're safe now. Please move in an orderly fashion." Wary-looking prisoners stumble down the ramp, some too weak to stand without the aid of others. The young Dr. Ziegler inspects them and silently directs most to go left and the remaining to go right. Hans makes his own selections, pointing a riding crop stiffly, as the gaunt faces pass him.

Erich is accompanied to the platform by an officer named Kleip. A girl steps off the box car crying for her mother. "*Rechts*," Hans shouts, flicking his crop at her to move right. A woman disembarking with the girl points to her mother, who is huddled together with a group on the left. The girl moves left but the SS guards push her back. She keeps calling for her mother, growing hysterical, which soon sets off a wave of panic among the prisoners. Hans regards the situation and then with seeming compassion indicates for the girl to join her mother. The girl runs into her arms, relieved.

An old man limps down the ramp clasping his chest. He sees the Red Cross vehicle and cries, "I need a doctor."

"To the left," Hans shouts above the pandemonium on the platform. "Someone from the medical block will look after you right away."

"Thank you," he says, with tears welling in his eyes.

"They aren't all bad," someone whispers from the group.

Erich steps up to Hans and salutes before handing him an envelope.

"You must be our wounded Wehrmacht."

"Yes."

"I have no use for you in my camp. Your lack of moral faith has cost us the East. It's people like you who will lose the war for Germany." As Hans turns away, he catches sight of a ghostly young woman coming down the ramp. "Rechts," he shouts to her.

A group of healthy looking men and women, including the pale woman, are led off to the barracks by a tired looking prisoner in a special guard's uniform. Dr. Ziegler points to the group of women, children, elderly and infirmed. "Quickly now. It's time to get washed before dinner. We must be clean to eat like civilized people." They are led away toward the factory and the chimneys pluming smoke. Ash falls like snow. The little girl, who walks with her mother, smiles and holds her hands out to the ash. "It's like winter, mamá."

Kleip directs Erich across the courtyard to his new office in the Inner Station. "Each of the barracks holds three hundred to four hundred prisoners," Kleip explains, grimly. "That's a total of sixteen hundred. With everything fully functional, Colonel von Flintz can dispose of one hundred and fifty a day. That's a thousand and five a week."

"We aren't talking about hay bales or an accounting ledger," snaps Erich, before catching himself and smiling.

"I know, sir."

They pass the well-fed faces of SS guards. Erich ventures to say something, anything -- to mask his horror. "Commandant von Flintz seems friendly enough."

Kleip stops and looks him in the eye. "He shoots prisoners if their beds aren't made perfectly flat."

"Come now—"

"This is no ordinary place *Herr* Hauptmann. Last week I watched Dr. Ziegler work on a patient." Kleip cannot hide the nerve twitching by his right temple.

"Go on."

"He had the legs of a birthing mother tied to the ceiling."

"Why the devil would he do that?"

"To test the effects of gravity on childbirth. She was left hanging upside down for ten hours, begging for the life of her child. She tried to pull the baby out herself. So Dr. Ziegler had her arms tied and weighted to the floor. The effect of gravity was correctly predicted by the doctor. It was fatal. For both mother and child."

"Impossible."

"Herr Hauptmann. I read your file. I know you were in Stalingrad. You are a soldier. Like me."

"Perhaps."

"God knows we've had to kill our share. Sometimes out of fear -- a fear that if we didn't kill our enemy our enemy would kill us. I'm guilty of that. I've also fought alongside men who loved battle. They weren't afraid to die because they felt their conscience was free of responsibility because of the exchange of life. We lay down so that they lay down. The logic is sad, but the principle of the exchange between soldiers remains sound. We're not saints, Herr Hauptmann. None of us ever claimed to be."

Erich's apprehension grows. When he approaches the prison barracks, he gags with the stench of decay. There is the sound of crying and moaning. Emaciated ghosts move in the darkness. A rainbow of armbands emerges from a doorway as prisoners are led away by a brutal-looking woman with shocking blue eyes and straw coloured hair. "Next year in Jerusalem," someone whispers. With his own eyes, he sees the yellow star of the Jews sewn on some sleeves as well as other patches. Violet. Pink. Red. Black.

"We've become colour blind, colonel. We are exterminating everyone. Political prisoners, communists, homosexuals, Jews, gypsies, the homeless, POWs. Soon we will be killing each other, brother against brother, until there's no one left. Then there will be peace."

Beyond any doubt, Erich now knows where his good friend Jacob Zimmer was taken all those years ago and what terrible fate must have awaited him. Bodies remain tangled in the barbed wire. Now it makes perfect sense why the prisoners sacrificed themselves. He bows his head and whispers to God why he has been allowed to live through the fires of Stalingrad only to be delivered to Übel.

20

ASCENDING THE MOUNTAIN

The hotel room was silent without the voice of the short-wave radio. Josef sat up in bed and looked around in search of the missing radio. Its shattered remains were scattered over the floor. He lay back and stared up at the ceiling, where a faint water stain roughly in the shape of the continents took form above. He saw Cuba somewhere below North America. It didn't exist on the stain map, but he placed it there, a tiny island crowded with boisterous *orishas*, spiritual possessions, archaeological mounds, rum and dominos. Josef's story didn't begin there, though. Nor did it start in Israel or with his birth at the Red Cross camp in France after the war. Perhaps his story began millions of years ago in the furthest recesses of the cave of genealogy. *Where did it end?* Or rather, *where did the past begin?* Josef remained troubled by Erich Hauptmann's arrival at Übel. Yet something within him had changed. Now Josef was seeking redemption for Erich as, perhaps, he sought for himself.

It was midday when Josef mustered the energy to escape his hotel room in search of some open space. He felt on edge. Loud sounds startled him so he stayed on smaller streets until he could no longer avoid the larger boulevards that crisscrossed Guatemala City. It was a busy time of day, the air cool and heavy with diesel. A creaky old woman slept on the shaded steps of an abandoned building, her head resting against the comfortless stone. Clouds of smoke drifted from a wood fire as a young *mestiza* slapped tortillas flat in her hands and lay them out over a skillet. Others sold fresh produce from baskets brought in from the countryside. In the alleys, spray-painted slogans called for the people to rise up and join the FMLN rebels. People pushed by Josef, their arms loaded with market goods, but he didn't resist. Instead, he moved as if against the strong current of a river, flowing this way and that, until he passed through the throngs. Several lorries crawled through the streets filled with armed soldiers, some tinkering with their triggers as they, in jest, took aim at people in the street.

He followed the highway as it curved up into the outlying mountains toward the colonial town of Antigua. But he soon decided to turn off onto a small dirt road and began climbing out of the chaos into the quiet hills. Up ahead, several children splashed around in a trickling stream choked with human refuse. In a moment, another young girl in *Kaqchikel* robes emerged from a series of hedges carrying a baby strapped to her back. She smiled and joined the other children playing in the murky cesspool, while squawking hens pecked incessantly at the dirt.

On the other side of the road, shaded by a dusty tree, a modest shop sold an assortment of packaged goods. A group of men stood around the shack talking, machetes gripped loosely in their palms or propped up against their shoulders. Some followed Josef with untrusting eyes, perhaps wondering -- with good reason -- what a foreigner was doing among them. Others, however, smiled and rattled their machetes in a welcoming gesture.

An ancient man rode by on the back of a sickly horse and was followed closely by a mangy dog with one tattered ear. The man, with a full tan face and prominent nose, tipped his hat to Josef and gave his horse a kick to nudge it forward. The beast responded with a half-hearted neigh and continued on down the path. As the sound of hooves receded, Josef slowed and grew mindful of each footstep.

After a few minutes, another path revealed itself. He cut through a grove of pine trees and toiled up a steep incline. It was here that he became aware of how lush the Guatemalan earth smelled. The twisting trail picked up speed as he moved along the edge of a sheer rock face. Down below, several trees clung to the cliff wall by their roots.

When he emerged through the brush into a clearing, he spotted an abandoned wooden structure that had been reclaimed by nature. The rotted roof, now collapsed, was covered with a fine green coat of moss, while vibrant plants grew in clumps all over the ruins. Nearby, an old man bent low and whacked the tall grass with a machete. A pig sat patiently tied to a tree by the man's side. Wordlessly, the campesino smiled and pointed Josef toward a giant rock overlooking the valley, somehow knowing what it was he was seeking.

From his perch, Josef followed the flow of cloud shadows drawing across the rugged landscape, the birds grappling with the ever changing winds. In the distance, *Volcán* Aqua towered above the crested ridges of the upper valley walls. All the weight that had been pressing down on Josef began to lift and he grew humbled by the vastness of his surroundings. It offered perspective, and he immediately thought of the words of Moses Maimonides, *And if the earth is thus no bigger than a point relative to the sphere of the fixed stars, what must be the ratio of the human species to the created universe as a whole? And how then can any of us think that these things exist for his sake, and that they are meant to serve his uses?*

Josef's eyes shifted from the limitless skies to the finite ground beneath him. For a time, he became lost in thought, reflecting how all the secrets imaginable were buried somewhere beneath the surface. He pictured the cave of genealogy in Sinai and the Mayan ruins of Tikal. He imagined the rise and fall of civilizations and the arrogance and feudalism that came with dominion and the desperation that haunted falling empires. In truth, it was hard for Josef to grasp just how much had changed since his days as an archaeologist excavating in Cuba.

As the sun arced across the sky, Josef gazed up once more at the birds circling high above and felt something approaching envy at the ease with which they moved. While they were free to fly any which way, he was chained to his earthly struggle with the old Nazi of Übel. He looked across the valley to the denuded hillside dotted with estates, sensing von Flintz's presence among the mansions. Josef knew he was coming closer but still couldn't be sure how it would unfold. All he could be certain of was that when the time came, he'd have to move swiftly and with ruthless force.

———

It was dark when Josef arrived at the main road entering the city. Street kids roamed the darkness, while an elderly man gazed at him with his hand extended for money. Josef placed a ten *Quetzal* note in his cupped hand but felt ashamed of his relative wealth. Up ahead, the street was filled with music and moving shadows. At the mouth of an Evangelical church, recessed in a store front, people sang and clapped. Josef moved toward the crowded doorway to get a closer look. A man at the pulpit screamed out prophecies, the audience chanting back in response to his calls.

It wasn't until he began speaking that Josef noticed Dimitri, the young aid worker from the *cantina*, standing next to him. "What's fascinating is that you'd think the Mayans here have lost their ancient ways. But if you talk to the people, they can still tell you the name of every deity that lives in the mountains and lakes. They won't tell you. But when they aren't here praying to Jesus or waiting for the apocalypse, they're out in the countryside leaving offerings to the Spirit of the Dead. The Mayans can't be destroyed. As long as the knowledge of their ancestry remains alive, their faith remains one with the land, even if someone else owns it."

"So they don't believe all this?"

"Of course, they believe it. They identify with Christ's suffering but that doesn't mean faiths are mutually exclusive." Dimitri stroked his thick beard then pointed to the swaying masses inside the church. "Look at it this way. While they practice this stuff, they're also protecting their history from dissolution. If they come down here from the hills, then the preachers won't follow them back up into the forests and rivers where their ancestral gods live. How I see it, religion is both a container of truth and the cup of illusion. Its truth resides when its essence is distilled. Illusion is found when we accept dogma and fear and mistake metaphor for reality."

"Let me ask you something, Dimitri. How can you believe in God when you see all this evil around you?"

"Can you blame a tree for murder?"

Josef shook his head.

"Then how can you blame God? God is as much a tree as anything else. Maybe God is just the name of all the things we can't know. Listen, why don't we go back to the *cantina* and have ourselves a drink. I'm returning to the jungle tomorrow and would love to talk. It's not every day I get to speak so openly. There are spies everywhere, even among the people I'm trying to help. What do you say?" They stepped away from the mouth of the church and wandered down the road in happy silence.

When they arrived at the bar, moths flapped and bumped noisily into the Coleman lantern hanging from the ceiling.

"They never learn, do they?"

"And neither do we," added Josef, raising the bottle of corn liquor. "*Salud*," he said, toasting Dimitri then the poster of the blond holding a bottle of beer. He tipped the liquor to the ground as an offering before pouring a generous glass for Dimitri. They threw back the fire water like cowboys from a John Wayne movie. Josef filled their glasses again, and they continued toasting until they had drunk themselves blind. "Tell me about Tikal and the Petén jungle," Josef slurred, trying to stay focused on Dimitri's foggy face.

"It's one of the most beautiful places on earth," he said. Then he grew sad, staring at the bottle in his hand. "But weird stuff goes on," he finally said. "Lots of people don't get out. It's easy to disappear. The forests are crawling with guerrillas, government troops, botanists and pot smokers who've simply decided to drop out. It's a blur of green; the senses can become deadened by the excesses. The jungle never sleeps. You'd never believe the racket the forest makes and the intensity that builds when you're confronted by such unending life and death. It'd blow your mind. It blows a lot of people's minds. They simply can't cope. A lot of people go mad down there, plotting out their little deluded fantasies."

"What kind of fantasies?"

"Some of it's fairly innocuous, you know – starting a commune and living off the land. Other fantasies are more dangerous. You know, they're playing God when they never could be. Those *cabrones* don't belong there."

"Who?"

"The military and the drop-outs. And then there are these covert CIA types. Who do they think they're fooling? All these old white guys in Hawaiian shirts poking around villages pretending to be on vacation. They're tinkering around with world politics, thinking they're so clever. Fools," slurred Dimitri, drunkenly.

"Not so long ago, I was at a *cantina* in the jungle when I overheard this American talking to some UCLA kids. He was bragging about being an employee of the CIA, taking part in some sort of operation. And these kids were giving him just the reaction he wanted. They were starry-eyed and asking him all sorts of dumb questions, which he gladly didn't answer. And these little punks excitedly began filling in the gaps. 'Oh,' they said. 'You must be involved in some sort of anti-drug campaign.' These kids couldn't imagine that this piece of shit was down there for any other reason but to save the world from bad men and evil drug lords.

"Here they were in the middle of a war zone -- because that's what Guatemala is right now -- and all they could imagine is that an American was down their busting some cocaine ring. They couldn't allow themselves to think that he was the bad guy -- spying on peasants, labelling them for assassination. Sorry, I'm running off at the mouth. I'm drunk and maybe a little depressed, because it's a river of madness with no end in sight."

"So why do you do it?"

Dimitri snickered to himself then shared his amusement. "You know, my dad grew up outside Amsterdam. He dealt with the humiliation of the Germans marching down the streets of Veesp. He was old enough to remember them confiscating all the bicycles to melt down and use to build more tanks for their war machine. To this day, every time he meets a German he asks, *When are you going to give my bicycle back.*"

Josef laughed into his glass.

"Yeah," Dimitri conceded. "It's kind of funny. It's his way of getting revenge. So to answer your question, maybe it's a human need to struggle against injustice. You know dominion is never complete. There'll always be resistance -- even in totalitarian regimes -- because the human spirit can never be completely broken. At least I want to believe that." He sighed. "I should probably get going. I leave for the jungle early."

"I'll pay."

Dimitri laughed outright and pulled out his pant pockets to reveal the lint collected in the bottom. He handed Josef a fluff ball.

"I'll hold onto this until you can pay me back."

"Deal."

As they staggered from the bar, Josef patted Dimitri's shoulder. "Do not go gentle into that good night."

"Rage, rage against the dying of the light," Dimitri called back, before disappearing into the shadows.

Josef staggered to a payphone across the street from his hotel and loaded it with coins. He was feeling paranoid, sensing he was being followed, and the alcohol wasn't helping. Could it be the man standing in the shadows of the alleyway? he wondered. Or perhaps the Indian family sleeping on cardboard under the awning of a closed store? *Orejas* -- ears -- were everywhere, listening, informing. He dialed home and waited, keeping a watchful eye on the street.

"Moon," he said, when she answered.

Asena immediately began to fume about Israel's invasion of Lebanon. "Daoud and Naseer have stopped calling. They don't even show up at the café to play music anymore."

"I'm sorry."

"We can't just go on oppressing them and throwing them scraps -- scraps of food, scraps of land, scraps of human rights." Her tone darkened. "Have you been talking with Saul?"

"Occasionally," he lied.

"Listen, Saul isn't the first guy I've met who acts like he doesn't give a shit. But I don't buy that cavalier crap. He does care, because he's an egomaniac. Saul graduated from the school of asshole. Top of the class. And there's something else -- he has been calling here. A lot. I think he's snooping for information."

"He's looking out for me."

"Well, something isn't right with him. Don't you see it?"

Drunk, Josef bit his lip and leaned his head against the phone. A beep warned that there was only one minute left.

He searched his pocket for coins but his pockets were empty. "Asena, I'm running out of time."

Asena persisted to talk about Saul. "I just don't trust him."

"I wouldn't have guessed."

"I'm serious. If he is Mossad like you think he is, then his loyalty is to the government, not you. That means he'll stick the knife in you if the job requires it."

"I don't believe that for a minute."

"Maybe this time around, he won't just string you up on a fence by your underwear." Asena sighed like his father used to, with the weight of the world pressing down on her. "I'm tired, *Sukkar*. I'm really tired. Call off your crusade and come home. This has gone on long enough."

"But I'm so close to finding what I need to know."

"Remember, I can't be married to a murderer."

"Hans has plans—" Josef sensed a presence behind him and glanced back. "I can't talk -- they're tapping the phones."

"Who?"

"I don't know if I'm going to make it out of here."

"Don't talk like that," Asena pleaded. "You're in over your head."

"It's Hans. He's unbreakable."

"Rope always seems strongest right before it snaps."

The warning signal beeped. "Moon, I've gotta go."

"Josef," she confessed, "when it comes to love, we're all fools."

21

A WORLD UNTO ITSELF

Inside the gates of Übel is a community and, like any community, it has its problems. But each person plays his
part to ensure things go smoothly -- at least that is what
they are told. Officially, Erich works within the *Politische
Abteilung* -- When he is not interviewing and filing prisoner cards, he is reporting to the Gestapo head, a cheery
fellow from the *Kriminalpolizei*. Despite going through the
motions of the job required of him, Hans von Flintz has
already accused Erich of doing less than nothing and told
him he was a total disgrace to the camp. Let him think what
he likes. If he feels he so terribly lost the Eastern Front for
Germany, why does von Flintz not go to Stalingrad himself
and fight the Slavs single-handedly? Erich would be more
than happy to give him the road map to hell. So he remains
largely absent from the processes of the camp; not so much
a cog in the machine as a fly trapped inside, watching,
powerless to slow the movement of the pulverizing wheels

and pulleys. The safest place to remain is locked away in his office, writing in his diaries and painting.

In recent weeks, in fact, he has experienced a strange medical condition that no doctor can properly explain. He no longer sees colour. No brilliant blues or reds or greens. Vibrant yellows and okras are now nothing more than the lifeless grey of the camp crematoria doors. Of course, when the austere busy little man Dr. Ziegler excitedly requested to examine him in his medical lair, Erich flatly refused, haunted by the stories told by Officer Kleip. Still he tries to paint in colour, but it is no use. So he only uses black and white pigments and fills his canvases with whirling shades of apocalyptic grey.

Übel is a strange universe, set apart from the outside world, functioning on its own time, rules, and reality. Even as rumours circulate around the camp of the Americans breaking through the front at Saint-Lô near the French coast and the attempted assassination of Hitler at the Wolf's Lair, Hans von Flintz still demands they push forward with plans to rid the world of Jews. Major Niehaus, a friend and comrade from Stalingrad who was also wounded and now stationed at Dachau, had heard that the one-eyed Colonel Stauffenberg planted a bomb at the feet of the Führer during a meeting, killing several senior officers. Furthermore, he said they had attempted a *putsch* in Berlin. What leaves Erich uneasy is that nothing outside the gates of Übel is certain. How can he be sure that the Americans have even broken through their front lines or that a *putsch* has taken place? Can anyone ever really know what is going on beyond sight? But somehow he does not doubt that those involved with the plot to assassinate Hitler will suffer a most terrible and agonizing end.

Doctor Ziegler is a nervous-looking creature and never stops moving. He keeps a staff of Jewish prisoner-doctors by his side and uses them as his instruments to experiment on other prisoners. Most of the Jewish doctors have already lost their entire families to the *factory*, so Erich asks Kleip why the prisoners collaborate.

"Because they think they still have a chance to live," he answers. And while Ziegler marches around the camp with his Jewish doctors, von Flintz's wife spends her days in the officers' barracks on hands and knees smoking cigarettes and digging in her private garden, humming as she plants tulips or prunes the bushes. It is as if she does not hear the gunfire or the groaning masses. Does she ever wonder about the smell that clings to the camp or where the ash in her garden comes from? Certainly not all from her cigarettes.

The Barber of Berlin runs this self-contained universe like a well-oiled machine. But even machines occasionally break down. That was why he had gathered a group of officers in his office a few weeks back. "The impossible has occurred," he announced. "The crematoria have broken down. We can't afford to slow down. We need labour squads around the clock digging trenches until the machinery gets fixed. *Topf of Wiesbaden* is sending some engineers from the company in a few days. But for now we need to figure out the most economical way to keep our termination numbers on target.

281

Berlin will not be pleased. We need every man available to control the chaos or we'll have a rebellion on our hands."

When he was dismissed, Erich crossed the courtyard, which was eerily quiet without the humming of the *factory*. A group of SS from Hans' office were standing in a circle, smoking cigarettes and drawing on pieces of paper, discussing something intently.

"We don't have the gasoline to burn all the bodies."

"It's a real problem," another said, more concerned with solving the puzzle than he was with his contribution to mass murder. "They won't burn without it."

One officer pointed at a piece of paper in his hand. "We could build a wooden platform inside the trench, stack the bodies, and use hoses to draw oxygen below—"

"That's stupid. It's too time consuming. Besides it won't get close to being hot enough," said another. "We've got to make sure the fire burns hot but not so hot that we can't dump more bodies." He tapped his cheek with a finger. "Perhaps we could use the fat collected from prisoners as fuel."

There was a general nod of approval. "Good idea," one of the officers said.

"I'm just doing my job."

"I'll make sure to mention your contribution to the commandant."

"Now with that little problem solved, gentlemen, it's time for a drink."

—·—

Stepping out of Übel's universe to wander into the neighbouring town of Stenedal is a gift. But it is strange to walk among civilians, who move through their days ploughing their fields and baking their bread while remaining so close to the mass killing. Leaving Übel is a little complicated, because returning to it is not like returning to a regular job. Emotions can be overwhelming; it is like seeing and smelling everything all over again for the first time. Now imagine Erich's wonderment and confusion of a weekend retreat with Marta not so long ago. As they sat beneath the shade of an umbrella having a drink, she held his hand and stroked his head, telling him she wanted to make a baby. She knew there was a war; she works in a hospital and sees the wounded every day. But somehow she was blinded by her own desire to be a mother. She wanted to create in a time of destruction.

Then she said she wanted to live with him at the camp. He thought of the blissful ignorance of Hans von Flintz's wife gardening with ash from the crematoria falling all around her, and he knew right away Marta could not be that person. She would not stand for the inhumanity. *Impossible,* Erich had told her. *I won't allow it.* Marta's posture stiffened. *But why not?* He admitted that it was no place for a lady.

"If it's no place for a lady, then certainly it's no place for a gentleman." She stood up. "You're the worst kind of liar. You lie because you think you're protecting me. But you're only protecting yourself from the truth. You're a villain."

Marta, of course, had been right. Marta has always been right. He is a villain and Übel is no place for men or even the most unruly beasts. From places beyond sight, voices, young and old, groan and cry. Sometimes, when the weight of misery is too heavy to bear, Erich also weeps.

But crying isn't enough. Inspired by Marta's defiance to the inhumanity, Erich is moved to act -- even just in a small way. He passes by the officer's kitchen, where he lingers by the back door. Then, when no one is looking, he steals a handful of apples. Calmly, he crosses the yard to the barracks housing the newest train load of POWs. The guards manning the entrance salute and open the door. Inside, it is stifling; the motley lot captured in Greece are shirtless and swatting at the circling flies. Wordlessly, Erich removes the apples hidden in his jacket. There is a look of surprise then distrust. He hands them out to the hungry men. Trick or no trick, the first prisoner takes a famished bite. The others follow.

—

It has been raining continuously for ten days and everything at the camp has slowed down. Guards and officers race between buildings, while the prisoners are sometimes left in the trains for days because the SS do not want to get wet. To get through these dreary days, most officers lose themselves in drink, trying to drown out the voices that mercilessly storm around inside them. Even Erich's dreams are filled with the hollow stares of prisoners, eyes that seek mercy. The killing takes a toll on the human soul.

Today, Erich has received a most magnificent gift from Major Niehaus at Dachau. The present was obviously stolen from the record collection of an internee at his camp, which leaves a bitter-sweet taste as Erich carefully studies the oily black surface of Debussy's Clair de Lune. When young Officer Kleip spots him carrying the record around under his arm with nothing to play it on, he soon acquires a player from God knows where and brings it to Erich in his office. Together, they sit in silence and listen to the delicate flow of melody and harmonics. They both grow emotional, having opened themselves up to the music and perhaps each other, neither of them escaping the moment without some tears.

All the music in the world, however, cannot cover up the decay. Erich has grown so weary -- haunted by a terrible dread every time he hears the chugging of the locomotive, brakes screeching and the sound of steam being released under pressure. He knows what is in those box cars and he knows Ziegler and von Flintz will be out there making their selections. At night, he is left feverish and sleepless, the drone of allied bombers flying high overhead. He spends the darkest hours praying that Marta is safe from harm. He would do anything to protect her from the hell that is boiling over. What terrible twist of fate has left Germany at the centre of such a nightmare?

He begins to compose a letter to Marta but then stands and removes a mirror that he has kept cloistered away for over a year. He hesitates, afraid of what he will find. But something compels him to face himself anyway; when he finally musters the courage, he sees a middle-aged balding man. He frowns. It was only yesterday, twenty-seven years ago, that he watched Julius vanish into the halo of light. They were both so young and careless with their lives. *I only wish*. No, he stops himself. Wishing is for children.

When he looks in the mirror, he sees many things. He has his grandfather's eyes and nose. Hans, in passing, has commented on this nose. He says it is the nose of the aristocracy but what he really means is that he has the nose of a Jew. He could have been one of them -- one of the faces in the masses lined up to enter the showers; they are killing everyone now. Suspicion is enough grounds for murder. The machine has become so large no one controls it any longer. Everyday more trains arrive with refugees. Greek and Polish Jews, French and Austrian Resistance fighters, Gypsies, Communists. Von Flintz walks around them, pointing to the ones who will go to the workers' barracks and those who will perish in the gas chambers.

There is a knock at the door. Erich quickly hides the mirror in a drawer, as Kleip walks in. He does not salute. "The commandant wants to see all of us in his office immediately."

"Christ, what does the barber want now?"

"I think it has something to do with the trials in Berlin."

"I'm not interested."

"He says everyone has to attend. If we don't, it'll be a judgment against us -- that we'll be as guilty as the men who tried to assassinate the Führer last summer. I think he's serious, Herr Hauptmann."

"He's always serious."

"We could get in a lot of trouble."

"I told you, I'm not interested."

When they arrive, two rows of chairs have been set up in von Flintz's office. They are given some brandy and are made to sit. Hans paces back and forth across the front of the room. He smiles a most cursed smile as his assistant Rudolf Wagner mounts a film reel and threads it through the projector. "You will be witness to the fate of those evil-doers who plotted against our beloved Führer. The same fate awaits anyone else who defies providence." Then, on Hans' orders, everyone in the room is plunged into darkness before the light from the projector flickers to life.

For an hour they watch the trials in Berlin of the conspirators, headed by Judge Roland Freisler, a tragically ugly man with huge flapping ears and a lumbering nose that rivals an elephant. Freisler used to be an adamant Bolshevik, admiring the heavy handed ways of the Russians during the Revolution. Everyone who enters the hall of the People's Court are subjected to Freisler's calculated rants and then sentenced to hang. All gathered in von Flintz's office remain silent with eyes fixed to the screen as Count Peter Yorck von Wartenberg and several others are escorted into the courtroom, dressed in collarless shirts and old dirty sweaters provided by the Reich.

Von Wartenberg, a lean and handsome man, stands before the former Bolshevik Freisler. Freisler looks at the cameras in the back of the room and asks, "Why didn't you join the party?" "Because I am not and never could be a Nazi," says the Count. Freisler glances back at the camera nervously.

"You mean you did not agree with the National Socialist conception of justice in regard to the rooting out of the Jews?"

What the young Count says next leaves Kleip clasping Erich's leg. "What brings together all these questions is the totalitarian claim of the State on the individual, which forces him to renounce his moral and religious obligations to God." Freisler cries out, "Nonsense!" But the Count continues, "I hope my death will be accepted as an atonement for my sins and as an expiatory sacrifice." Freisler is enraged and orders the Count be removed from the court. Von Wartenberg is still speaking as he is dragged from the courtroom. "By this sacrifice, our time's distance from God may be shortened by some small measure--"

"Stop the film," Hans von Flintz shouts from the darkness, and the projector light dies. People begin to stand, but he orders everyone to sit and shouts for Wagner to load the next reel.

The next movie is what von Flintz really wants them to see -- the true face of Reich Justice. A group of convicted conspirators are led through the courtyard of *Plötzensee* prison and into a room with eight meat hooks fixed to a giant steel beam overhead. The executioner parades around and makes jokes about the conspirators, some of whom were once proud generals of the German army. One by one, the condemned men are stripped to the waist. Count Peter Yorck von Wartenberg looks resolutely toward the audience gathered.

Nooses made of piano wire are fixed around their necks. Hans looks dazzled as if watching a display of fireworks. As the executioner is about to string up Count Peter Yorck von Wartenberg, Kleip whispers desperately, "I don't want to watch."

Erich stands. "Let's go."

Kleip stands, too. But Hans stares stony-eyed into the darkness and barks, "Sit, you fools."

Kleip moves to sit but Erich grabs him by the arm. Others in the audience begin to stand too, as the men responsible for planting the bomb at the feet of the Führer are strung up grotesquely by piano wire. Erich leads Kleip toward the door.

Hans is livid. "Hauptmann, you goddamn traitor. I know you've been stealing food to feed the POWs."

Some of the other officers are still standing, their backs to the screen.

"Sit down," Hans spits, "or I'll have you all shot."

The others sit. Kleip and Erich leave anyway.

"We shouldn't have done that. We're going to get in trouble," Kleip says, his voice trembling.

"We're all in a lot of trouble already."

———

It is Spring -- a time of renewal, yet there is only decay. Things around Übel have taken on a new heightened madness. Bombs are dropping around the camp. The allies are advancing, crushing Germany's haggard armies that are tired of fighting and dying. Still, von Flintz demands more prisoners be gassed each day. The only good news that has come in recent months is that Judge Freisler of the People's Court was killed when an allied bomb dropped through the roof of the courthouse, squashing his miserable life. But that is no consolation for the news received from Marta today that their apartment building had been struck by a bomb in the middle of the night. Miraculously, the walls collapsed around her bed and left her unscathed. Perhaps the next time she will not be so fortunate. And so it was with such bittersweet emotion that he received the news of her pregnancy. To stay safe, she has gone to live with relatives in the countryside.

The weather is cold and damp, and no number of blankets can keep the chill from penetrating the Inner Station. To pass the time, Kleip gives him a copy of Bram Stoker's *Dracula*. But who needs to read about imaginary vampires and werewolves when there are real monsters running around killing innocent people? Erich remains in his office painting and listening to Debussy. He pauses and crosses the room, pulling his desk out from the wall. On hands and knees, he etches into the brick wall a line marking another day in purgatory. He covers the etchings with the desk and returns to his canvas, painting using black and white oils. Blue skies are grey; so too are sunsets and sunflowers. As he applies brush strokes to the canvas laid out on his lap, he is startled by a bang and a muted cry. Then a desperate whisper escapes from down the hallway. Something compels him to find the source of the struggle.

Another bang. He follows the sound down the corridor until he reaches von Flintz's office. He stands before his door -- staring at it. He can hear another violent burst and a muted cry. He touches the door, his body alert. Then, he swings the door open. Hans has his pants around his ankles and is raping the pale young woman from the train platform. She is laid out on the desk as he holds a knife at her throat. For a beat, he does not see Erich. Then, sensing another presence in the room, he looks up. "Get the hell out!"

Erich steps back unnerved. "Let her go," his voice low and threatening.

Hans points the SS dagger in Erich's direction. "Get the hell out I said!" Erich takes another step back. His eyes mist over with rage. He lunges at Hans, pulling him off her. He falls backward, his dagger knocked free to the ground. By the throat, Erich drives him into the wall and thrusts him to the floor. His hands are gripped around his neck squeezing tightly.

Von Flintz gasps and curses Erich but is unable to fend him off. It would be easy to take his life right now, Erich thinks, but he releases him. Behind Erich, the young woman still cries. Hans steps around Erich, grabs the knife from the floor and clutches the young woman. He motions toward her throat with the dagger but instead lops off a length of hair and shoves her to the floor. He storms out, dropping the knife but still holding the lock of brown hair pinched between his fingers.

Erich covers the girl with his jacket. She averts her eyes, ashamed, as if it is her fault she has been raped. He carefully helps her off the floor and walks with her back to the barracks.

"What's your name?"

"Sarah," she whispers.

"Don't leave the barracks. If anyone comes back for you, tell them Colonel Erich Hauptmann has ordered you to stay put. I won't let anything happen to you, I promise."

As Erich walks back to his office, careful to avoid the view of the pluming chimneys, Hans charges at him and drags him behind the Inner Station. Von Flintz has the eyes of a wild man. With a hand, Erich clutches his face and swings him around, thrusting his head against the wall. Erich presses himself close against his ear and whispers, "Keep your hands off the girl! If I ever see you around her again, I'll kill you. I swear to God!"

"You cowardly piece of shit. From the moment you stepped into my camp, I knew you weren't like the rest of us. You cross my path again and it'll be you I send up that chimney."

———

It is late now. As he stands before the mirror and buttons his coat, a most fantastic peace finds him in his place. The struggle is no longer from within. The struggle is now between men. With certainty, Hans already has plans to kill him. But tonight it is Erich who will be the hunter. He turns away from the mirror and sits at his desk.

April 17, 1945

Dearest Marta,

I wish that I could speak to you face to face. It is with such bittersweet emotion that I received your letter today. The news of your pregnancy fills me with tremendous joy and sorrow. I wept when I read your words. More than anything, I want to be there with you and be a father to our child.

As I survey the camp, the stench of death hangs thick in the air. I see with open eyes the righteousness of the bomb that blew up the map room at the Wolf's Lair. It comes to me so clearly, as clearly as memories of the men on the Eastern Front conspiring to rebel against the slaughter. I am embarrassed that I thought them unpatriotic. In fact, it was the most patriotic act I can imagine. It comes as clearly as Count Peter Yorck von Wartenburg hanging from piano wire and the executioner telling jokes as the last gurgles of breath were choked from the Count's righteous body. It is ever so clear to me now. Sometimes resistance is only symbolic, but sometimes symbols can be more powerful than swords.

I have learned that cowardice has less to do with a fear of death than with a fear of life and compassion. That is why I feel strong knowing that I must confront SS colonel Hans von Flintz, though I will take no pleasure ending his life. That would make us the same. I am making my escape tonight and, if I have any fortune left at all, I will make it safely back to you in the coming days. Do not cry for my unlucky soul -- perhaps I was born in the wrong time and place. Perhaps I chose the wrong path. I have walked my days in hell. That is the days not spent in love with you, not drawn away by hatred. You carry precious life within you now. Nurture that life with all of your love and please forgive me. I have failed you so many times. This pains me more than you will ever know.

I cannot bear the thought of a world without us together. But if I cannot hold you again, then perhaps my sacrifice in the name of justice will free my soul to dwell with you in happier times. Your grace flows unendingly within me, and in my imagination I kiss you a thousand times. Perhaps you will resurrect my memory from time to time for the seedling that blooms inside you. Maybe you will come to understand how my blindness turned to sight in my final days.

While you walk this earth, be my eyes and ears, my breath and spirit. You will be my vision and I will continue to grow long after I am gone. I only hope that in some way my final act will be payment for all the wrong I have done in my lifetime. I love you for all times.

Erich

———

The vision ended as if in mid-sentence, between his plotting and his final fate against the barn door. So many questions remained about Erich and that fateful night he went off to commit his final act on behalf of humanity. Obviously, something went terribly wrong, because he lay buried in Stenedal while Hans von Flintz still lived as a free man in Guatemala City.

Beneath the stream of water, Josef scrubbed himself with soap like he once had with the sacred herbs of Palo. He felt a strange sense that approached pride for Erich Hauptmann and his decision to protect Sarah. Josef dressed and from under the mattress withdrew the SS dagger that Erich had buried for safekeeping in the wall. He was staring at it, wondering if he was actually capable of murder, when Saul called. They talked for a time, and it soon became clear that Saul had been drinking.

"So, how goes your search?" Saul slurred.

"The pieces still aren't fitting together."

"How so?"

"Well, you've got Hans, who is still full of piss and vinegar and seems well connected. But his two lieutenants are old guys. I'd guess former low ranking SS men. One of the guys -- Max -- has been helping me get closer. You know, to get on the inside—"

"Please don't tell me he reminds you of your dad or any shit like that."

"I don't know what it is. I think he's tortured. There's remorse there."

"So now you've gone all Helsinki Syndrome on me."

"Saul, you of all people should believe in redemption."

"You know," Saul said, "My father was a real *q'ábr'zl.*"

"Saul, show him some respect. Your dad was no doormat. God rest his soul."

"When I was a kid, I watched him get beat up in the street."

"By who?"

"Who the fuck knows. My dad wasn't like his brothers, who brawled with Nazis. He was a bookworm who thought he could be nice to everyone. He believed everyone's heart was pure, if you just wiped the grime off. I was humiliated for him and I went crazy. Imagine a nine-year-old taking wild swings at three grown men? My father just sat there on the pavement watching. He didn't even defend me. Afterward, he tried to look me in the eye. But I couldn't do it. I couldn't look my own father in the eye. It was pathetic." He sighed into the phone. "Do you want to know what the problem is with the world, Josef?"

Josef didn't answer.

"I'll tell you. It's the Garden of Eden."

"You've been drinking too much again."

"We've got terrible role models, my brother. The snake convinces Eve to take a bite of the apple."

"So."

"So then Eve gets Adam to take a bite. You're still not following, are you? All that education, and you still can't think on your feet. God gets pissed at Adam when he finds out about the apple. Adam points the finger at Eve and Eve blames the serpent. From the beginning of time, no one accepts responsibility for anything."

"Are you telling me you want to repent?"

"I own everything I've done. You know, Josef, you never gave me any credit. You always thought I was just an enforcer, but what I do requires brains."

"So tell me, what do you really know about Israeli involvement in Guatemala?"

"I know some of the guys that trained President Rios Montt's men for the coup. Beyond that, not much."

"You mean, you don't know? Or you can't say?"

"You want to believe you and I are so different. But we're not," he snapped. "Jews are no better than anyone else -- it just happens to be *our* tribe. We do what we have to do to protect our own. You know in my line of work we pull back the curtain on people, revealing how fucked up we are as a species. Actually, I think you'd appreciate that part. I've seen how brave people can be but also what chicken shits they can be..." Saul's voice trailed off.

"The Nazi knows about Asena. I don't know how, but I can't have that. You hear me? Because if anything happens to her..." Josef stopped himself from speaking, a rage boiling up inside. "He killed my parents, Saul. Now it's his turn."

"No. No. No, J. The timing is all wrong. Don't underestimate these guys. Asena will be lucky to find some of your teeth after they're done with you."

Josef hung up.

22

THE PLAN

The late afternoon air was unpleasantly cool and dry, the sun shrouded in a dense patch of cloud that had stalled near the horizon. As Josef passed a kiosk selling newspapers, something stole his attention. He felt a heaviness in his limbs. It was a blurred picture of the bearded American, Dimitri, on the front page of the *Prensa Libre*. The Spanish headline read, *Foreigner Killed During Apparent Robbery*.

Josef's head swam with disbelief. How was this possible? He needed to think. He needed time to remember the details of last night. The article said that he was shot at close range sometime after midnight while walking to his hostel. The article questioned why a foreigner would be out after dark and blamed him for his lack of *sentido común*, common sense. But the article said nothing about what they possibly could have taken from him. Dimitri had nothing. Josef had seen the inside of his empty pockets.

In time, Josef collected himself and hailed a cab. As the driver pulled out, he immediately scrutinized Josef in his rearview mirror. Then he blurted out, *"¿De dónde viene?"*

"Belgium."

"You never hear about Belgium, never," he replied, in Spanish.

Josef said nothing but stared out the window at the decaying city.

"What's in Belgium?"

"Nothing," Josef answered, feeling distant from himself. "Just fields, war memorials and a giant atom. We keep a low profile. We aren't like the Americans or Japanese. We like to blend into our surroundings like those insects you have in the jungle. The ones that look like twigs."

The driver didn't seem to be listening at all, sighing as he drove through the slums and over the bridge into Zone 15. "Just the same," he said in a lowered tone, "some say foreigners are building machines in the Petén jungle that are powered by humans. They feed on them. Of course, it's only rumours and I don't believe rumours, especially any told by Indians living in the forest. Those people aren't like us; they don't understand the city. They walk everywhere and don't even have shoes or use electricity. So no," he said, as if his assertion had been questioned, "I don't believe there are machines in the jungle that eat people."

The taxi wound its way up the road into the outlying foothills. "I believe in God, Christ and Salvation. These things I believe. All the rest is Indian talk, nothing else."

People-eating machines in the jungle? Von Flintz's estate passed in a blur outside the window.

"*Para!*" Josef called out.

The driver hit the brakes hard, slamming Josef into the seat in front. Josef paid the cab driver and stepped beneath a tree, watching the taxi vanish down the road. For a time, he remained motionless, trying to conceive of the loss of Dimitri. His gaze shifted from the road to Hans' mansion. He noticed the Guatemalan security guard from days past had been replaced by a Germanic-looking man in his twenties, a gun strapped to his waist. Josef took it as an ominous sign.

Hans cleared his throat. "Come now, stop admiring the view," he said, standing on the other side of the gate. "We have lots to discuss."

Josef remained beneath the tree for an instant longer then followed the old Nazi's gesture inside the gate.

"So have you heard what our friend, *El presidente*, is up to?" von Flintz asked, as they walked through the garden.

"I haven't kept up with the news."

"Voluntary ignorance is a far greater sin than stupidity."

"You have a point."

"Of course I do. I always do," he said, with a laugh. "Our guardian, Rios Montt, has started a program forcing peasants to patrol for communist guerrillas in the countryside."

"Interesting."

"It's transformative. *The Civilian Defense Patrol* may not sound like much, but these conscripts are forced into direct combat with the enemy. Think about it. You're turning slaves into soldiers for the cause. You see, you put them to work and the fruits of their labour is their own demise. You're impressed, aren't you? I can see that." Hans grinned and ushered Josef through the front door. "You want hypocrisy? Guatemala has it all. The American congress bans military aid to us, and the CIA gets it to us through you people."

"The interests of the people are never the same as the government," Josef stated, matter-of-factly.

"My boy, that's all fine and well, but there's a lot you don't know about this country. And perhaps about Israel, either. I know you don't think you need to know much about politics. After all, you only sell arms. You don't tell people who to shoot. But I need you to think a little more broadly for a moment—"

"He's coming."

"Who is?"

"The hangman."

"The prosecutor from Israel?"

Josef nodded.

"How much time?"

"A day. Maybe two."

"So we must move quickly." He directed Josef to a seat at the dining room table and poured him a drink. The old Nazi sat stiffly in a giant wooden chair, with lions' heads perched at the ends of the arm rests.

"You know Josef," he said pointing back and forth between them, speaking confidently like the *commandant* of Übel. "Max and I used to do this, talking about the great achievements of the past and the next rise of the Front. But he's old now, up here," he said, pointing to his head. "Now I will say this: I have watched you and Max over the past weeks, and I can see how deeply loyal you are to him. That shows great character, Josef. Great character. But revolutions can't be waged by tired old men. They need the balls of the young and the brains of the seasoned leader. You see, the average person does the obvious. Like hide things under their bed. What kind of fool would hide something there?"

Josef let slip a grin of recognition.

"Don't they know it's the first place people will look?" continued Hans. "People like us, we never make that mistake, because we aren't ordinary men."

Hans leaned back in his chair, both hands gripping the ornate lion heads. "Did you read the paper today?"

"I know. Voluntary ignorance is a far greater sin than stupidity." Then Josef remembered the picture of Dimitri on the front cover. "Yes, as a matter of fact, I did."

"Shame about the American, isn't it?"

"I would imagine."

"It's always difficult when you lose one of your own."

"I wasn't aware he was one of us."

"One of YOU."

Hans looked at Josef curiously. "Well," he said, clasping his hands, "the American didn't know us, but we certainly knew who he was." He tossed down a photograph of a brutalized body with most of its head missing.

"This Dimitri was getting the peasants tied up in knots about plantation wages and working conditions in the Petén. These are the kinds of international Marxists I want to be rid of once and for all."

"So you killed him."

"Not exactly." He leaned forward and smiled wryly. "I took a little ride last night with a couple of G-2 sharp shooters. My sight, you see, is growing poor, my hands a little shaky."

Josef clasped the steak knife set before him.

"I'll be honest with you -- I never lie -- I see no need to. I like you, but I don't trust you. Not at all. You are, after all, an arms dealer and an Israeli. And with your military training, I'm sure you could take that knife and stab me in the chest. But I trust your eyes. That's why I invited you here, to be certain your eyes didn't betray any other intent you may have." He wagged his finger. "If you were deceiving me, I could read it in a second."

From the cabinet behind his chair, Hans removed a bottle of wine and placed it on the table. "It's a very special wine. I've been saving it for an occasion like this. You may not know it, but today is a monumental day."

Josef smiled but was filled with dread.

"The history of the world, my boy, has always been tumultuous, moving us this way and that. Revolutions and counter-revolutions. Loyalty, betrayal, new chapters constantly being written. It doesn't matter that it happens here or in Bolivia or even in Germany, for that matter. What matters is that it happened and it changed us."

Von Flintz passed the bottle to Josef. "Would you do the honours?"

The bottle came from an Italian vineyard -- 1938. Perhaps it was a departing gift from the Vatican after hiding there like so many other Nazis at the close of the war. With a resounding pop, Josef pulled the cork free and let the wine breathe before pouring a glass for the colonel and himself. They made a toast, and Maria arrived with a side of beef.

For a time, they ate in silence before Hans looked up. "You know, Josef, if I'd found anything in your eyes that betrayed you at the barracks, I was going to kill you right there. It's that kind of conviction and trust in my own judgment that has allowed me to accomplish so much in my lifetime."

"Why did you choose Guatemala?"

"Let me to tell you something about this country. You know the national symbol is the Quetzal. Do you know the myth behind the bird?" The old Nazi didn't wait for a response, his eyes gleaming with fire. "Well, in Mayan mythology the quetzal was known as the Plumed Serpent, the creator of the world. When the Spaniards came and conquered the Indians, they wiped out 20,000 of them on the battlefield. The quetzals descended to earth and covered the dead, staining their feathers with the blood of slaughter. As you can see, Guatemala has always had a bloody history.

"But don't make the mistake of thinking my job is an easy one. No, my work is cut out for me. I must arm the military and intelligence with an ideology they can use to act on. I've seen first-hand what an army does without the proper ideology. I advised part of the campaign in Argentina, but I left. It was a total disaster. Their efforts to cleanse the country of intellects was laughable, because they were running on only bits and pieces of ideology. There were rumours that psychiatrists were bolstering the morale of the guerrillas so a campaign began to eradicate therapists. It was illogical hysteria without a meaningful direction. Pure and simple stupidity. An embarrassment, in truth."

Hans took a bite of meat and continued talking as he chewed, "I don't want to bore you with the details, but let's just say a problem still exists in Guatemala because the military, though anti-Communist, isn't ideologically bent in our immediate direction. And there's another problem. The army ranks are bloated with Indians. First, I'll worry about rooting out the Bolsheviks and then I'll worry about the cancer in the military. I have a plan, a realistic one." He appeared to size Josef up. "Do you want to know what it is?"

"Absolutely."

"It's a second coming of *volksdeutsche*, the German pioneers," he said. "General Barrios had encouraged the first wave of Germans from Europe at the turn of the century to run the plantations, and now I've begun to organize the next wave. It'll mark the second rise of German dominance as a historical force in this part of the world."

"Do you think it's realistic that millions of ethnic Germans will move here?"

Von Flintz's eyes flashed with rage. "*Ach*, Josef, do you think I'm so stupid that I'd organize something doomed to fail? Please give me some credit."

"I do."

"Good," he shouted. "Because I can't have someone questioning me every step of the way. Do you hear me?"

"Hans, I only ask, because I have to understand all aspects of your plan. I know you didn't wait all this time to launch a doomed campaign. That's not like you. You're absolutely thorough. I know that about you."

Just now Blondi, his great white Alsatian, trotted into the room and sat beside Hans. "The sooner we set up a foreign presence, the sooner we can enact the final phase of my plan."

"How?" A sickening knot twisted in Josef's guts. He studied the scar on Hans' neck, the arrogance held in his erect posture and the steadiness of his ageing blue eyes.

"You say I need to lay low while your *friend* comes to investigate?"

"Yes."

"Excellent. We'll take a little trip. I want you to see how a civilization can be remembered after so many centuries. Then you'll see what greatness we have planned."

23

EL PETÉN

The rugged Guatemalan mountains floated by beneath the twin engine plane. As Hans read the *New York Times*, Josef gazed from the window, unable to think beyond the plans he imagined the old Nazi had for the country. The pilot, an American in his early forties, sat comfortably in his seat, occasionally talking loudly above the sound of the plane's engines. He smiled with his big teeth, telling stories of flying sorties in Vietnam during the war. From his unapologetic accounts of bombing villages inside Laos, it appeared he was not at all pre-occupied by moral questions. *As long as he got paid.*

In time, the endless crags and valley slopes submerged beneath a sea of dense jungle. The plane tilted and descended through patches of cloud. Deep brown rivers snaked their way along the tropical floor. In the distance, the fabled city of the Mayans appeared like a swatch cut from the velvet green fabric of the wilderness. The earth rose up to meet the plane, the runway still nowhere in sight. They glided low above the forest canopy, and at fifty feet, the paved runway sped by. The plane touched down, skipping along the tarmac until it slowed and came to a rest.

"This is just a quick stop. I want you to see this."

"No black hood treatment?"

Hans didn't laugh.

When they emerged from the Piper, the intense humidity struck Josef hard. In no time, his shirt clung to his exposed ribs, which was not lost on von Flintz. "*Ach*, you need to eat, Josef. You look like a withered Jew."

"I didn't realize you read English," said Josef, pointing to the *New York Times* tucked under the old Nazi's arm.

"I had to for dealing with the CIAs of the world. You know the English speaking world is probably the most un-educated anywhere. Language," he said arrogantly in broken Hebrew. "*They knowing nothing of them.*" Then Hans waved the newspaper before Josef. "We made the American papers." He pointed to a small photograph. "Our friend Dimitri is fa-mous. The Americans are launching an investigation into his death and already it's creating ripples in Congress. There's talk about human rights violations and extending military sanc-tions against Guatemala."

"You aren't worried?"

"Why should I be? As we speak, G-2 officials are at the prison finding two convicts guilty of the murder. We launch a thorough investigation and find a murder weapon with their finger prints all over it. A crime committed during theft. Politics doesn't enter into it. Ambushes and kidnappings happen all the time. The Americans won't even step out of the airport and we'll have their men handcuffed and ready to go. We wash our hands clean and the Americans go home."

"Case closed."

"Case closed. And, you see, the whole thing was my idea – the problem and the solution. Killing the American was a fun little experiment to see how our U.S. friends would react. Predictably, of course. You may ask yourself how I have survived all this time. And I'll tell you. I've made myself useful to people. Powerful people. With my advice and connections, they get richer. They hold onto power longer. Never underestimate the power of the gatekeeper, Josef. That's why I've never felt the need to hide. Being indispensable can make you very popular and, I might add, very wealthy."

With that, the old Nazi raised a machete and led Josef along a rutted road before entering the thick of the forest. A fine cobweb mist clung to the trees. Josef grew aware of everything around him. Just as Dimitri had described, the sounds rising from the jungle were stranger and more intense than anything he'd ever experienced. Ceiba trees towered alongside the sleek *Pimienta Gorda* tree, while the Strangler Fig wrapped its thick vines around its host. A spider monkey suspended above, limbs spread, clung to the branches. Below, industrious leaf cutter ants cut a path across the jungle floor, carrying their burdensome load of leaves above their heads like tireless workers.

Inside this natural cathedral, the old Nazi's breath laboured as he hacked his way through with the machete. It was an unnecessary effort with the trees so far apart. Von Flintz looked back, puffed his chest and smiled. "This is the work of real men."

Like a vision, the forest opened and revealed the ruins of Tikal. It was a dream first echoed in the texts he had pored over in Cuba, but nothing prepared him for the grandeur of the Mayans' most famous city. The scaling heights of Temple I and II faced one another over the Great Plaza, capped by small chambers and platforms where rituals and human sacrifices had undoubtedly taken place. The stelae lining the open courtyard appeared to tell the story of the Mayan City in both pictures and ancient text.

They lingered for a moment. Hans touched a stela and murmured to himself, as if reading braille. "Very interesting," he finally concluded.

"I didn't realize you could decipher hieroglyphs."

"I'm a man of many talents."

From the central courtyard, the North Acropolis appeared as a labyrinth of vaulted rooms spanning Tikal's immense history. Kings dressed in their finest costumes once paraded around the royal palaces made of stone and lime.

"You probably don't know this but Tikal was lost to the jungle for centuries. The wilderness had literally swallowed the city." He paused for dramatic effect. "So much can be concealed here."

The old Nazi directed Josef toward Temple I, the Temple of the Giant Jaguar, a lean steep monument that begged reverence. He beckoned Josef to follow him to the top; but not ten steps up, he paused breathlessly. He stared up and then nervously back at Josef. With a grave nod, he took another trembling step and stopped again. For perhaps twenty minutes, Hans continued on in this way until they reached the crown of the temple. In the near distance, several temples peeked above the jungle canopy. Beyond, an unbreakable view of forest and sky.

"Do you realize," von Flintz said, "how many died on Mayan altars? It's impressive. Hundreds of thousands -- maybe even millions -- over the years were sacrificed to the gods, for the greater glory of the Mayan civilization. Tell me this, Josef. How is it that after thirty-seven years Germany is still being condemned for the death camps, but the same people who condemn us come here and marvel at the Mayans' great achievements? They say, 'see Indians weren't savages, they built great civilizations.' They fail to mention all the slave labour that went into building these glorious empires and the hearts ripped from the bodies of the condemned. The Germans were saints compared to that."

For an instant, Josef felt the sensation of pushing against von Flintz until his weight no longer resisted, falling like a heavy sack off the edge. But Josef remained still, his sight fixed on his parents' killer.

"We could once again drench the temple with sacrificial blood," said Hans.

"Whose?"

"Why yours, of course," he said with a grating laugh.

"I'm not sure the groundskeepers would appreciate that."

"I'm making a joke, Josef."

Down below, tourists in khakis and hippie garb were now arriving. They spread over the ruins like ants, scurrying around snapping photographs.

Hans trembled as he gazed over the edge of the temple. From this angle, the temple steps appeared as a vertical drop. Unwilling to admit his fear, he began to descend, sliding down step by step, bracing with his hands. Unlike the SS colonel encountered in his visions, Hans appeared to have grown fearful of death with age.

For the next two hours, they explored the ruins, wandering along trails cut through the forest, where small temples remained hidden beneath earth, shrub and vines that grew from their sloping heights. They came across various Mayan artefacts, including a circular stone altar in which Hans took particular interest. It detailed the preparation for a human sacrifice -- the prisoner laid out on his back, four priests holding his arms and legs, a fifth preparing to cut the prisoner's chest open with a long blade.

"You see, Josef, blood sacrifice is as old as mankind itself. It wasn't a fanatical lust for blood that drove the Mayan priests to make humans sacrifices. They understood that these blood offerings were required for the continuance of their culture. I'm sure they thought it was an unpleasant task, but they did what they had to do for the greater good." He rested a hand on Josef's shoulder. "Western religion is founded on a man who was going to kill his son to prove his faith in God. Do you realize that? Of course you do.

What more proof do you want that murder is sanctioned by God? A lot of people -- blind people -- want to believe these images of violence in our history are aberrations. I assure you they aren't. They represent the foundation of our beliefs. Until we recognize this, we will remain stricken and confused about the essential role of violence and destruction in the health of society." Hans smiled and studied the stone altar for countless minutes and then led Josef back toward the airstrip.

———

The plane was in the air no more than ten minutes before it began to descend. With a sharp finger, Hans pointed below to a village clearing carved from the forest. "Gone," is all he said.

"What do you mean?"

"We made them disappear."

"Everyone?"

"One hundred and twenty men, women and children."

"And no one noticed?"

"Of course they noticed. But everyone assumes it was the Guatemalan military. That sort of thing is commonplace. And who are they going to run to? The police? Besides, what's another one hundred and twenty lives in a war that's already claimed one hundred thousand. *Ach*, I've never understood why people are so horrified when kids are killed in war. People say, *What kind of monster kills children?* This kind of moral outrage has always amused me. You see, I don't see it as the act of the monster...I see kids as future adults and the children of my enemy become my enemies. So kill them while you can."

In the middle of the afternoon, the pilot took them by jeep to the gates of an enormous compound deep inside the forest. The camp was surrounded by three outer coils of barbed wire, while the inner perimeter was protected by a high electric fence and watch towers every twenty yards or so. A sign on the first of two gates read: *Peligro. Experimentos biológicos.* Químicos *tóxicos.* Danger. Biological experiments. Toxic chemicals.

The compound appeared deserted but for Hans, the pilot and a servant, who silently opened the gate.

"Where is everyone?"

"Our manpower is better served elsewhere until our operation goes into action. Besides, no one can enter or escape this place." He smiled proudly. "This is our best kept secret. You're one of the first to see and, if you're lucky, you may actually make it out alive."

Josef smiled thinly.

"Where's your sense of humour today?"

Hans directed Josef to a brick room outfitted with a mahogany chest, a mirror, and a turn of the century canopy bed with mosquito netting hanging around it like a bridal veil. "Josef, do not wander the camp alone," he warned. "It's still under construction and I can't be responsible if something happens to you."

"What's this all about?"

The old Nazi ignored his question. "I'll come get you in a little while," he said. And with that, Hans closed the door and left Josef alone.

But Hans never returned. So in the late afternoon Josef crept out of his room and began exploring the camp. The site was perhaps two kilometres long and wide. With sickening clarity, Josef recognized it from his visions. It was a replica of Übel, only transplanted four decades and five thousand kilometres away from the original site. In the near distance stood a number of chimney stacks, and at the far end of the grounds was a dense stand of jungle. He walked between the long barracks made of brick and then found an unlocked door and entered. There were hundreds of bunk beds stacked three levels high and 30 beds long. The mattresses were stuffed with straw. Josef could almost imagine the haunted faces staring up at him from their beds, too weak and hungry to stand or resist. He remained motionless, absorbing the meaning of the old Nazi's madness.

After what seemed to be an eternity, Josef entered another long brick building with giant wooden support beams crisscrossing the ceiling. It had counters and, by its size and position among the other buildings, it appeared to be where new arrivals were to be stripped and their clothes taken away and burned. Further along the corridor stood a large windowless room with two dozen barbers' chairs. Heads were to be shaved before the prisoners were taken through another door to the showers for cleaning. At the end of the hallway were shelves piled with grey prison uniforms. This design seemed impossible and naive but, in truth, this orderly nightmare -- of barber chairs and gas showers -- had already worked. In Birkenau. Treblinka. Bergen Belsen. Übel.

Josef followed the corridor outside and then underground to three large gas chambers sealed with steel doors. Here the line ups would grow outside the doors, the anxious people sensing something was terribly wrong. He hesitated then entered one of the chambers. Inside the acrid smelling room, Josef felt the distinct absence of life. He heard people moan and children cry. This was the future designed by SS Colonel Hans von Flintz.

Josef silently closed the steel door and moved toward the building with the chimney stacks. Outside the mouths of the ovens, the walls were covered in thick black soot. Josef swung open the door to the crematorium. Inside, there was a pile of skulls, large and small, blackened bone splinters, and ash. It was all that remained of the villagers that von Flintz had made "disappear."

24

CONFESSIONS

Sometime after dark, Hans von Flintz still had not come to fetch Josef. So he mustered the energy to make an appearance in the dining room in the building next door. When he arrived, Hans was sitting at the very end of a long table, eating by himself. The shutters on the barred windows were open wide and allowed the rattle of the generator at the edge of camp to disturb the silence.

"I trust you found your way around," he said, without looking up from his plate.

"So you wanted me to discover the camp," Josef stammered.

"I brought you here, didn't I?"

"Who else knows about it?"

Hans shrugged.

"The U.S? Who? Israel?"

Hans sighed heavily. "A dozen men. That's it. The circle is necessarily small. And yes, for now only Germans -- and you."

"But someone had to have built it."

"*Ach*, do I have to spell it out? Those villagers! They were hired to build a research centre in the jungle. That's what they thought, anyway. After it was completed, we need to test operations."

"Two birds. One stone."

"No witnesses are the best witnesses."

"But what if someone escapes from the camp and speaks?"

"No one will believe them."

Hans was still chewing when he pointed an accusing finger at Josef. "You need to eat. Have some wine." Josef regarded the platters of rice and meat before him as one looked at an insurmountable obstacle.

"I learned early on that for a lie to succeed it had to be so spectacular and so detailed that everyone would have to believe you. Josef, I know as a Jew this may not seem sane, but I assure you it is. Don't feel alone -- you aren't the first Hebrew I've worked with." Then he added, "This here has nothing to do with the Jews or the past. It's about the future. The conspiracy is far greater and more sinister than anything the Semites could have concocted. The communist hoards must be stopped."

It was all quite implausible. It seemed likely that Hans von Flintz had lost his mind. No sane man could create such madness and still speak sanely about it. And what kind of Nazi would bring a Jew inside his nightmare and not expect to be killed or at the very least turned over to the authorities? For Josef, it was impossible to fathom how he fit into von Flintz's plans.

"There's lots to consider here," said Hans, talking and chewing. "We can't overcrowd the facilities. That's important. Very important. Otherwise we risk the spread of disease or revolt. Too many people to feed while they're waiting can cause disturbances. We can't allow for anarchy. This thing has to be very methodical and we need contingency plans every step of the way. For instance, what if the humidity of the jungle slows the furnaces?"

"Collect the prisoners' fat and use it as fuel," said Josef, drawing from Erich's vision inside Übel.

"And what if the machines break down completely, food runs short, and the prisoners become rebellious and threaten revolt?"

"Poison what little food is left and distribute it among the prisoners. And whoever is left, shoot from the guard towers."

"Clever. And if the machines run smoothly, as I'm confident they will, we can march the Indians right into the gas showers. No need to feed them. No need to clothe them."

Hans' face became flush and his language looser as he polished off a second bottle of wine. "Those were great times," he said, caught in a moment of revelry, as if speaking to the ghosts of his past. "*Ach*, they'd brought us to our knees, Josef. We couldn't breathe. We had no more air to breathe. They would've sold that to us too if they could've. But we were reborn and brought the war back to the traitors who had betrayed us. And for a time we were the undeniable rulers. No one can take that away from us. No one. We destroyed the libraries and churches and the newspapers. We destroyed everything that opposed us. We became a way of life. And that's how you win, my boy. Not by violent coercion, but by convincing people that what you want is what they need. Answer me this -- why did university professors, lawyers, doctors and school teachers walk into the gas chambers like obedient sheep? Their sheer numbers could've overrun us. But they didn't. Why?"

Josef remained silent.

"You're not a thinking man tonight. Let me answer -- we led them to believe that if they did as we said, they'd still have a chance to live. If they died, it was their fault, because they didn't follow our orders to the letter. We were Gods, Josef. Do you know what that means? Soon you will. We could do what we wanted without judgment, without fear of reprisal. That's what it means to be a God.

"There is so much evil in the world, so much to be cleansed. I believe in freedom. Do you know that? Freedom from the tyranny of a communist world that would take away our personal freedom. Imagine that? No personal freedom so that we couldn't walk down the street and say what we want. Guatemala is a testament to my work-in-progress. We can carry on as we please now that the Bolsheviks in this country are being subdued. I'm providing a freedom that most people are unaware of. They can't see that what I'm doing is saving them from the perils of a Bolshevik republic, one that controls not only the body but the mind.

"We all must make sacrifices of ourselves for the greater good," he confessed. "That is our burden. But the important thing to remember is that civilizations constantly rise and fall. And they fall when they are sick -- and sometimes we must help tear them down. History demands it of us. I am fulfilling a duty that is greater than the sum of our parts. To purify and build an altar worthy of man's glory. And if in the end we breathe new life into our civilization, then all the pain and loneliness we have suffered has been worth our sacrifices."

"Are you planning to kill all the Indians?"

"Must you be so crude? Of course not. Why, who else would pick the coffee and harvest the fields or sweep the streets? Surely not Germans. No, I've already figured that three to four million will have to be spared to keep our export markets happy. Hard foreign currency is the name of the game. Man can't survive on ideas alone. Economics powers the machine."

The old Nazi quickly sank into shadow, the lines of his brooding face now more deeply pronounced. "I remember when I was a boy. Maybe five or six. I used to throw stones at birds -- I quite liked it -- but I never hit them, though, because they'd fly away from the fields behind my aunt's farm. But one day I hit one. I ran into the tall grass looking for it. I'd knocked it out of the sky as it flew off among the flock that'd taken off. It probably thought it had been safe flying in the middle of the group.

"Even as a child, I had so many questions about why that particular bird had been selected. Who determined it was time for that bird to die? As you can see, I was very bright. At that age, I realized it was destiny -- in the same way the

Great War took my parents, in the same way I avenged my parents' murderers. I'm not going to lie to you," he said abruptly, before pausing to comb his white oiled hair with an open hand. "During the war I worked at a camp. And do you know who chose the destiny of so many lives?" He stood and pointed a thumb at his chest. "I walked among the wretched and decided the fate of thousands. I stole that power from God. In my hand, I grasped His lightning bolt, and for Germany I helped cleanse her of everything that was vile and evil."

He looked toward the door and the steely pride with which he spoke melted away. After a deep sigh, he sat. "So, here I was a young boy excitedly searching for my first kill. When I found it, its head was torn off. I was fascinated. My heart beat fast and I actually tasted blood in my mouth. I took the mangled creature back to the farmhouse to show my aunt. And do you know what she did?"

Josef shook his head.

"That awful bitch hit me and told me not to kill. But I hated her, everything about her -- the way she smelled, and her wretched voice that would tell me every day how fortunate I was to have such a good aunty to look after me because her sister and her sister's husband were dead. So the metallic taste of blood remained in my mouth."

"Why did you choose me?"

"I'm an old man," he said, without hesitation. Then Hans pointed to his head. "Not up here. But the body will ultimately betray the soul and I don't want all my work to be in vain." Hans drank another glass of wine. "And you know Max is finished."

"What do you mean?"

"Cancer of the pancreas."

"He never said anything."

"Max has always been something of a silent martyr. He turned yellow before he even mentioned it. But enough about him, God rest his soul." Hans locked eyes on Josef. "We, Josef, are similar. You see, men like Reinhard -- if you can call them that -- take the easy way and leave the hardest work for last. For us, we work hard from the very start and then enjoy the fruits of our labour."

"But why me?" persisted Josef.

"Why not you? That was the beauty of Germany in our day. Ordinary men could become gods. We belonged to a higher order. You can't do that alone. You need a group of people around you to help realize the dream. My son was to be my heir," he said. "But there's something else." The old Nazi stared at Josef with the eyes of a possessed man. "I had a prophecy, a prophecy that a young Hebrew would stand to my right as I ascended to the heavens. I think you know who that person is. I knew you were coming. I just knew it. Now it all makes sense."

His eyes narrowed and suddenly he stood. With an air that approached regret, he directed Josef from his chair. Von Flintz led him like a condemned prisoner down the hallway to an open door. The old Nazi took him down a flight of stairs. In the stifling darkness of the basement, Hans stopped and prompted Josef to walk ahead. He drew up close behind. There was the sound of keys as Hans reached around Josef, one hand resting firmly on his shoulder. He pulled open a heavy steel door and pressed him forward.

There was the metallic ring of a safety catch being released. Every detail of the moment became crystal clear -- Hans' heavy breath, the damp smell of earth, the lingering fear of what forever remained concealed by the darkness. The slow creak of a gun being cocked left Josef deaf with fear. He was succumbing to the pistol, succumbing to Hans' will. Just as Erich Hauptmann had failed to exact justice, Josef sensed his own impending doom at the hands of the Nazi.

Then, all at once, Josef was blinded by a light.

When his eyes adjusted, he saw Hans fiddling with a Luger. A brassy smile appeared across his face when he saw Josef look toward his altar. "I knew you'd be impressed," he said, waving the Luger toward his shrine.

Inside the vault was a collage of objects. Hans had created an altar that stood in perfect opposition to Asena's altar. Where there had been a Menorah, there was a Swastika. Where there had been a Buddha meditating, there was a photograph of von Flintz holding a whip. Where there had been a picture of Asena's family, there was a portrait of Adolf Hitler. Where there had been a Crucified Christ, there was a neat lock of brown hair. Another shelf elaborately adorned with red velvet seemed conspicuously empty, as if an object was missing.

"What goes there?" Josef ventured to ask.

"Someone's heart," he replied, stroking the scar on his neck reflectively.

"When I'm finished with mine, I'll let you know," said Josef, as he gazed at the lock of Sarah's hair and the empty space reserved for a human heart.

"You know," Hans said, unable to conceal his thoughts. "I didn't want to be a leader. I didn't. But it was my calling. People believe in the words I speak. And I believe them, too. So when they call me a prophet, I say, yes, I am a prophet. And I will lead the people. But I can't do that alone." He pointed to Josef, before leading him from the vault.

When they returned to the dining room, Josef remained standing. Hans unbuttoned his shirt and lifted his arm, wavering on his feet drunk. "Look at this. This is my proof." It was a small tattoo with his blood type and the double SS lightning bolts. "After the war, some tried to erase it. They wanted to obliterate the past. But not me, not me for one second. To erase it would say I've something to hide, something I should be ashamed of. I'm ashamed of nothing I've done. Nothing. My conscience is clean."

Hans dropped back into his chair. Only now did he seem to recognize that something had changed. "You don't seem with it, Josef. The forest does strange things to people. Go. Get some rest. I'll talk to you tomorrow." He picked up his glass of wine and waved Josef away like a fly.

—⁃—

When Josef was certain Hans von Flintz had gone to bed, he removed the SS dagger concealed in the lining of his bag. He needed to assure himself that the old Nazi hadn't uncovered it while Josef was exploring the horrors of the camp. With his worries dispelled, he dropped the insect net suspended above the bed and listened to the forest -- beating, clicking and pulsing with life. Insects crawled and fluttered around the netting. As he closed his eyes and sank into bed, many forms appeared to him, though one notion captured his attention: to return to the final day at Übel before von Flintz's empire of death collapsed.

He focused on his breathing, growing more and more relaxed. Random images poured through the open window of his mind's eye. Then the vision sharpened and the images merged and began to flow. It was the final sequence of Erich's life. Josef closed his eyes and dreamed of Erich, as if it were himself. He sped through as Hans raped Sarah, her eyes squinting in pain. Erich threw him off and drove Hans into the wall. He led Sarah away by the hand, concealing the SS dagger he had stolen off the floor. He fell further back, penetrating Erich Hauptmann's mind. Josef was now thinking his thoughts, unable to separate himself from Erich or his story.

His sight shifts around the desolate brick office toward the image of the Führer in his knight's armour. SS colonel Hans von Flintz has already commenced his round up and murder of all remaining prisoners at Übel, but he is running low on

Zyklon B and has begun the mass executions along the camp perimeter.

It's early morning and Erich hasn't slept in two days; he wants to be awake when it all comes to an end. He steps out from his office and hears the guns and sees the bright flashes as artillery pounds the area surrounding the camp. With the stolen SS dagger clenched in hand, he moves through the corridor with the silent resolve of an assassin. The cries of families being separated and their final moans of agony between life and death are drowned by the rattle of machine guns.

As he approaches the firing line, he hears a struggle behind the barracks. He cuts back toward the sound of muted cries and sees Hans whipping her -- whipping Sarah viciously and clawing at her rags, angrily fondling her breasts. The colonel doesn't hear him coming, as he steps up behind him, emotionless and determined as the sun. A barrage of artillery explodes. Hans turns, and for a moment, they're illuminated to one another then cast into darkness. "*Ach*" is all Hans manages to say, because he has no time to act. In a single motion, Erich grapples Hans by the face and slashes his throat with the dagger. Blackness is followed by another quick succession of mortar rounds. In the flash, he see von Flintz's eyes open wide, as he clutches his neck. He can't speak, choking on the blood spilling from his open mouth. His legs buckle and he falls to his knees as if in prayer. For a moment, the Nazi remains there, gurgling, before he tumbles, his life draining away into the earth.

Erich draws Sarah away and places his coat over her shoulders. Each time the machine guns rattle, Sarah clings to him whispering, praying for it to be over. Along the corridor of the Inner Station, soldiers and officers push by one another carrying armloads of documents out to the courtyard. The massive bonfire fed by the constant stream of camp papers is dwarfed only by the smoke stacks pluming smoke. If he doesn't do anything about it, the evidence of all that has happened here will soon be erased.

He pushes his way through, clenching Sarah's arm, until they reach his office at the end of the hall. He sends her through and closes the door quickly behind them, locking it in case they're discovered. Sarah shivers and recoils as he approaches with a blanket. "You're safe with me," he tells her. Sarah nods, tears streaming down her pale cheeks.

On his knees, he breathes heavily, clawing at the wall with a chisel, digging deep into the brick. He grips his file along with that of Dr. Ziegler and Hans von Flintz. It has always been their job to record their deeds -- but destroy the prisoners so that none may bear witness and live to tell their stories. The ground heaves as an artillery shell lands nearby, sending a beam crashing down from the ceiling.

Erich clutches a handful of his favourite sketches and places them in his file. He removes the cover page to Hans von Flintz's file and on his photograph strikes a black line across his throat. He places the SS dagger and the three personnel files inside the niche, locking history away for the future. He replaces the freshly mortared bricks and turns to

Sarah. "When it's over, this is where you'll find them," he says, pointing to the wall. "Please do this for me."

She nods.

He grabs his diaries and steers his way through the mob in the hallway, gripping Sarah's arm. They move like shadows across the courtyard. Officers continue to gather around the giant funeral pyre fed by the camp documents. Some of the SS are emotional and sing old German songs from their youth. Several shells land directly on the Inner Station, sending the guards scurrying. Prisoners continue to be shot along the length of the barbed fence; Dr. Ziegler is shouting for the guards to reload their machine guns.

Through the dust, they run away past the furnaces and beyond Übel's iron gates. They crash through the meadows, heading in the opposite direction of the pursuing sun. He has a single wish and that's to be a bird and fly away, but the time for running is almost over.

Shells land around them, blowing the last living things to pieces. As he holds Sarah's hand, he feels life in the warmth of her palm. Then something happens -- the colours which had vanished from his sight are now returning. The flowers are bright yellow, their stems a vivid green. He clenches her hand more tightly as they run, filled with the strangest sense of hope. In his other hand, he clutches the diaries. Maybe if he is caught, his captors will understand from his confessions that he too is just an ordinary man.

When they reach the deserted streets of Stenedal, he knocks on the old wooden door of a farm house. The young man, Jon Küssel, peers out and looks at Sarah curiously before vanishing behind the door. He reappears moments later with a handful of clothes and, for a moment, their eyes meet. Jon steps forward and hugs him. Then, in fear, Jon shuts the door.

Erich turns to face Sarah and retrieves several diamonds and gold pieces from his pocket. *She is just a girl*, he thinks. *Not my sister or daughter or even my niece. Just a girl caught in a man-made disaster.* He gives her the diamonds and gold and silently points for her to seek shelter. The Allies will be here soon to liberate her. Sarah looks at him and steps forward as if to press her lips to his cheek. But then she becomes confused and simply vanishes down the street.

He grasps the bundle of clothes and darts through the empty yard. In a moment's time, he finds himself unbuttoning his coat, tearing through his soiled shirt and pulling down his trousers. It's strange that in these final moments, as the rope runs short, his thoughts continue to unravel. His soul is ready but his flesh still yearns for life.

A noise from behind steals his attention. He turns to see the hardened faces of the enemy. They drag him through the dirt, kicking chickens out of their path, and throw him against the barn. He begs the officer to be merciful but the American points a condemning finger at his German uniform. "I wish to repay my debt," he whispers, "with blood." He raises his hand to offer his testament, his diaries, but they think he salutes Hitler.

Everything recedes into a point on the horizon. There is no escaping this moment. He sees Marta smiling down on him as his sight is reborn in the hospital. His grandfather sits at the kitchen table reading aloud from *Arabian Nights*; Julius stands on the rock that warm summer day, whipping his fishing line out into the river, the light dancing on the river like stars.

His body remains utterly exposed to the bullets that emerge from the fiery barrels aimed at his chest. Jon's mother cries out as he is struck. He touches the brilliant colour of blood with a hand and marvels at how perfect a canvas the body truly is. All the revelations are no use now. He falls with eyes turned up toward the morning sky.

He is now separated from his body but not his sins. In his lifeless hand he holds the books he has carried with him for so many miles. The Americans leave his body for the crows. Then judgment.

25

ASCENSION

When Josef awoke before dawn, Erich Hauptmann was still there, flickering like the dying light of a candle inside him. Night filled the room with dark impenetrable shadows, yet he saw clearly as he had years before in the darkness of the Palo altar in Cuba moments before the ritual sacrifice. Hector had taken the glistening blade and slit the chicken's throat, draining the ink-thick blood on the *nganga* to feed the hungry dead. From the bag, Josef removed the dagger Erich had used in his attempt on von Flintz's life.

Outside, it was much quieter without the rattling of the generator; he was certain Hans had already awoken. With the starlight fading, Josef crouched low and peered in through von Flintz's window. A candle burned on the mantle. The old Nazi was awake, standing before a mirror, shaving with slow ritualistic intent. Something shining on the bed caught Josef's attention. It was an SS dagger.

He stood back from the window, a blanket of heat clinging to his skin. A building tension grew in his chest, as he knocked on the door then stepped beneath a tree. For a moment, he remained at an unsettling distance from himself.

Hans appeared at the doorway dressed in black silk pyjamas, hunched and shrunken with age, wiping his face clean with a towel. Josef remained sheltered beneath the tree, only a few feet from where the old Nazi stood. Hans greeted him with mild cheer and smoothed his hair down. Josef stepped from the shadows and embraced him.

"I couldn't sleep."

Hans hadn't even released his warm grip when Josef struck at his throat like a cobra.

"*Ach*, what's got into you, man?" Hans threw his head back defiantly, as Josef drew the dagger to his throat. Just as the old Nazi yelled for help, the generator kicked on, drowning his pleas. In the single moment that the generator stole Josef's attention, Hans pushed the knife away. Josef lunged for his shadow but he was already on his feet, running toward the forested area of the compound. The colonel vanished into the thick fold of trees. Josef's feet sped beneath him then disappeared into the tomb-like blackness of the jungle. He could hear him up ahead, panting and stumbling wildly, twigs snapping beneath his heavy footsteps.

The Nazi ran toward the high fence at the edge of the camp and looked around confused. He touched it, but it sparked and sent him jumping backward. Immediately he doubled back, skirting wide along the electric coils of barbed wire, looking for a way to escape. Josef was getting close. In the near distance, he saw the shadow of the crematoria. Hans gasped for air and glanced over his shoulder. Josef was now only a few steps behind when Hans broke into the clearing and dashed for his door. He grasped the handle, but Josef pulled him back and dragged him to the ground. This time, he had him and forced the knife against his ragged neck. Von Flintz clawed at him, but Josef was delirious with revenge. He saw the bomb planted at his parents' feet.

Kill him, said a voice. *He doesn't deserve to live*. Josef resisted the voice though pressed the knife more tightly against his neck so that the skin grew tight and was about to split. He was gasping and twisting in agony, and Josef could feel the life slowly passing from him. Greedily, he took more, seeing himself at this moment doing God's work, following His voice as surely as Abraham had when he took his only son to Mount Moriah for sacrifice. Josef grew afraid of the fierceness welling up from some inconceivable place he'd never before dreamed he possessed.

A door creaked open. Josef looked up. The pilot stepped out from a doorway, his gun trained on him.

"Step back or he's dead," Josef warned.

"Just shoot him," said von Flintz, "I don't care about my own life."

Josef choked him hard. Von Flintz let out a yelp and wheezed: "Tyler. Put your goddamn gun down. Do what this maniac says."

"Get your plane ready. We're taking a trip."

"It's too dark," the pilot said. "The runway isn't lit."

"Then we'll die together."

When the lights of the town of Flores appeared up ahead, the pilot banked the plane and began to descend toward the blackness of the forest, the ruins of Tikal glowing in the faint light of dawn. Without the aid of runway lights, the pilot effortlessly lined the plane up and dropped below the tree line, touching down on the tarmac without the merest shudder.

Beneath the pilot's seat, Josef found a length of rope and used it to bind von Flintz's arms behind his back. With the remaining length of rope, he tied his legs loosely together so that he could only shuffle. Josef tightened a dirty oil rag around the Nazi's mouth. Still dressed in his black pajamas, von Flintz gave a muffled protest, as Josef hauled him out of the plane.

"Good landing," he called back to Tyler.

The pilot shrugged and gave a cocky big-toothed smile. "I flew more night sorties in Vietnam than I can count and could have done this one in my sleep."

"I don't need to warn you not to circle back, because he'll be dead before you touch down." Tyler nodded with resignation and began fiddling with knobs, preparing his plane for take-off. Hans seemed disgusted by the pilot's lack of loyalty.

When the sound of the plane's engines faded and its blinking lights had melded seamlessly with the stars, Josef dragged von Flintz away from the landing strip. The old Nazi stumbled around. Josef had to use all his strength to keep him on his feet, as they entered the darkness of the forest. After countless minutes navigating his way around the enormous pillar-like trees, Josef marched his prisoner into the Great Plaza of Tikal's North Acropolis. He dragged Hans toward Temple I then removed the gag from his mouth. Only now, standing at the base of the temple with its steep narrow staircase, did the colonel seem to register where he was.

Josef pulled on the rope, as if the old Nazi was a mule, and began dragging him up, step by step.

"You deranged son-of-a-bitch. You've lost your fucking mind."

Josef looked toward the top, dragging the burden of the Nazi's weight up the shallow steps of the Temple of the Giant Jaguar.

When they reached the temple summit, Josef placed him on his stomach, his arms and legs still bound together, and pulled the Nazi's head up from the stone by the hair. Von Flintz winced in pain, but Josef didn't care, feeling vicious and drunk with the certainty of his power, knowing there was no limit to his command over the colonel's life and death.

"Great men think alike," von Flintz gasped.

"Words are meaningless now."

"So you say. I was going to bring you here, too."

"You're insane, old man."

"We're both sane. That's the problem. The prophecy I spoke to you of—" He motioned for Josef to ease his stranglehold so he could speak. "What I told you wasn't the whole story. Yes, I knew that a Jew would appear and I would bring him to the camp. Then I was to sacrifice him…you…up here to ensure the success of my plans."

"So you'd reserved a place in your altar for my heart. Thoughtful."

The old Nazi managed to smirk, before Josef rolled him over so that his chest and heart were laid open and exposed like the inscription on the Mayan sacrificial altar. Josef kneeled above, the SS dagger gripped in both hands. What happened next only took a few seconds. History began to unravel. Josef descended through time where he had been reborn a thousand times, maybe more. The archaeology of the cave was nearly complete. He raised the knife high above his head, aiming it directly at the Nazi's chest. He wanted to watch the blood flow. God warned Cain not to be mastered by his rage. Now Josef, descendant of Cain, threatened to transgress. His head swam. Hector whispered that the head the *orisha* Obatalá had given him had grown too hot.

Suddenly, in the lair he was confronted by Cain, son of Adam, who lived nine hundred and thirty years. Josef descended backward through the darkness of the cave. Hans flailed, and Josef gripped the knife even tighter, his arms shaking with the explosive tension that begged to be released like a guillotine.

Cain left the Lord's presence and settled in the land of Nod, east of Eden. "What have you done?" said the Lord. "Hark! Your brother's blood that has been shed is crying out to me from the ground."

"Am I my brother's keeper?" Cain responded to the Lord.

The Lord said to Cain, "Where is your brother Abel?"

Cain had slain his brother. Descending. This sin was second only to the first in the Garden. Hans panted. Josef loosened his grip on the knife, uncertain of his resolve.

"*Ach*, kill me," Hans gasped. "You can't. That's your problem. You don't know what the meaning of life really is. If you did, you wouldn't hesitate to kill me. Instead, you stupid creature, you're tormented by the prospect of suffering. Life is suffering and meaningless. Take the blade and end it."

"Am I my brother's keeper?"

Von Flintz hesitated. "No."

Josef's body stretched long, the blade raised even higher above his head, ready at any moment to unleash the wrath and plunge the dagger through his ribs and pierce his pumping heart. Hans stared up from beneath Josef's powerful stance, his eyes wide open in dread.

The sound of distant thunder couldn't distract him. Josef continued to travel back through the cave of his ancestry. He descended toward the first sin in the Garden and then beyond the duality of oppositions that created She and He, Us and Them; a duality that forced Adam to distinguish himself as something apart from Nature and God. Josef closed his eyes, ready for the next revelation. Silently, he arrived at the back of the cave. But the end wasn't as it appeared -- it was merely the end of time. In an instant, he was there with all his mothers and fathers and it was in this place that he found unity with all things. The world existed within him and he existed everywhere in the world -- in the trees, in the light of the sun.

He had journeyed to Eden where time fell away and he shared the cave with all existence. He couldn't kill Hans von Flintz; his life wasn't for Josef to take. Then, just as Josef began to surface, the trees below the temple shifted. The thunder grew so loud he no longer heard the jungle. Now the trees blew like the final tempest and everything was being swept away. A single light pierced the gathering mist. The horizon tilted and shifted as Josef tried to look through the circle of blinding light that was now fixed on them.

The helicopter hovered just above, suspended only meters from the sloping point of the temple. As three ropes dropped from the helicopter, Josef flipped von Flintz on his stomach, pulled his head back and lodged the SS dagger tight against his throat. Masked men slid down the ropes and took up positions on all sides. Josef was trapped, the circle drawing tighter, guns pointed at his chest -- the same intolerable fate that had befallen Erich Hauptmann.

From behind, a familiar voice shouted above the thundering whirl of helicopter blades. "Put the knife down."

Josef kept the knife at his throat, preferring to die in defiance of G-2.

"*Ach*, this madman is trying to kill me," Hans cried out. "Shoot him. He's crazy. I order you to shoot this maniac."

The voice from behind bluntly told Hans to shut up. "Come on Josef, put the knife down."

In his confusion, Josef loosened his grip then tightened it again. "You should die for everything you've done."

The voice was shouting again, this time impatiently. "Put the knife down." A man stepped before him. "Josef, put the knife down," pleaded Saul's shadow.

Josef was reeling, trying to put the pieces together. Then his disbelief gave way to clarity. He turned to Saul, "So *this* is the length of your reach?"

"Further," Saul boasted.

"You know this man, colonel?" said Hans. Comprehension played across his face. "*Ach*, the lion is jumping sides. So now you're my judge when before you were my henchman. I guess the world never runs out of surprises, does it?"

Saul shrugged, making no attempt to hush the old man. From the stone, von Flintz craned his neck and gazed toward Josef with a smug side-long glance, as if once more he was victorious.

"What the hell?" Josef looked to Saul for an explanation then released the knife from the old Nazi's throat. Almost immediately, a masked man stepped forward and yanked Hans to his feet.

Saul spoke into a walkie-talkie, "Hit it now."

From the direction of von Flintz's death camp in the jungle, a flare streaked through the darkened sky like a meteor. An explosion lit the dawn. More flares hit the camp, followed by enormous fireballs that shook the earth.

"You used me," said Josef.

"Everyone uses everyone. We killed two birds with one stone. We got what we needed and you got what you needed. A win-win."

Hans watched the fire in the sky, witnessing the dissolution of his dream. He clenched his jaw but managed a smile. "Ah, the miracle of causality. Who could have predicted the first war would create the perfect conditions for the second and that would spawn the birth of your homeland and the oppression of the Palestinians?" Hans looked amused. "Who knows what seeds you've just planted with your actions."

"Shut up," Saul barked.

As the rope around von Flintz's feet and hands were cut, Josef referred to the old Nazi by his real name and withdrew his photograph from the Übel dossier in his satchel.

"But how did you know?"

"Erich Hauptmann helped me."

"That's impossible," said von Flintz, startled. "He's dead." He glanced at Josef's hand then recognized something. "That-that's my dagger."

"The one used to rape Sarah; the one Erich tried to kill you with."

"You couldn't know that." The old Nazi seemed confused and stared at Josef with the eyes of death. But in a moment, clarity passed over him and he smiled knowingly. "Yes, Hauptmann tried to kill me, too." He made a sound and sliced at his throat with a finger. "He didn't succeed and neither did you. You're just like Erich was -- a hopeless coward."

Saul and another masked agent tied a rope around von Flintz's waist and signalled to the helicopter hovering above to start the winch. As von Flintz began to rise from the temple like a black angel of death, he looked astonished as if his prophecy of ascending to heaven with Josef at his side had somehow been fulfilled. He shouted his last words. "You think you could kill me? You can't. Only I have that power."

A faint smile played across Saul's face. "So you didn't have the balls to kill the old Nazi, after all."

"I held his beating heart in my hand. I had the power to take his life -- and I gave him life. I gave his life back in a way he never dared on the selection platforms of Übel. That, Saul, is true power."

Up above, there was a commotion. Hans was bouncing like a puppet on a string. Something glistened in his hand. Josef glanced down. The SS dagger had disappeared from the temple stone. Hans was smiling, before the last threads of rope gave way. He released the knife and fell silently beyond the platform of the temple. The dagger rattled on the temple mount while the dull sound of weight hitting the earth gave away that Hans von Flintz had met his end.

"Nice way to end the hunt," Saul grinned.

Josef wasn't amused and didn't hide it. "How could you have worked with a goddamn Nazi?"

Saul ordered his men back into the helicopter before he spoke: "I don't keep track of all that high level shit. You know that's not my style. But we had to help the Americans after the Congress imposed an arms embargo on Guatemala. Billions of dollars and our political ties with the US were at stake. The situation was much bigger than me. Than any of us."

"Bullshit."

"Josef, you know politics is a dirty business. You just have to follow the money. Hans was the point man for the Americans...to keep the commies from coming further north. The CIA warned us not to touch him until they were done with him. But when we learned his camp was coming online in a matter of days, the rules changed."

"Unfucking believable. Asena was right about you. You probably would sell me down the river, if you needed to."

Saul found that amusing and picked up the SS dagger, playfully popping it up off his elbow before catching it with his other hand.

Then it came to Josef.

A sick feeling washed over him and, at once, the ground was pulled from beneath him. He tumbled forward but Saul grabbed hold. Josef knew it now. The truth had been revealed as clearly as daylight destroyed shadow. "But how-how could you, Saul?"

"How could I what?" Saul was still smiling when he met eyes with Josef.

Josef now understood that his parents had not only uncovered an aging Nazi living in Guatemala but had also come to learn that their own government was protecting him. And that was why they had been silenced.

"How could you kill them?"

"Who?"

"I know it was you. You planted the bomb."

Only a flicker of recognition crossed Saul's face. Josef pushed up against Saul's imposing frame. He knew it was futile. He knew Saul could kill him with a single blow. Still, Saul dropped the knife.

"It was an accident."

"An accident, Saul? This isn't, '*I slipped and fell and mistakenly blew up your parents.*' I saw you with my own eyes." Josef shoved him harder; Saul accepted the blow, glancing back to see how close he was to the edge.

"Hold on, Josef. You don't understand."

"I do understand, Saul. I do. That's the problem."

"They weren't supposed to be there. You know that. It was six in the fucking morning. They shouldn't have been there."

"You shouldn't have been there." Josef was struggling to breathe. "My God. What have you done?"

"I was following orders. Your parents...They had information they were never meant to find about the Nazi, and the CIA refused to give up the old man. It sounds fucking ridiculous, I know, but they were getting too close. We were ordered to do it. Just to spook them. That's all. We didn't want to, I swear to God."

Josef was shaking, crying. "You did it anyway."

"Listen to me. He was going to get taken out just as soon as we got the go-ahead from the Americans. We had tracked down the Nazi bastard back in '75, but the US didn't want him touched. I fed you information so you could find him yourself, because I couldn't. I wanted to right some wrongs, but I had my orders -- you understand, right?"

"You. Fuck."

Cornered, Saul turned on Josef: "Who just saved your ass? Me. If it had been up to my superiors or the goddamn CIA, you'd already be dead and disposed of and that cretin would still be waltzing around, a free man. I just stuck my neck out, risked everything, because you're my brother. You've always been my brother."

"You have to go. Before I do something terrible." Josef shoved him, though Saul held his ground.

"Josef—"

"Go. Now," Josef growled.

Saul looked back regretfully then climbed a rope into the belly of the helicopter. Josef stood on the stone platform of the temple mount, rocking back and forth in the gale-like winds as the helicopter tilted and whirled away. He approached the edge and stared down at the hollow shell of Hans von Flintz. From the temple mount, Josef retrieved the SS dagger, studied it one last moment, and tossed it into the thick of the forest.

The thunderclap of the helicopter receded into the distance, before being swallowed up by the sound of the jungle. With it, Josef felt the knot of rage loosen ever so slightly. He looked out at the orange haze gathering along the horizon, a deep turquoise sky resting above. Josef took a deep breath, followed by another. Then he let go and cried for his parents, cried for Saul's betrayal. With haunting clarity, Josef also recognized that Saul had taken orders from his own government.

Josef would blow the whistle, that much he knew, but he was under no illusions: his government would offer up a sacrificial lamb -- some mid-level player, maybe even Saul -- to pay the blood debt. The real power would remain in place.

––––

Atop the Temple of the Giant Jaguar, a calmness came to Josef -- an absolute quiet amid the chaos of past moments, days and years. In the upper reaches of the temple, several birds were perched, waiting. He sat cross-legged, watching the sun reveal the Mayan city cast in shadows. As the sun climbed into the pure morning sky, he felt the intensity of life building within him -- feeling centred and a part of everything.

In the deepest sense, Erich Hauptmann's story had become his own and was now as much a part of Josef as his hands or eyes. He had searched and searched how it was possible that Erich came to possess him in his visions. In the letter from Cuba, Hector had written that it was not for Josef to understand how Erich's visions had found him. *The Dead have their ways*. The important thing was what they would reveal. In the breeze that sent the clouds chasing overhead, Josef sensed Erich was being released, set free to be carried out to the open sea.

The sun rose stronger. Asena, the sun, smiled down like the fiercest love. Perhaps Asena had known all along about the nature of his journey -- about Saul's ultimate betrayal, what was hidden in the cave, and where his discovery would lead him. But like all wanderers and shamans, she understood that he had to make the journey alone, to uncover for himself the mysteries that had remained buried, so he would be ready with unfaltering faith to embrace the lessons learned from experience. He pictured Asena's altar and recognized with absolute faith the wisdom her shrine possessed. At this moment, it felt as if the world rotated around this one immovable spot, focusing all of its energy through him. He was *Lucero Camina Mundo Busca Sendero Encima Entoto*, Morningstar World-Walker Searches For The Path On Earth.

The birds perched above took flight. Looking up toward the low ceiling of billowing clouds, Josef saw his parents and sensed they were a part of him but did not possess him as Erich Hauptmann once had. For the first time in his life, he imagined himself reborn as a bird. Josef closed his eyes then allowed them to spring open, sending him soaring up through the white and grey clouds. He felt the warm face of the sun against his wings as he rose high above the wilderness of El Petén, which closed in around the Mayan ruins of Tikal like an impenetrable cloak.

ABOUT THE AUTHOR

Robert J. Brodey is an adventure travel writer, photographer, and an avid long distance trail runner. He has spent much of his life exploring the world, and when he isn't travelling, he is often planning his next adventure. His work has been published in numerous national and international publications, including The *Houston Chronicle, Toronto Star, Globe and Mail, Outpost Magazine,* and Costa Rica's *Adrenaline Factor* magazine. *Josef's Lair* is his first novel. He lives in Toronto, Canada. You can find him online at www.cloudgazer.com or follow along on Twitter @RobertBrodey

DISCLAIMER

Despite the long list of wonderful and knowledgeable people who have read and commented on this book along its twenty year path, I remain solely responsible for any and all creative and historical oversights.

With the exception of some very well-known historical figures, all other characters are pure works of fiction. The death camp, Übel, is also fictitious but based on historical accounts of other camps created by the Nazis.

Where I have been able, I try to remain faithful to the religions and cultures described within these pages. However, I have taken some creative license when I felt it would not compromise the values of the religion/culture.

ACKNOWLEDGMENTS

First off, I would like to thank editor extraordinaire Michael Schellenberg, who provided valuable notes for the final redraft of the manuscript. I would also like to extend my gratitude to those that have read various stages and chapters along the way, including: Ana Serrano, Joel Gregorio, Kathleen Scheibling, Riley Adams, Michelle Gibbs, Leah Jaunzems. Jo Saul, Samantha Sherkin, Maureen Holmes, and Lara Arabian. Aussi, un grand merci a France Simard for her input on the visuals for the project.

A very special thanks to José Esnobol and his family, who provided me with a doorway into the powerful world of Cuba and Santería during my visits there in the early 1990s.

Love and respect to my wife, Lara, and son, Sevan, my parents and sibs (Michelle, Andrea, Deborah, and Simon) for encouraging me every step of the way. To my nieces and nephews, Quinn, Jaime, Michael, Emilia, Alexander, Amanda, Matt, my bro-and-sis-in-laws, cousins, uncles, as well as my vast Armenian family, including Lena, Maro, and Jiro Arabian, Araxie Robertson, and the rest of the Toronto, LA, Lebanon, and Syrian contingent. To John and Pat Hatton, who inspired me to pursue anthropology, holism, and the love of all things natural. The book is also dedicated to my grandparents, my uncle Steven Vise, and relatives who endure in memory and continue to inspire.

A special thanks to Michelle and Gary Gibbs for their flexibility in the workplace so that I can be a responsible parent but also continue living my dream of travel writing.

Friends are so often inseparable from family, so I dedicate this book to that great swath of family and friends that have populated my life from my earliest years. To Rita Verba, a survivor in every sense, and her children and grandchildren. To Susan Lee, Jason Robinson, Jordan Cheskes and family, Kumail Karimjee, Sarah Elton (y las niñas), Michael Carter and Ivy Lim-Carter (who were there when the story was born), Annie Mandlsohn, Salima Pirani, Claire Harvey, Scott Enns, Marlisa Budihardjo, Alarice Jones, Kim Li, Ray-Ray Deslandes, Stevie Sardella, Pui Sim, Lily Ng, Sonya Woods, and the whole Sim and Jones crew, Ian and Joanna de Souza, Patrik Witzmann and Deanna Shinde (Aki and Toyo), Kate Cassidy and Christopher Sealy, Juan and Nicole Baquero, Wudasie Efrem, Dereje Demissie, Sarah Kurita, the extensive Jarvis posse, Tara Darrall, The Joneidi sisters, Andrea

Brockie, Kevin Allen, Jacqui Bryan, John and Susie Grondin, Rose Chalker, Kara and Guillermo Del Aguila (y chicas!), Eric Larson, The Zumbados (Costa Rica!), Paul Drumonde, Ori Levy, Cam Drynan, Asha DaCosta and Santiago Rincon Gallardo, Rosa Mesa, Andrea Grant and the Trinity, Romelle Espiritu, Cash Lim, Andrew Alzner, Biren Gurung, Sameena and Khusbu Shrestha, Ingrid Jones, Thomas Bollmann, Harpreet Khukh, Chris and Jonathon Fitzpatrick, the Potvin boys, Mia Sheard, Boza and Peter Sperr, Ralph Fox, Nahid Sachak, Selia Karsten, Veena Verma, Pierre Brun, Victoria Moreno, Rodrigo Moreno (y la familia), Edan Gomez, Löys and Alison Maingon, Alanna Marshall, Matt and Deborah Robinson and Team Outpost, and the good people at Gibbs & Associates. A big thank you to David Reed, my high school English teacher and a great inspiration to so many young minds.

Given there are so many other wonderful people to commit to paper, I will have to take solace that you know who you are.